Soul Riders

THE LEGEND AWAKENS

HELENA DAHLGREN

TRANSLATION BY
TARA CHACE

Andrews McMeel
PUBLISHING®

The Great
Reservoir

CRATER OF JOR

Ashland

Valley of the
Hidden Dinosaur

NORTHSHIRE

CENTRAL JORVIK

Firgrove
Village

GROVE

South Link

MISTFALL

Jorvik City

Dundull

RN JORVIK

Other *Soul Riders* books
by Helena Dahlgren

Jorvik Calling

There's no trick to being brave—
if you're not scared.
                    —Tove Jansson

1

There was a special spot in Lisa's heart with room for just one thing: the horse Starshine; brave, beautiful Starshine, with his soft muzzle and perfect, near-floating gallop. Fearful young Lisa had had such a rough life so far, and Starshine had gotten her back into the saddle again. Now that she thought about it, this spot had been filled for a long time, so much longer than she would have suspected. Ever since her childish preschool drawings of a gorgeous white horse with an unusual blue-tinted mane, this spot— this place in her heart—had tempted her, beckoned to her, with whispers of moonlit rides, dizzying adventure, and the kind of pure, uncomplicated love that you can only feel for an animal. This was the whisper that had brought her to Jorvik, to Starshine.

Of course you can love people, too. Lisa knew that. But somehow loving people was always harder. With people, there were always other considerations—so many other complex considerations.

Conflicts, arguments, demands, everyday life. People wore on each other. They were either misunderstood, said the wrong thing, or said something they might not be able to take back.

Loving a horse, on the other hand, was simple—that was really just unconditional love. And Lisa had learned that a person could grow and gain courage from this kind of love.

But Starshine wasn't here now. He was gone, kidnapped, and it was up to her and her friends to find him. She had cried so many tears, of sorrow and fear, panic and dread. She didn't have any tears left anymore. All she had left was simply the knowledge that they *needed* to find him. Which was how she came to find herself standing there, outside of the Dark Core complex. It towered over her like some sinister giant. In the gentle wind a wilted, yellowish-brown piece of grass tumbled forlornly past. A dry red leaf blew off a tree and landed on the cover of a well. Otherwise it was completely and utterly quiet. Almost too quiet.

But at the same time, it felt as if a hundred pairs of eyes were staring at the back of her head as she snuck through the fence into the seemingly deserted industrial area. Maybe it was more than a feeling. She had not been here very long, but she had seen enough to know that people could turn up from any direction at any time.

They might come off the frothy, black ocean. Or from any of the winding staircases and hallways. Or from the copper piping that reminded her of large, glistening snakes.

And then a few hours ago: from the sky had come an enormous helicopter with *him* in it.

Mr. Sands. Just his name, just the thought of him, made her skin crawl. When he stepped out of the helicopter, he had stood there for a while beneath its swirling air currents with his inscrutable black eyes focused on something above the helicopter pad. Lisa knew that there was no way, not from that far away, but from her hiding spot on the water tower, it felt like he was looking straight at her, through her.

He must still be in there. She hadn't seen him come out again, hadn't seen anything at all since she came down from the water tower and onto the grounds.

But she knew that she had to be on her guard.

She clenched the bolt cutters she had just used to pop open the fence. They weren't much of a weapon, not if the big workers in the green outfits she had seen go in the front door earlier turned up and grabbed her. Or if he did. Lisa shuddered. But the bolt cutters were something solid to hold onto, and that helped her hands stop trembling for now. She hurried across the grounds, not really sure where she was going. The big building—that was actually several buildings that flowed together—was like multiple islands in an archipelago. It reminded her of some evil knight's fortress, only made of steel and sheet metal instead of stone. There were thick pipes that led down into the ground here and there, as if they were sucking something out of the earth. It was easy to imagine the pipes branching out below the surface into a vast, snaking, underground universe. Who knew where it all ended? Lisa looked around and spotted several strange little buildings—various sheds for storage, some kind of a pavilion with paint flaking and a ramshackle cupola on top. Deserted? They appeared that way, but she could be wrong. She had to remind herself that she had been wrong before.

For example, she had believed she would get to ride Starshine during the fall break adventure and that her father would be waiting at home. The idea took root in her again, the one that had not left her since her father had left to work the night shift and had not come home again.

What did they do to him? Where is my father?

Her eyes burned as tears began to well up. But she couldn't fall apart now; she couldn't let herself think too much about her father. She had to have faith that she would find him, of course she would. But first she had to find Starshine. She needed him in order to accomplish the rest—his warmth, his strength. At the same time, there could be other possible leads here, she thought. Important pieces to the puzzle that could maybe—her heart fluttered in her chest—lead her to her father.

9

She tried to shake off the grief growing inside of her and returned to scanning the large industrial area.

The complex stretched along the coast like a dark lava field of asphalt and concrete. Smoke rose from the tall smokestacks sticking up out of the ground here and there.

There was a string of doors lined up in front of her when she reached the first wing of the building, but only one of the doors was ajar. Finally, an easy decision. She pushed open the heavy, metallic-green door. It slid open with a creak like long fingernails on a chalkboard. She winced at the sound and then she crept in.

Darkness. She fumbled around, feeling for a light switch, running her hand over cobwebs and wires. She wondered to herself, Didn't anyone ever clean this place? Apparently not. She had expected a big industrial facility would be more . . . orderly?

She took in the stuffy, dusty air, searching her scent memories—hay, dung, warm horsey bodies. Could she smell anything familiar, any kind of trace of Starshine?

But what did she have to go on, really? Doubt welled up in her as she stood there in the darkness. At best, coming here was a long shot. At worst . . .

No. She didn't want to think about that option.

Lisa sneezed and kept fumbling around until she found a light switch. One bare bulb hanging from the ceiling crackled and then came on. In the sickly greenish light, she saw that she was in a storage room. There were cardboard boxes, order lists, and big moving dollies with several boxes stacked on top of each other. She crept through yet another door—this time she avoided any creaking noises—and found herself in a long corridor. It was quiet aside from the distant, muffled sound of machines humming.

Mostly she wanted to just break into a run. She wanted to keep moving, investigate every nook and cranny of this enormous building.

Each door, each flight of stairs could bring her closer to Starshine. If he was here, of course. She tried to convince herself not to be too hopeful. This was only one of the places that Linda, Alex, and she had pinpointed as a potential hiding place for Dark Core. You could hide a dinosaur in that place. That's what Alex had said about the industrial complex back when everything had just been dots on a map and not real life yet. She had laughed back then, in that slightly intermittent Alex way that Lisa had grown so fond of.

Lisa missed Alex's laugh. She missed her friends—because they were her friends, the best friends she had ever had.

The only friends she had ever had.

Alex, Linda, Anne. And then Lisa had arrived, new to their class and to the stable. She had never dared to dream before that she could have a best friend, let alone three best friends.

She had scarcely been on the island of Jorvik for a month. Even so, so much had already happened. If she wrote everything down in a short story, maybe for English class, her teacher would probably accuse her of being unrealistic. Or he just might praise her imagination.

There were so many unanswered questions, but Lisa didn't have time for them, not now.

She forced herself to sneak farther into the building, slowly but surely. The hum was louder now than it had been in the storage room. The air felt charged with electricity, as if the atmosphere itself held a charge. She heard the sound of heavy footsteps above her. Lisa stopped, holding her breath, listening anxiously. Then she heard something new that crept into the rhythm of the sounds along with the footsteps.

Something familiar.

Could it be . . . ?

No, impossible.

Then a loud, piercing whinny echoed through the dark corridors, and Lisa no longer cared whether she was detected. She ran, ran, ran toward the hope of Starshine. Her cowboy boots echoed on the hard floor until she was no longer rushing forward. She was stuck. Something compact, baggy, and rough had hit her and stopped her legs, which wanted to keep running. It felt like her heart stopped, too.

She had just enough time to see the DC logo on the green cloth before she collapsed.

"Is this the right way, Meteor?" Linda asked.

The first light of dawn was just barely visible. The trees in Pine Hill Forest rose out of the dark cloak of night, slowly greeting the day. The whole world was gradually awakening, still clinging leisurely to the cool silence of night. One lone girl on her horse rode through the chilly morning forest.

The shadows that fell over her were dark blue. Not even the birds were singing this early. It would be easy to take a wrong turn and get lost riding in this silence, Linda thought. This was the sort of silence that belonged to thick drifts of fresh snowfall, not an autumn forest. A muffled, bundled-up silence. Each time she opened her mouth to talk to her loyal horse, who was walking along the scrubby forest trails, she thought her voice sounded more uncertain, more childish somehow. Obviously she knew that Meteor could not answer her, but he was the only one she could talk to now, the only one who could make the horrible, stifling silence go away even for a moment.

"We should have stuck together, Meteor, all four of us, just like Herman said. I have such an awful feeling that something is going to happen soon, something really terrible. And I know we're the only ones who can stop it," Linda said.

Linda didn't know exactly how her ability worked. Yet. She couldn't choose which small glimpses of the future came to her, nor could she distinguish the dreams from reality. Possibly because reality was increasingly starting to seem more like a dream.

Meteor stumbled over a large rock. Linda lost her balance and almost fell off but successfully grabbed Meteor's thick, white mane. She could feel the heat from his body. Her fingers grew damp from his sweat.

"Sorry, pal," she said. "These aren't exactly like the riding trails around Jorvik Stables, but it shouldn't be far now."

Meteor pricked up his ears. Had he heard something that her human ears could not detect?

Linda, too, listened attentively now. Was that a faint birdsong that she heard in the distance?

"What is it, Meteor?" she wondered and stroked his soft, shaggy neck.

But of course Meteor did not answer her. Instead he broke into a trot on the trail. Linda noticed that the narrow forest trail had suddenly begun to open up into a big clearing and that something light and sort of flowing could just be made out through the dense, dark spruce forest.

It was the pale shimmer of the new moon, just visible in the lavender-blue morning sky. The moon seemed to be suspended, poised unusually low in the sky. She felt like she could almost raise her hand and pluck it from the sky. In the faint gleam of the fading moon, she saw the silhouettes of flapping bird wings. There was a heavy fragrance of flowers. The fresh, cool forest scent was gone. This was a completely different sort of smell that made her think of unfamiliar places and hot nights, more southerly latitudes.

She looked at the moon and a feeling blossomed in her that was just as familiar as it was unexpected.

It felt like clearing a tall jump with Meteor. Meteor whinnied unexpectedly. Linda blinked hastily. Suddenly she was overcome by the strange feeling that she was being watched. Invisible eyes burned into her back.

Should she turn around and stare straight into the whites of the monster's eyes?

"What monster? There's no monster," she reassured herself quietly, without actually believing it.

She did not turn around and simply urged Meteor onward. He carried them away from the forest at a gallop, away from scornful, watching eyes. With every galloping step, the feeling of being watched drifted off behind her. She let Meteor slow his pace and straightened up in the saddle. She wouldn't arrive at her destination for hours.

The sun was breaking through the clouds. Morning had arrived, and with it the feeling that anything was possible. True, she missed Alex and her friends, but she did have Meteor, her bestie who understood her better than any two-legged human in the whole world. Together they were unbeatable. She thought about the secret mansion waiting to be discovered. Pine Hill. What if Starshine was there? Or at least an important clue that could help her find him? Maybe it wasn't likely, but *what if?* For a moment Linda allowed herself to picture Lisa's joyful smile as she came riding in on Meteor with Starshine beside her. Her heart swelled, moved by the thought.

Oh, Linda, how will I ever be able to thank you?

She suddenly felt free and easy, alone with her horse on an early, crisp, clear fall morning, out on an adventure that had only just begun.

Whatever awaited her at Pine Hill Mansion, she was ready for it.

Alex remembered the magic. She couldn't feel it now, but she *remembered* it: how everything flashed and sparkled, the lightning bolt that had guided her. Jessica had collapsed on the ground in front of her as Alex had held her hand out in the air. She wore the necklace with the lightning bolt pendant as she rode Tin-Can through the chilly, deserted countryside in Winter Valley. As she headed for Cape Point, there were no more lightning flashes and no pink, pulsing beams of light anymore. In front of her were only empty plains and sharp, rocky outcroppings that seemed to say, "Stay away! Don't go any farther!" Everything here was gray or grayish-brown, like an old photograph that had lost all its color and luster. Alex felt like the loneliest person on Earth. She was completely cut off from everything and everyone—except for Tin-Can, of course.

"It's just you and me, guy," she said and picked a leaf out of Tin-Can's mane. "Always."

There was something about the solid grayness up here that made a person's courage dissipate away on the cold winds. The previous night's rains had left the ground wet and mucky. Mud splashed up onto Tin-Can's thick fetlocks. She decided that the next time she stopped she would have to pick out his hooves carefully, brush the mud off his fetlocks, and rub ointment into his pasterns.

She lightly touched her pendant. It was far too cold this morning. When the lighting came before, the metal grew so hot it had left a burn mark at the base of her neck. It had hardly had time to heal.

What did this mean? Was the magic gone?

There was so much she didn't understand yet.

Everything felt muted in the cold morning air, almost like she was riding underwater. A viscous stiffness had taken over her arms and legs so that everything moved in slow motion.

She let Tin-Can trot for a while and tried to remember what, exactly, she was on her way to do.

"Save Starshine?" she said tentatively. Tin-Can neighed, a muted, rumbling sound from deep in his throat.

"Save the world?" she said and sat up straighter in the saddle. Tin-Can neighed louder now.

"Glad that's all cleared up," Alex said, ruffling Tin-Can's unruly mane.

She let him switch gaits, speeding up from a trot to a gallop as she thought about Anne. Out of the four friends, Anne was the one she couldn't get out of her mind during this long ride. Why hadn't she talked to the other three before she left? And where had she gone? Even more importantly: Where was her horse, Concorde?

Anne with her glossy hair and her steady eyes. Was she ready for what awaited them now?

Was Alex ready herself?

Heading out separately had been the wrong choice. She knew that now. They needed to be together, unified. Right now they were weakened, spread out across the entire island. At best.

Epic fail.

But once you had made the wrong choice, what could you do besides keep going?

So, she kept going, because that is what a Soul Rider does.

Alex longed for the lightning, for SOMETHING, something that would lead her in the right direction, away from her worries and the watching eyes of the beasts of prey that lay in wait in the shadows. She had felt their eyes upon her in the forest that morning, right from when she'd awoken from her uneasy dreams. It was so cold, so lonely. Not even Tin-Can's warm, furry body could warm her up.

Some seagulls sailed across the rain-laden sky. It wasn't far to the water now. Down at the harbor, you could just make out the light from the cargo ships beyond the bay. That was where she was headed.

"Come on, Tin-Can," Alex said, the hesitation gone from her voice.

The dark clouds in the sky flashed, suddenly a dazzlingly white. Then, just as quickly as it had appeared, the lightning was gone.

2

Anne could not remember when the world had turned pink, becoming pulsating and distorted. She knew only that she was not in Jorvik anymore. Time and space had dissolved. Days might have passed . . . or was it actually hours? Minutes?

Years?

The new unreality loomed around her there in Pandoria in the form of purple mushrooms. Yes, "unreality" really was the right word for her surroundings. The mushroom formations seemed to sort of sway in the air, forming a garish fireworks display of pink and purple shades. The sun shone, mercilessly bright, directly into her eyes. The ground swayed beneath her as she crept forward on all fours, toward something that in another world— her world—might have been a stream. Big, sparkling pink cliffs cut a sharp silhouette against the horizon. They looked like giant gemstones. Maybe there was a name for pink gems like that. Anne couldn't remember.

She tried to stand up and fell over. She stood up and tipped over again. Finally, she managed to get to her feet, but her legs just barely held her up.

What am I doing here? she thought. No matter how hard she tried to remember, she couldn't. It was as if she were inside a gigantic, brilliantly colored centrifuge, spinning helplessly around and around, faster and faster. One time when Anne was little, she had ridden a roller coaster at a fair. She had gone on the ride again and again until the whole world was spinning and she threw up. There hadn't been anyone to hold her hair out of her face then.

Is that where she was now? Was she ten years old? Did she hear the same music from the spinning carousel horses?

The horses, Anne. Stay by the horses.

Did she smell cotton candy? Did she need to vomit?

Where had her mother gone?

The horses. Don't forget the horses!

But she forgot, she forgot again. The forgetfulness was soft and cozy, and so easy to fall into. She fell again, couldn't remain upright. There was something about the ground, the air, the light, the colors. Everything was strange. It felt wrong and she didn't belong here.

And yet . . . At the same time, she was *supposed* to be here, wasn't she?

There was something she was supposed to do, something important. Wasn't there?

"Please," she whispered to herself as tears ran down her cheeks, "FEEL something, anything at all."

She felt nothing, heard nothing. She could not smell anything. Had the smells remained on Jorvik? But things were spinning. Everything was spinning so much that she wanted to throw up, but she could not. Her body didn't seem to work the same way here. She was not built for this world. It was drawing the life out of her. Soon she would not even be able to think anymore. The thoughts that did come to her just pulled her even deeper into the bewilderment. Nothing was logical.

Confetti, she thought. *Pink cotton candy everywhere. In my ears, my eyes, my mouth. No thank you, Mom. I don't want any more. Please, Mom, no more cotton candy.*

Anne felt sick as she fumbled her way along past hazy, pink pools and small floating islands of barren rock. She tried jumping between the islands, like when she was little and used to play Don't-Touch-the-Floor in PE class. The air felt lighter than back home in Jorvik, as if the gravity was different. Everything was impossibly pink.

She was alone here, but inside her hopelessly spinning, dizzy head, things were starting to feel tight. Her mother was there, and that light gray carousel horse.

The horse is important. Don't forget the horse!

And now Alex was there, too . . . or *here*? Alex stood in front of her now in muddy riding boots, looking triumphant. Or was that not Alex? No, that had to be Alex. The bolt of lightning that hung around her neck flashed and made her light brown hair gleam pink. Her eyes looked completely black when Alex looked down at Anne where she lay huddled like a rag doll on those sharp, pink rocks. Around them the purple water was bubbling and fizzing. The shadows that had only been an inkling before grew longer and deeper. The shadows crouched down over Anne and Alex.

"This was a mistake. *You* are a mistake," Alex hissed into her ear, and Anne felt her warm breath dissolve the very last remnants of resistance in her weak body.

"You went off alone," Alex continued. "Just as well. No one else wanted to ride with you anyway. We kind of have other things to think about right now besides doing our hair. Girl, you need to get your priorities straight."

Anne raised her head and blinked skeptically, her eyelids feeling sticky. She heard what Alex said, saw her there in front of her—but *was* that really Alex? The Alex she knew would never be so mean. Self-important or noisy, sure, but never mean.

"Who are you?" Anne whispered faintly.

The answer echoed dully through her throbbing head, but she did not dare believe it, did she?

The anti-Alex. That's not Alex.

The Alex figure faded away before her, becoming a part of the pink shadows. She gratefully slipped back into the dark, sluggish unconsciousness, into a sort of trance, but somewhere deep inside the drowsiness, someone called to her.

Or, not called . . . but whinnied.

The horse, Anne. I did say that he was important.

"Concorde?"

3

At the top of the castle of steel pipes and winding hallways, Mr. Sands maintained one of his offices. You would think that a man in his position would have chosen the best view, but his office looked out over a sooty, dilapidated industrial area a long way from the city. The smoke from the smokestacks shrouded everything in haze, giving the sky a dirty, sulfurous yellow cast. In that light, Mr. Sands looked like he was at least a hundred years old.

The truth was that a hundred years wasn't even close. Now, the sickly, gritty sheen lit up every wrinkle and furrow of his face; every year showed, like the rings of a tree. He sighed and turned away from the window and his own reflection. He nodded briefly to the figure dressed in white who had crept into the room and come over to stand beside him without a sound.

"You're just in time, Katja," he said and sat down at his desk.

Katja still did not say anything—she just looked at him with her big eyes. They were so light gray that they looked almost completely white, like a corpse.

Mr. Sands leaned over his massive oak desk and spoke into his speaker phone. The reception was bad. It sounded staticky and words dropped out or were cut off.

"Generals, are you there?" he barked right into the microphone. "Sabine? Jessica?"

On the other end of the phone line, in a forest grove by her big, black horse, Sabine made a face and vigorously rubbed her ear.

"We're here, boss, but the question is if our eardrums are," she replied grumpily.

"Doubtful," mumbled Jessica, who was riding close to the cliffs between Cape Point and Anvil Bay seeking better reception. She sat still with her back straight and looked out at the ocean. Her face was tense and expressionless. The others' tinny, staticky voices were drowned out by the noise of the waves.

Katja smiled. Something happened to her eyes when she did that. It was clearly visible now: her eyes were milky white, not light gray.

"Generals!"

Mr. Sands's voice was like the crack of a whip.

"I want a status report," he continued. "What's the news?"

"One of them seems to be on her way to Cape Point," Jessica said, adjusting her hairnet. "I imagine she's headed for HQ. Obviously I'm planning to give her a warm welcome."

"Excellent," Mr. Sands responded.

"Try to stay on your feet this time, would you?" Sabine interjected. Jessica could definitely hear her triumphant smile and for a second it was like a fire flared up in Jessica's eyes before she sniffed dismissively. She would have preferred not to be reminded of what happened the last time she and Alex met, the disgrace of being knocked over by a little stable girl with lightning around her . . . No, she didn't want to think about it. She would never have thought that was possible.

"And the one with the glasses seems to be on her way to Pine Hill Mansion," Sabine said, tossing her long, dark hair. Khaan, her horse, stretched his ears back following a sound from the trees. Sabine squinted her dark eyes but saw nothing. She sighed, hoping to wrap up the call soon and ride on.

"I'm assuming the third general has everything under control," Mr. Sands said in his raspy, sandpapery voice, with a furtive glance at Katja.

"Of course," Katja said and smiled her nasty, vacuous smile again. "It will be a true pleasure. I CAN show her the horse, too, can't I?" she added, suddenly acting like a little girl pleading for candy.

"The horses must be sacrificed. You know that very well. They are needed to liberate Garnok once and for all," Mr. Sands said slowly, almost thoughtfully, as he regarded Katja. "But why not use the horse we already captured as bait to lure the last of the horses here?" he added and smiled, a real sinister smile.

"But we have to wait until all four of the horses are captured, don't we?" Sabine said. "They can't be sacrificed to liberate Garnok until then, right?"

"That's right," Sands confirmed. "To succeed we need all four of them, or technically their magical energy . . . That's why they need to be sacrificed. And it must happen soon, while the Pandorian flow is favorable. Therefore, it is important that you locate the girls and their horses as soon as you possibly can. In other words, we have one horse in captivity, and one in Pandoria. Now the two that remain need to be captured and brought to the lab for preparation before the sacrificial ritual."

"And the girls?" the three generals wondered in unison.

"The only thing that interests me is the capture and sacrifice of those horses. If you capture the Soul Riders or put them out of commission, that's a bonus. Then they can't try to save the horses or cause problems. These Soul Riders are far from skilled . . ."

"Concorde—my Starbreed," Jessica added with a weak smile. "I believe he is almost ready for transport from Pandoria to captivity now."

"Good. You have my permission to use the portal at HQ to get to Pandoria," Mr. Sands replied.

His pale, white spider fingers move rhythmically in the air, kneading some invisible object, slowly and artfully.

"Is there anything else you want, boss?" Jessica wondered over the staticky phone line.

Mr. Sands looked like he'd swallowed a lemon. "Yes, Jessica. I have indications that someone came to Pandoria to rescue the horse . . ."

"Then there's less time than we thought," Jessica said, half to herself, and urged her horse onward. They rode away from the coastline and into the forest. She was forced to duck to avoid the branches but rode decisively ahead through the wild surroundings. "I have to get to Pandoria before any of the others do. I do not intend to fail, not this time," she added grimly. "Never again. Whoever is poking around in Pandoria . . ."—she pictured Anne's face in front of her—"I promise I will destroy that person, and it will be a real pleasure to do it." Jessica was quiet for a few seconds. "I suppose I should find some reinforcements. I'm going to need to take care of the other girl who's on her way to Cape Point as well as the intruder in Pandoria!"

Mr. Sands looked out at the industrial area where the burly workers in green were bustling around.

"I'm sure you'll do fine, Jessica. Sabine, on the other hand, I'm of the opinion that you do need extra resources," he said, staring hard at the microphone on his desk. "I'll arrange for a vehicle so that the horse you need to pick up—the one that seems to be heading for Pine Hill—can be transported here as soon as possible."

Those spider fingers again, they were moving faster now. He smiled to himself as he thought about what was to come. When he sacrificed the four horses, that would release enough energy to liberate Garnok. He had met Garnok several hundred years ago and had been granted eternal life then so that he could successfully accomplish just this: the liberation of Garnok. Although for him, personally, it may have been more important to get revenge for what the people had done to his Rosalinda. He intended to put right what had been done to his beloved. And he, John Sands, would make her queen the day he became king. Because once the liberation had taken place, Garnok would leave the planet, and John Sands would remain as the most powerful person on Earth. With eternal life he would be able to build an empire of money and power such as had never before been seen before. Not to mention taking revenge against all the pathetic people. It would be a real treat.

But time was of the essence now. He got up from the desk and stood by the window for a bit. The reflection that met him in the extremely clean pane of glass revealed an exhausted man, an aged man. Everything was intensifying as Garnok grew increasingly impatient. Soon time would run out on John Sands and all his dreams. In other words, failure was not an option. Never! He clenched his fist in his jacket pocket and turned away from the reflection in the window. The next time he saw himself he would not be able to detect any new signs of aging. Starting now, he thought, it would all go according to plan. He would appease Garnok and save himself. And all would be his.

He sat back down, straightened the red bow tie he always wore around his neck and said guardedly, "I really hope that everything is clear for you now, generals. I have a visitor to deal with . . ."

4

Her legs were stiff and her tummy was rumbling by the time Linda finally rode up the hill that led to the vast Pine Hill estate. The mansion looked down at her with its dark, empty holes for eyes. It felt more like an animal than a building; like a raptor with outstretched wings waiting to sink its claws into its prey.

Could a house have a soul? If so, Pine Hill Mansion's soul was dark and defiant, Linda thought—a lost soul.

"You need to stop reading so many scary stories, Linda," her aunt was always telling her. "The world is awful enough." Right now, she felt like maybe her aunt had been right. It was just a house, not haunted at all—right?

An abandoned house, obviously. She looked around for tire tracks, cars that had possibly been tucked away out of sight, any form of presence other than the dark, silent house. But there was nothing. It seemed like no one had been there in a long time.

But possibly the stables? Almost all of the old estates and manor houses in Jorvik had at least a stable, often more than one. She should walk around and take a look, let Meteor catch his breath and munch on a little hay.

As soon as she had looked around a little, her tummy started rumbling again. She thought about the glass jar of cookies that

Herman had given her. They were in her saddlebag, waiting to be eaten. Soon, but not now. She looked at the garden. Even now, on a clear, sunny fall day, there was something dark and menacing about it. The thick, overgrown hedges and scraggly trees seemed to be reaching out toward her and Meteor like long, outstretched arms. Next to some twiggy bushes there was a dilapidated pavilion, full of leaves and cobwebs. But closer to the sinister-looking mansion, the garden seemed to become denser. Along the walls of the building, the dead garden appeared to start turning green again. Right near the high stone staircase that led up to the front door, the plants were resplendent; deep red roses climbed up the mossy wall. *Were roses really in season this late in September?* she wondered.

Farther into the garden, toward a greenhouse that seemed to connect to the actual mansion, there were birds singing. Linda could see them: canaries, hummingbirds, cockatiels—exotic, brightly colored birds from other latitudes. Their breathtaking sounds made her chest ache, because they were so beautiful and because their song awakened a strong longing in her. She wished she could share this moment with someone, she realized—with the others.

She wondered whether once everything was all sorted out, once everything had been resolved somehow, would the memory of these birds in this amazing garden fade more quickly because she had experienced it alone?

She looked around cautiously before climbing the stone steps to the front door. The handle made no sound as she tried to open it.

Locked, obviously. She wouldn't have expected anything else. But a building of this size must have many doors, she thought. Best to look around a little more. She led Meteor closer to the greenhouse, closer to the birdsong.

The base of the greenhouse was made of brick, with big glass panels to allow in sunlight. She remembered that this style of greenhouse was called an orangery, because you could grow orange trees in them. She ran her hand along the brick walls, following the birdsong. And then she saw it. There was a broken pane of glass, and that was where the birdsong was filtering out. An enormous, urgent impatience erupted inside her. Should she . . . ?

True, breaking and entering wasn't part of the plan, but this was almost too good to be true.

The birds kept singing as Linda and Meteor neared the broken window. Her heart felt heavy and light at the same time as she led her horse toward the dark, hidden building. The broken pane of glass drew her in. She stopped, pausing to think.

If only the others were here, she thought, then they could have made a decision on this together, the Soul Riders.

In the library or in the stable earlier, when they had discussed all the strange things that had happened, everything had felt so simple. The plans were no more than theories. Everything had been warm and cozy despite all the awful things that they had faced. Safe—at least it had felt that way. Kind of like riding a roller coaster, a sort of controlled fear. You could turn off the computer at any time, fold up the map, or close the book. There was so much they didn't understand, but they could talk to each other about it. Everything they discovered they had discovered together, as a group. Being alone the way she was now was a completely different situation.

Yes, they should have stuck together.

But the others weren't here. Linda was alone with her horse, who was looking at her with his ears pricked forward, his shaggy coat soft against her cheek. She stroked his chin and played a little with his beard, the beard that made him look like an old uncle.

The full-bodied horsey scent became all the more intense when it was mixed with her salty tears. The loneliness and feeling of missing her friends weighed on her as she leaned forward and whispered:

"What do I do, Meteor?"

The sun reflected off the green rosette windows of the orangery. The broken glass glistened.

Linda took a step forward, allowing herself to be blinded.

5

As Alex and Tin-Can rode toward Cape Point, the winds had eased up. It was a brisk, clear, sunny fall morning. The view of the little coastal community wedged between the high waves and the even higher rock formations was marvelous, but Alex didn't have time to admire it—or to rest, for that matter. She was stiff and exhausted, and a bit worse for the wear after a night in the woods. A long shower and a heaping plate of eggs and bacon would hit the spot, she thought.

"Ah, well," she said to Tin-Can, patting his sun-warmed coat. "If you can manage without a shower, then so can I. It's the back-woods life for us!"

She decided to stay and buy breakfast from a café in the village before she went on to Dark Core's headquarters by the abandoned shipyard on the coast just west of the village. It was never good to face evil on an empty stomach. And she had money since she had been saving as much of her scholarship money as she could the last few months. Plus, she usually earned a bit of money when she helped Herman with repair work on all the dilapidated machinery that was parked in the Jorvik Stables garage. One of the stable managers usually let Alex babysit for her daughters as well. Unlike the other girls at the stable, Alex didn't have parents who could afford to help out. She liked earning her own money and she tried not to waste it. If there was anything she had learned by this point, it was that she always needed to have a buffer to fall back on, just in case . . .

She didn't want to finish that thought. Not now, when the sun was sparkling on the unimaginably blue water and she had a beautiful horse to ride. Or two? Because there was probably a chance that Concorde was at HQ, too. But what would she do if it turned out the horses were being held captive there? She would have to deal with that when it happened. If it happened.

The sun, the crisp air, and Tin-Can's happy snorting cheered her up. She watched the residents of Cape Point start leaving their homes, biking to work, and going to the store to buy bread. Although she was still looking down at them from a distance, she felt a sudden, fierce tenderness toward these unknown people in the village below. It felt wonderful to know that soon she would be among people again and see how everyday life was chugging along.

The little white houses reminded her of sugar cubes set against the sparkling sea. She would soon be there.

Sure, it would have been better if they had been together now, all four of them. But things were the way they were, and Alex was used to managing on her own. She was a real lone wolf, not by choice, but by necessity. Although there was ample freedom in being on your own. She could do what she wanted to do, run at her own pace. She didn't need to change herself to suit other people. No one owned Alex—well, with the possible exception of Tin-Can.

Could a person be truly free without also being lonely? Was that maybe the downside of freedom? Her thoughts jumbled up like dark, sticky threads. She tried to move on away from them; she wanted to return to the tingling feeling in her stomach she had just felt when she had looked down at the little coastal village.

Her phone chimed. Alex pulled it out and saw that the screen was filled with missed calls, text messages, and voicemails. Apparently she had not had cell coverage in the forest and now a flood of them were arriving as she approached the village. Now the tingle in her belly had returned. Maybe one of these was from Linda? Or Lisa?

The butterflies in her stomach quickly turned into a heavy stone as she listened to the first message.

"Hi, Alex honey, it's Mom. I need to borrow a little money from you for food and rent. Just this once. This is the last time, honest. Will you please call me? Mommy loves you, hugs and kisses."

Beep. New message.

"Uh, yeah. This is your mother again. Just wondering if you got my message. Call me. Love you!"

Beep.

"Sweetie, you could answer when someone calls you, couldn't you? Do you think I like doing this, begging my own daughter for money? Please call me back."

Alex sighed loudly as she tried to shake off the cold feeling that always took root in the pit of her stomach when her mother called. Neither of them particularly enjoyed having a sixteen-year-old help support the family, but they didn't have much choice, either. Her mother used to work as an assistant nurse at the retirement home in Jorvik City. She started right after school and worked there for many years. But she had injured her back from all the heavy lifting and couldn't work anymore. And her disability did not cover much. It didn't cover much at all. The idea was that her father would help out with food and rent. However, he unfortunately showed up about as often as Santa Claus. He always brought some unnecessary present and was filled with completely unreasonable apologies that her mother somehow always accepted because she still held out hope that he would come back for good. Alex had stopped feeling disappointed in her father. She didn't feel anything anymore. It was easier that way.

With a whole gang of hungry kids in the cramped apartment at home in Jorvik City, the refrigerator was a sinkhole. Alex, who mostly lived at Jorvik Stables, where Herman had arranged housing for her, usually went home and restocked their supply of milk, bread, cheese, and frozen pizzas as often as she could. But her little brother James drank two cartons of milk a day. He was like a baby animal. Oh, it would be so nice to be younger sometimes, Alex thought, and then sighed. How wonderful to just be able to glide along and not worry about what tomorrow was going to be like. She was tired of being the backup mother. Before she texted her mother, she permitted herself to imagine how a conversation between them might go, a *genuine* conversation, where she said the kinds of things that she was normally afraid to say out loud.

Do you know what? I can't be responsible for all this, for all the rent and food money, for having to be the backup mom for the whole family and having to serve everyone all the time, even though you're so packed in there that I have to live at the stables. And you know what, Mom? I know you've done the best you can all these years. We love you. You know that, right? Soon the boys will be bigger and they'll be able to help you, too. We can deal with this. But, Mom, right now this isn't working. I can't take on this much responsibility, and you are actually the grownup. There has to be some other way.

Even in this imagined scenario, Alex was not able to choke back her tears. She wiped her eyes on her sleeve. What good was lightning and pink magic when she couldn't help her family with everyday life?

"Ugh," she mumbled. "Now I feel guilty, Mom."

It was always like this. Alex tried to escape from the responsibility, to put the responsibility back where it belonged, on the adult's shoulders. Because she wasn't actually the parent here. She was just a kid, and kids shouldn't have to bear so much responsibility. Deep down inside she knew all of this. But in spite of everything, she loved her mother and wanted to help out.

She only had one mother, her own mother. And yet at one time, back before the fatigue and all the disappointments had taken their toll, there had been a different mother. She remembered what her mother was like before her dad had left. Back then, her mother had still been able to do it all—a happy, young, vibrant mother, with Alex's caramel-colored eyes and strong arms. That mother had always come to the stable with her, helped lug hay bales around and polish saddles. That was the mother everyone used to fall a little bit in love with, because her energy and warmth were so strong that people were drawn to her, to bask in her warmth.

Her mother was still in there somewhere, inside the frazzled, impoverished, sickly woman. It was for that mother's sake that Alex wrote this text now.

"Out riding with Tin-Can for a few days! But of course I'll help out. We'll figure it out when I get back!"

If only Alex had not been so preoccupied with her phone and her mother. If only her tears had not spilled over and left her eyes blurry, made the world around her shrink and disappear. Then maybe she would have noticed that she was no longer alone. The fact was that she had had company ever since she and Linda had left Jorvik Stables. First there were two of them, just like her and Linda. Then they split up, riding like shadows, each following her own girl. They followed them the whole time, like evil twins in an enchanted mirror. And Alex's shadow rode back at a safe distance, controlled, every movement perfectly timed.

If Alex and Tin-Can breathed in harmony and enjoyed mischievous pranks together, Jessica and her horse breathed a taut, compact darkness. Jessica's back was straight as she sat in the saddle and her big, coal-black horse chomped eagerly at the bit as they walked along following Alex and Tin-Can.

"That little toy horse keeps up a better pace than you do," Jessica muttered. Her horse rolled the whites of its eyes and tossed its head impatiently.

"Yeah, I know," she said. "When it counts, you're the fastest. But now it's a matter of maintaining just the right pace and you're not so good at that. Me either . . ."

She furrowed her brow in irritation. This whole little excursion felt a bit pointless now that she had already confirmed that Alex was on her way to HQ, just as she had thought from the beginning. If anyone had listened to her, she would be in Pandoria right now instead of following the girl who had made her collapse like an old dishrag the last time they had seen each other.

That last bit was hard to accept, but it was true.

Alex had the power of lightning inside her. Jessica had not counted on her already being so strong.

On paper it had all seemed so simple. Kidnap the horses and delay the Soul Riders. Release the magical energy and liberate Garnok from captivity. End of assignment. How hard could that be?

Apparently harder than she had assumed. They had underestimated the Soul Riders.

Her goal now was to get to the Portal in time. She had to deal with the girl who was mucking around in Pandoria—it had to be Anne, Concorde's protector. After that the pursuit would continue until all four horses were captured and sacrificed to liberate Garnok. Then she could relax. If she even remembered how. She had come so far from who she had once been, from the place that had once been hers and would be again.

She closed her eyes, released her earthly body, and dreamed of the dark star, remembering a different gravity, another universe. That was where she needed to get back to. Everyone wore masks here. Nothing was what it seemed, herself least of all. But being in disguise came at a price. Sometimes she thought she could feel her true self slipping further away from her. What even remained? Who was she here, on the island of Jorvik?

Her white jodhpurs chafed against her skin. She hated being stuck in this body. When Garnok was finally set free, she needed to be as well. She needed to be herself again.

Yes, Jessica longed to return to the dark star, back to her life beyond a body, beyond the earth. She dreamed of black and silver. She dreamed of finally being home.

She had to abruptly let go of her dream. There was no time for dreaming just yet. Instead, she cantered along so as not to lose Alex and Tin-Can. They had to get to the magical energy. Without it, Garnok could never be freed.

Garnok . . . he was restless now. You could hear his rage if you listened carefully. Jessica's horse pricked up its ears and whinnied. Just then a muffled roaring sound rose from the bottom of the ocean. Jessica nodded, as if a question had just been answered. Then she rode on after Alex.

6

The echo settled over the vast industrial facility and Lisa finally
dared to move again. What kind of a place was this? With trembling legs, she worked herself out from whatever it was that had
made her trip. Then she saw that it was a pile of clothes made of
the same stiff, green fabric she had seen the Dark Core factory
workers wearing. That was it.

And yet. Only a moment ago she could have sworn that the
bundle of clothes had eyes, arms, and legs. It seemed to have strong
muscles that had pulled her down toward the cold, concrete floor.

She looked around the dark hallway. Everything was dead quiet,
aside from the noise of her heart beating as fast as a jackrabbit.
Had she imagined that horse noise just a moment ago?

Lisa closed her eyes and pictured Starshine, the two of them
galloping together, so perfectly in sync that it felt like they shared
one body. It was impossible to determine where Starshine began
and where she ended. She saw his gleaming white coat, his blue
mane and tail, her dream horse. Oh, how she had dreamt of him,
had heard him call! Now he was hers, incomprehensibly, truly *hers*.
Or he certainly should be, but the kidnappers had beaten her to
him. She rubbed her eyes to forestall the tears. She had no time
for tears. She had to rescue Starshine, and she had to do it now.

Maybe they were hiding him here, in this strange fortress of pipe-work and sheet metal . . .

Soon she reached a long, winding spiral staircase that led her up higher in the building. She climbed, closing her eyes, gulping, and clutching the handrail.

Come on now, Lisa. Starshine needs you.

She wondered how he was doing, if he was in pain, if he was scared.

"I'm coming to help you, my beloved friend," she mumbled and then took her last trembling steps up the stairs. The monotonous sound of metal on metal echoed through the vast machine room she was in now. She saw stainless steel benches everywhere with various tools on them. The windows had bars over them. Were they to keep people from getting in—or out . . . ?

She crept along, terrified that she would run smack into a green uniform with a big, mean guy inside it this time. This place was huge. Lisa felt like she was drowning in loneliness, becoming small and timid. What would she say if someone discovered her? Did she have a cover story ready? An excuse, even? "Hi, I was just standing here with my bolt cutters looking around. Nothing to see here! Oh, by the way, is Carl Peterson here? He works here."

Oh my God. This was not exactly your usual "visit Dad at work" sort of scenario! How could she dare proceed when she didn't have any idea what awaited her?

Farther into the room, which was bigger than her entire house, she saw a big, rusty iron cage. She snuck toward it with a lump in her stomach. Wasn't there a similar awful cage that Linda had shown them in one of her books about Jorvik? Yes, she was almost certain. It had said that the cages were used by evil horse thieves to trap the wild horses on the island.

Starshine was back in her thoughts. Overwhelming worry squeezed her pounding heart. She scarcely dared to imagine what kind of experiments they conducted in here. Is this where Frankenstein's monster had finally ended up?

There was a glass jar on the workbench closest to the cage. At first glance it looked empty, but when she went closer, she saw that there was something white floating around in the clear liquid. It looked like a large hardboiled egg with something cloudy in the middle. "Equus 237: Specimen 2" was printed on the jar's label.

Equus, Latin for horse. Lisa started to feel sick.

She turned the jar around as she fought against her nausea. She jumped up, her hand covering her mouth.

An eye stared back at her from inside the glass jar.

Heavy footsteps and loud voices filled the room. An army of men dressed in green came in moving stiffly and jerkily toward the workbenches, as if they were remote-controlled. Lisa quickly crawled under one of the workbenches and hid. She was trembling all over after what she had discovered in the jar. The eye wasn't blue like Starshine's, was it? *Please, don't let it be blue.* She feared her thumping heartbeat and heavy breaths were probably audible throughout the whole vast room. It felt like her breathing had taken over her whole being. What had she gotten herself into?

Oddly, no one seemed to notice her, though. One by one they marched into the laboratory and positioned themselves at the workbenches like obedient dogs. *Are these people really human?* she wondered with a shiver. She felt a gust of wind as one of them moved past the workbench she was hiding under. He came so close that she could have stretched out her hand and touched his leg.

Breathe, try to breathe.
Breathe, but not too loudly.

Lisa wished she could sing. Music always had a soothing effect on her. It had served her well in hard times, after her mother's death. When she was new to Jorvik and the thought of horses made her body ache, music had helped her breathe again, let her dare. She wanted nothing more than to be able to sing right now, but the music wouldn't come to her, not even in her head. The room was completely silent aside from the muffled clang of metallic instruments.

Starshine, I need you. Just as much as you need me.

There was zero view from her hiding spot on the floor. All she could see were big shoes and green pant legs. The booming metallic sound from the machines had a rhythm. She soon knew the melody, because everything has a melody, even monotonous work. Hidden under the workbench surrounded by those thumping machines, she could think of nothing but Starshine. In her thoughts they were riding through Everwind Fields. Starshine's gallop was smooth and comfortable. She leaned forward and inhaled his warm horsey scent. Oh, how she missed that smell. In her imagination it was everywhere, not just in her nostrils, but in the air around them, in the ground, in the windblown trees that suddenly started to sound metallic.

Minutes passed and then hours. The memory of Starshine kept her company the whole time. She thought about how they hadn't had a chance to jump yet. How wonderful it would be to swoop over an oxer with him. She thought about flying on horseback, because that was how it felt, the lightness that filled her when she sat on Starshine. The rest of the world faded away for a little while, until he received his evening hay and it was time to go home.

After an eternity, the workers started to shut down their machines for the day. The throbbing, rattling melody of the work was gone. Starshine, too. With a crackling click, the last worker turned off the lights and closed the door behind him. Everything went dark. Lisa was totally and completely alone. And she was cold.

Her body was stiff. How long had she actually been hiding?

Something white lit up in the cold, silent darkness. Lisa was so cold she was shivering now. It was an icy cold that she had never felt before, not even during the winters in Norway. The chill cut right through the marrow of her bones. She stood up and wrapped her arms around herself to warm up.

But it was as if the cold became even stronger when she stood up. It was radiating from above, suspended from the ceiling. She looked up. The ceiling must have been a good fifteen feet up, she guessed.

And yet . . . impossible: There was a young woman dressed in white sitting up there. Her hair was as white as the cloak she wore. Even her eyes shone milky white in the darkness. Then the girl slowly turned her head and stared right into Lisa's eyes.

Now it wasn't just the paralyzing cold that crept into the very fiber of Lisa's being. No, it was the opposite of everything that was good, everything that was life. She could feel Lisa Peterson draining out of her as she stared helplessly at the girl on the ceiling. The music, the cowboy boots, the horse models that stood lined up in her bedroom when she was little, yes, even her red hair. All of the color was gone. Everything was black and white. She could not stop shaking.

Death, Lisa thought.

Yes, that must be it. She could not stop shivering. All of her other feelings had disappeared, the will, the spark of life. Everything that had been Lisa was gone. She had felt something similar when her mother had died: the total absence of light, the emptiness rattling around inside her, everything else so quiet.

This had to be death she saw up there on the ceiling.

"Almost correct," the being said in a loud, clear voice. "My name is Katja, but for you I will be death."

Lisa shuddered, feeling the sleepy cold nothingness suck her in again. She collapsed on the floor. With her shoulders trembling, she squinted up at the ceiling, but the girl in white was gone. Once again she was alone in the shut-down industrial building. Had the girl even been there, or was Lisa just seeing things? Was this her lively imagination running amok again?

She got up. Her legs were wobbly as she hurried out of the room, continuing out into yet another corridor. She hoped it would lead her closer to her objective, closer to Starshine.

7

"Concorde!"

Suddenly Anne was wide awake. The sticky cotton candy sensation was gone. She moved unencumbered now over the little pink islands that together formed the world of Pandoria that should not exist.

A non-world.

An un-world.

A grotesque dreamworld of neon-pink water and purple clouds.

The rules were different here. Everything Anne had learned about everything that was solid or liquid, up or down—she had to forget all of that and relearn everything. It was exhausting. With every step, she felt how the forgetfulness, the sticky, bubble-gum-pink sleep tugged at her with its gooey strands. She did not know how she was going to manage here. She only knew that she had to somehow manage, for the sake of her beloved horse, for the sake of the others, and for the sake of the Soul Riders.

Now she knew what this world was called. How could she have forgotten?

Maybe because it was so easy to forget things here.

What else had she forgotten? Every time she blinked, every trembling breath she took carried her further and further away

from Anne von Blyssen, daughter, big sister, dressage rider, classmate, and stable friend. Anne loved glitter and popcorn with butter. She had twenty-seven different nail polish colors. Her favorite
one was called "Purple Rain." She had read every single one of her
mother's old horse books, and when no one was looking she did
goofy dance moves to Justin Bieber. She had a little brother who
always woke her up too early on the weekends, but she loved him.
She read him bedtime stories at night and stroked his unbelievably
soft coltsfoot-yellow hair until he fell asleep.

Her best friend and confidant was named Concorde. She had
won more ribbons and trophies than she dared to dream. But the
best thing about Concorde was not that together they made such a
great team in competitions. It wasn't his gallop transition or piaffe.
No, the best thing about Concorde was that . . . he was her friend.

She reminded herself of all of these things as the harsh pink
light tried to blind her. She managed to hold onto who she was
for a brief moment, convulsively clutching hold of the little puzzle
pieces that made Anne *Anne*. Then they were gone. Now she was
just a lost girl who was far away from home. Maybe she could possibly remember her name if she really tried. Unfortunately, she just
didn't have it in her. The power of all the strange, pulsing, glittering,
swooning things surrounding her was just too strong. She couldn't
resist. Among the intensely pink meandering waters were green,
orange, and black vines swaying back and forth. She stared at
them, as if entranced. Seconds passed, or maybe hours; she wasn't
quite sure. The plants danced their sleepy, swaying dance.

But she remembered. She remembered the place.

"Pandoria," she whispered to herself. "You're here, Concorde."

She proceeded forward.

The shape of the landscape slowly changed. The water, the
vine-like plants, and the little islands that she had been forced to

navigate her way between before were gone now. Instead a long rocky bridge spread out before her. It led out to a large island, the closest thing to a mainland she had seen since she came here.

The bridge was pink, of course. What else would it be? Anne rubbed her eyes and wished she were colorblind. The garish colors grated on her, disturbing her whole body.

Someone called to her, a hoarse female voice that she vaguely recognized. Why did her stomach turn itself into nervous little knots when she heard that voice?

Anne, come here.

She closed her eyes, just for a brief instant. When she opened her eyes again, she found herself on the other side of the bridge, in front of a big, temple-like building.

It brought to mind pictures she had seen of the Acropolis in Athens, only clad in a techno, hot pink. Behind the tall pillars— she thought they were called columns—she could just make out a pink marble floor extending back behind the entrance, all the way into the cool, silent building.

Maybe it had been a temple at some point, Anne thought. But that would have been a long time ago. The building, like this whole world, seemed deserted, uninhabited. Aside from the shadows that fell over the columns . . .

The shadows that were coming closer now.

In here, Anne. A hiding spot.

A hiding spot? But what was she hiding from?

What—or who?

She heard the voice again now.

The shadows, Anne. I can help you hide from them. You trust me, don't you? Surely you know who your true friends are now?

Forget Alex. She is false through and through, not to mention Linda and Lisa. Do you even know what they say about you when you're not around? How they laugh? You're a joke to them, a princess, nothing more.

Now she knew whose voice that was. Her stomach twisted into knots again, a tangle of glacial panic. She pictured herself in front of Concorde's stall. The dark-haired girl's look of triumph as the lifeless horse faded away on the floor of the stable. Her own roar, rising from her throat when she understood.

What did you do?

Jessica.

How could Jessica possibly reach her? Here? Anne turned around in a wild panic. She saw nothing. She was still the only one here, alone in this awful new world.

No, she thought. *Don't listen to her.*

But then she spotted a statue outside the entrance to what she now, for want of a better word, thought of as a temple. The blue, soothing color was a restful oasis among all the loud pink. He was just as small as when she had met him at the Secret Stone Circle, and the dreamy look was the same. There, in the cold stones, the stars can be divined, the banished galaxies and visions of what will be. All of the things that he had talked about when they had first met were before her now, and she could hardly believe her eyes or ears.

Yes, that is a really nice statue. It does him justice.

"Fripp," she said. "What are you doing here?"

Those big stone eyes stared inscrutably back at her.

Come.

Jessica's voice, again.

What are you waiting for? Better times? Forget it. The time is now.

The time was now. Anne was startled. Concorde!

You can forget Concorde, too. He's going to die here, and there's nothing you can do to stop it.

Why was Jessica talking so loudly? Why did it echo like that in her head?

Why was she suddenly unable to stand up?

Anne collapsed, crying. This was impossible, she managed to think. Then she saw something sparkling pink just out of the corner of her eye, below the temple.

Just what I need. More pink sparkly stuff, she thought, shaking her head weakly.

But something made her raise her head and look in that direction. And then she saw it. There was a big, tiled swimming pool with a trampoline and a long set of stairs leading down into the sparkling pink water.

Anne recognized that pool. It was the von Blyssen family pool back at home in Jorvik City. She had swum in it more times than she could count. In one of her earliest memories she was floating on a gigantic inflatable crocodile with her dad. Her mother was sitting on one of the chaise lounges, watching. They were heading toward the deep end of the pool and Anne felt herself growing tense—she didn't know how to swim yet. But her father had his arms around her, warm and safe, and she splashed her feet and laughed. Her mother picked up the camera and took a picture. That picture was in a frame in Anne's bedroom. Is that why she started thinking of the pool now?

She heard her mother's voice mixed with Jessica's. Her mother sounded bubbly and sort of watered down, as if she were beneath the surface of the water. It was hard to understand what she was saying, but Anne was able to make out a few words.

Toward . . . the water . . . carefully . . . you . . . won't make it . . . little sunbeam.

There was movement in the pool. The water swirled in time with the words. Anne felt dizzy. What kind of inverted world had she wound up in? This was just *too* messed up.

And yet: the water tempted her, pulling her closer, like gravity. At home in the pool in Jorvik, the water sparkled turquoise blue. Here the water was a bright, pulsating pink. Otherwise everything was the same. She knew her way around. She was at home here. This was where she was—Anne.

But could she trust herself here in Pandoria? How could she even know if she was herself when the water was so pink and talking to her?

It's just a mirage, she thought. *Like those oases in the desert right before you die of thirst.*

From inside the temple, Jessica continued to call to her. Her voice was darker now, with the tone of something ancient. She sounded almost like a crazed preacher. Anne felt the little hairs on the back of her neck stand up. Jessica's words almost knocked the wind out of her.

There's no point, Anne. You are doomed to fail. Your friends are not your true friends, Concorde is going to die, and you are just a scared little rich girl in over your head. Come to me and you won't have to feel so lonely.

Lonely. Yes, there it was. Anne felt lonely. She always had. And she had never really known who her real friends were, who she could really trust.

Not until now. As Jessica's voice grew louder and rougher, so did something inside Anne. She pictured the others in front of her: Linda, Alex, and Lisa. She thought about how they would chat with Herman in the stable, about how they were special, chosen. Soul Riders.

Together. They should have been together now, united at the Secret Stone Circle with their horses. How could everything have gone so awry? Or were the others there at the Secret Stone Circle? Together, without her . . .

Jessica laughed. Anne noticed that her laugh echoed over those pink rocks, but nothing happened to the water in the pool. The surface remained as still as glass, despite the noises Jessica was making. She couldn't get to the pool! For some reason, the pool belonged to Anne and her life in Jorvik.

She mustn't lose that. If the pool went away, then the last remaining part of her would, too. She couldn't explain it, but she knew it was true.

"Laugh all you want," Anne said in Jessica's direction. "You can't beat me. Not here, anyway."

She saw how her words created little waves in the pool in front of her. She nodded in satisfaction and leaned out over the water.

Jessica's voice ebbed away. All she could hear was the peaceful lapping of the water. Anne looked deeper into the pool, gazing into her own reflection—and then she saw something else. There was something at the bottom of the deep end!

Something light gray and big, motionless. Glossy hooves.

"CONCORDE!" she screamed. Before she had a chance to contemplate what would happen if she dove into a mirage, into something that was not there, she jumped into the pool.

8

Go inside.

Linda could not shake that thought. She could actually try to get in here, through the broken pane of glass into the orangery and then from there, she hoped, into Pine Hill Mansion. Cautiously she crept closer and then stopped right beside the hole, sizing it up with her eyes. It was very big. She could probably crawl through it if she was careful.

Beyond the shards of glass, it looked dark and oppressive. There was a musty smell from the dusty plants inside the orangery. The birds were singing a melancholy song that made her heart feel so strangely heavy again.

"What do you think I should do, Meteor?" Linda asked, petting him. Meteor kept munching grass. A strand of drool dribbled down over his little goatee, onto the palm of her hand, and it was totally green and slimy.

"Great, thanks for that!" She laughed and let him carry on munching. "Will you be all right on your own if I go in there for a minute? I'll be right back. You stand guard, OK?" she added and hugged her horse, who raised his head to look at her. Was it just her imagination, or did he look stern, almost disapproving in some way?

"Yes, yes, I get that you don't think it's a good idea, but we need to save your pal, Starshine. He might actually be in here somewhere. Who knows? Here, there, anywhere, you just keep grazing and I'll be back in a minute."

Meteor snorted and tossed his head vigorously so that his long white mane shook.

"I know, buddy. You don't like being left on your own, but I promise I won't be long."

She kissed him on his white blaze, closed her eyes, and inhaled the scent of slightly sweaty horse. *The most calming scent in the world*, she thought. That horse smell, full-bodied and salty, a combination of hay and sweat, safety and soil. It anchored her. Even now, in a strange, scary place, it had the same effect on her as it had back home at Jorvik Stables. The tension in her body relaxed. She breathed normally again.

Meteor exhaled warm air through his nostrils. She blew back, and then he sighed and exhaled again. They would usually do this for a long time in the stall. The trust game, the bestie test. A horse only blows back when he feels safe.

Linda wanted to stay here. With Meteor. Every fiber of her body screamed this to her, to stay here. It felt so wrong to leave him on his own. Meteor seemed to sense it, too, because the cozy, relaxed horse was gone now. No more bestie games. He scratched at the flagstones with his hoof and pulled back his ears, showing his big, yellow teeth in an ugly grimace which might have made her laugh under other circumstances. Instead, she pulled away now, feeling the uneasiness that crept down her spine.

"You really don't want me to leave, do you, Meteor?" she whispered, her voice breaking. She stroked the bridge of his nose to calm him down. Then she scratched him under his chin, in his little goatee. He usually loved being scratched there, but not now.

She looked into his eyes. The whites of his eyes were showing and his old, safe, friendly gaze was gone. She felt a pang in her heart. She thought of Starshine and Concorde, of how indescribably horrible it would be if anything happened to her beloved horse.

Could she really leave him here alone, at Mr. Sands's house? Her heart raced and she was dizzy. She felt cold and sweaty. Meteor's response was starting to rub off on her, as had happened so many times before. The mood and the energy bounced back and forth between them. They shared a symbiosis, she and Meteor; they depended on each other.

She patted him until he eventually calmed down, until his ears relaxed and Meteor's safe, calm look was back. But the situation still did not feel good. Deep down inside, the thought nagged at her with uncomfortable certainty: this was a bad idea.

But then she thought of the visions she had had, of dark, cold water rushing down, the panicked screams of people and animals. She thought of the horses that had already been captured and injured, of Lisa and Anne, who had lost their horses. She had to help them. She did not *want* to, but she actually *had* to. She owed that to the others. What if it turned out that Starshine had been here somewhere at Pine Hill all along? Would Lisa ever forgive her if she found out that Linda had never even looked around?

She clenched her hands into fists, and chased away the fear and the clammy, sweaty feeling with her breath. She thought—just like she had when she and Alex were on their way from Jorvik Stables, heading out on a journey they knew very little about—*sometimes you had to, even though you didn't dare.*

"Sometimes you just have to, Meteor," she said, her voice break-ing. He was resting his big, warm head in the crook of her arm. His head was super heavy as she tried to release herself from his cuddle hold, which they so often wound up in back home in the stable. It almost felt as if he was resisting. She sighed deeply and kissed him one last time on the nose. Then she lifted the reins over Meteor's head and led him over to the stairs. He whinnied, loudly this time. He did not want to follow her, refusing to budge until she coaxed him by making kissing sounds and pleading.

"I'm sorry, Meteor," Linda gulped, "but it's for your own good, in case you get scared. You have to stick around, buddy."

She tied him by the reins to a railing very close to the main entrance of the mansion. She didn't usually tie Meteor up, but something made her do it this time. He seemed so anxious—what if he ran away?

Her horse made a sound deep down in his throat, making it clear that he did not like this development. It was as if he was trying to say: *Me, tied up?! I thought you knew me better than that, Linda.*

Another pang raced through her heart. Logical thoughts could not make it go away. And she certainly couldn't tie her worries to a stair railing and leave them behind. She felt awful just tying him up like that, like a cowboy in some old western. What if he man-aged to get away anyway? Plus, she was *so* not a cowboy. Her worry filled her trembling legs, accompanying her to the greenhouse where she finally turned her back on her horse, calling, "I'll be right back, Meteor!"

He neighed in response.

Meteor's scent and warm breath filled her as she climbed through the broken pane of glass and stepped inside. It was a tight fit, so tight that she almost got stuck and she could feel herself starting to freak out. What if she got stuck right here?! Before she had a chance to think, her reptile brain stretched one of her flailing hands out to brace herself against the glass. She screamed as she cut herself on the sharp ragged shards.

"Ouch!"

Blood slowly dripped onto the glass. In the afternoon sun, the bloody glass shimmered like a ruby. Surely it looked worse than it was, Linda thought. Just a little cut.

Nice job, master detective. Now your DNA is all over the place! She cursed a little at her own clumsiness. Then she hurried on, through all the dead plants and frightened birds in the greenhouse. At the back, past all the withered greenery, she saw a door hanging by just one hinge, maybe the gardener's old door. And sure enough, the door led right into the dark house. Linda disappeared into the shadows, leaving the scents and sounds of the orangery behind her.

What Linda didn't know was that just then, a sound came from the forest—a sound that made Meteor flatten his ears back and stomp uneasily . . .

A big Jeep pulled into the driveway at Pine Hill Mansion. One by one, the Dark Core workers, all wearing the same green uniform, streamed out of the car, resolutely silent until they spotted the horse still standing and grazing peacefully a little way away.

"Hey, they're giving 'em away!" one of the men laughed, but was interrupted by a sharp voice from inside the woods.

"Silence! Do you want us to be detected right away?"

Dark clouds drifted over the estate. The shadows from the tall trees grew longer and longer. A young woman emerged from the shadows riding a majestic, coal-black horse. Both horse and rider exuded darkness and elegance, radiating a sultry, quivering sense of menace that made all the men in green fall silent and stand up straight.

Sabine and Khaan had arrived at Pine Hill.

9

Linda was glad that she had packed properly. Otherwise she would not have been able to sacrifice one of the extra shirts from her backpack, a white T-shirt she needed to use as a bandage now. The laceration on her hand was still bleeding quite heavily, but Linda pulled the cloth around it tightly to stop the bleeding.

"Should have brought the first aid kit," she mumbled to herself and tugged the bandage even tighter. She bit her lip to keep from making any noise. Her arm throbbed, a dull, aching pain that seemed to have a pulse of its own, a life of its own.

This building seemed to have one of its own, too. She was inside the mansion now, coming first through the greenhouse into what she guessed had at some point been the gardener's residence. Probably not that long ago, she thought. She fumbled along into a sort of atrium with a door that led her into a long corridor. Thank goodness the door was unlocked. Finally, a little bit of luck.

But, boy, was her arm really hurting now. She fished around in her backpack to see if she had anything that could help, down under the books and the sack lunch. Nothing.

"Newbie mistake," she whispered and tied a tight knot to secure the end of the bandage.

She thought back to the morning when she and Alex had decided to go for a ride. Had that really only been a few days ago?

It felt so long ago now. Her aunt had still been asleep. All of Jarlaheim had been quiet and still as she grabbed her backpack and snuck out. Something had pulsed inside her then, too, she remembered—an insistent, throbbing sensation that made her heart beat faster.

Here, in Pine Hill's dark, unexplored rooms, it just hurt. But it was the kind of pain that could be ignored, Linda thought. She just had to think about something else, not feed the beast. She checked her bandage one last time. It was a lot redder than she had hoped. With a grimace, she adjusted her backpack and groped her way along through the stuffy, claustrophobic darkness. She opened door after door along the hallway and peeked in. There was a bedroom with the curtains drawn and a white sheet over what might have been a mirror, possibly a wardrobe. And then a sitting room of some kind. There were white sheets over the furniture in here, too. A crystal chandelier hung over the covered table. She snuck into the room, feeling for the light switch. She turned the light on, but nothing happened. The electricity must be disconnected.

"Wonder how long this place has been empty?" she muttered to herself.

Farther in it was so dark that she had to feel her way forward with her hands. In the end she was forced to pull out her cell phone again and use its flashlight. The building smelled abandoned, like dampness, decay, that sad, musty basement smell. She had seen pictures of this place from back in the day. At one time Pine Hill had been the most beautiful estate in all of Jorvik. There were still traces of its glory days in the ornate fountains that no longer flowed in front of the mansion, in the high, vaulted ceilings, in the marble floors that she cautiously tiptoed across.

She encountered the same sight as she opened door after door: white sheets draped over big pieces of furniture; dust that swirled around in the musty, stuffy air; pulled curtains; an aching silence. Whenever there was even the slightest sound, it shot through her wounded arm and made her wince.

A rattling sound.

Linda jumped, looking around. Were there mice here? No doubt there probably were.

Or maybe it was just the house, she thought. Old houses always make weird noises, sighing and groaning like tired, old men. She hurried on. A stubborn voice inside her told her to be careful, but not to hesitate. So she kept going, moving deeper and deeper into the house, which was starting to feel more and more like a labyrinth. How was she going to find her way back out?

She kept on going. Several of the rooms that she checked were even empty. Finally, she came to a room that was unlike all the others. It appeared to still be in use. A study, she thought, as she regarded the large desk made of solid wood with papers and books strewn across the top and stacked in piles. Or a library? The walls were covered with bookshelves that reached almost to the ceiling.

Linda shivered as she stepped into the room. It was cold in here, surely twenty degrees colder than the rest of the house had felt. On hot summer days this room must stay cool, like a lovely refreshing swim. Today the cold reminded her of a crypt. She pulled her jacket tighter around her and walked over to the desk. Where should she start? There was so much to explore, and she didn't know how much time she had. She randomly picked up a few of the books from the various piles.

"*Garnok: Truth or Myth?*" she read aloud. She flipped through to the first chapter and started reading.

Rumors were rampant in the 1800s of a sea monster near Pinta Bay that dragged ships down to the depths. The beast had a name: Garnok.

The few who survived the shipwrecks had suffered tremendous distress and described a colossal sea monster that stole the sailors' souls. It was a routine occurrence for sailors who said they had come in close contact with the monster to be brought to the hospital in Jarlaheim to be treated there. One of them, a young seaman named Arthur Machen, spent his whole life there and wrote the horror story "The Terror of Pinta Bay," which became popular among local teens. Unfortunately, no copies of the short story survive for posterity, as all existing copies were burned during a book burning initiated by a Free Church society called Friends of the Light during the great church-sanctioned purge of unwholesome and morally questionable reading matter in the 1930s . . .

"Idiots," Linda mumbled, putting her hand to her forehead. She reluctantly set the book back down and kept exploring. *The Early History of Jorvik, Realm of the Clouds, Dimensional Travel . . .* That last book showed a fair amount of wear, appearing to have been well-read with illegible comments in the margins. One attractive volume, bound in soft brown leather, drew her attention. A diary? She picked the book up and flipped to the first page.

Property of John Sands.

She shivered. It was dark in the room, so the flashlight she found on the desk came in handy as she put her phone away to preserve the battery. She started to read the ornate handwriting. The farther she read, the more underlined sections she saw. The complicated, old-fashioned handwriting grew larger and larger, and harder to make out.

August 18, 1798

Rosalinda was very beautiful when I visited her tonight. Beautiful, but weak. Her fever has risen and none of the good doctor's treatments or medicines seem to work on it. She has a nasty cough as well. She managed to sit up with me for a little while. Her hand was so soft and warm in my own.

I am a fool, I know, but I couldn't help imagining how her left hand would look with a ring on her finger. Instead of wedding bells, I fear that a completely different sort of bell will toll soon. She is leaving me, and it is all THEIR fault. If only they had not made those terrible accusations. If only they had not flung her into the icy waters to see if she would float. If only they had not treated her so harshly even after she turned out to be innocent of witchcraft . . .

Yes, I hold them all responsible for her illness, and now I fear that it is much worse than the doctor says.

I am afraid . . . oh, I cannot write it! I cannot! My dear, dear Rosalinda, what have they done to you?

August 30, 1798

Today Rosalinda asked me if I believe in the afterlife. I replied that I believe we will see each other again, she and I. We will be together again, and we will be very, very happy. She smiled then and closed her beautiful eyes. Every time she falls asleep, I am afraid that she will never wake up again.

Strange dreams. Strange thoughts take root in me. Some are so black as night that I can scarcely describe them. They come from the bottom of the sea, these thoughts, from a darkness vaster than our Earth.

I have almost begun to welcome them.

September 2, 1798

The word arrived earlier this evening. She is no more, and neither am I. Everything is blackness.

September 12, 1798

A strange voice has started talking to me. I think it is coming from the ocean floor, from my odd dreams and poisoned thoughts. The first time I heard it speak to me directly was at Rosalinda's funeral. The low number of mourners was downright unacceptable given that at one time Rosalinda's family was one of the most respected on Jorvik. I sat at the front with her mother and sister, in the end not in the role of loving fiancé. But everything was too late. Everything was wrong. The darkness was everywhere, even within me. Maybe that was where the voice came from. I heard it just as I placed a red rose—one single red rose for eternal love—on my beloved's casket. At first it was no more than a whisper, but after everyone else left the church as I lagged behind, I heard the voice more strongly. It was in the sacristy, and there was no doubt that it was speaking to me.

"John," it said. "Follow me and everything will be yours."

I no longer have any other desire than this: to get my beloved back. Maybe the voice can help me?

Linda read on with a tear running down her cheek. She quickly wiped it away, a little ashamed of her reaction. Mr. Sands as the grieving fiancé with genuine human emotions?

"I need to pull myself together now," she muttered, trying to drive away the images of the red rose on the coffin.

For the first time she felt something reminiscent of sympathy for Mr. Sands. So did he make some kind of agreement with Garnok— the voice in the dark—because he wanted his beloved back? Linda thought that was a motive that she could understand.

She picked up a framed black and white photograph of a young John Sands in uniform. He stood leaning on an old car with one elbow. Could it be from the 1930s, maybe? Linda suddenly remembered that she had seen the picture before: in Jorvik's digital archives at the school library.

"Who are you really, John Sands?" she whispered. "And *where* are you?"

Linda flipped through several blank pages in the book before she found the next entry.

January 4, 1810

The years pass. While my Rosalinda molders away in her coffin, I remain the young man I was that fall when I lost her. Soon only her bones will be left. Soon even the worms will no longer remain with my darling.

I understand now that she is lost forever. No witchcraft in the world can bring her back. But surely I could experience love again? Garnok forbids me from forming close ties with other people. I must be his faithful servant.

Does he not understand that I, too, need companionship? An eternity without Rosalinda—without love—is not worth living . . .

Again Linda was forced to flip past a number of blank pages. As if years had gone by, but there had not been anything to write down, she thought. This thought suddenly made her feel sad. In the end she found one last page with writing on it.

October 31, 1815

Today, on Samhain itself, I bury my hope at the bottom of the sea. There it can roar and make noise along with HIM, whom I will one day free to restore to his proper dwelling place. When that happens, I will be the mightiest in all of Jorvik, maybe even on Earth. And when everything is ashes and fire and the little humans are screaming, then I will laugh and think of the moment when all that was warm and good in me died with her.

Linda's heart hurt to read that entry. So this was what had happened. This was where he had lost hope and the last of his humanity. Would she have acted any differently in this same situation?

She pushed that thought aside. She was a Soul Rider, a champion of the light. Mr. Sands was a tool of the dark, and he had been that way for HUNDREDS OF YEARS. You always had a choice, though, didn't you?

At any rate, there was no doubt that Mr. Sands believed what he wrote—and what Linda had read was worse than any horror story. So was Mr. Sands using his position as CEO of Dark Core to free . . . a monster?

She wished her friends were here so they could discuss this together. Even completely unimaginable things are easier to deal with when you're not all on your own.

She remembered how they had talked together in the library after that first time they saw Mr. Sands out in the school's parking lot. He had been talking to Sabine then. Evil Sabine, whom people were wise to watch out for. Sabine, who suddenly felt like something so much worse than a mean classmate. Something about the way she carried herself, the way she moved, lithe and catlike, almost predator-like. It had been as if a cloud had covered the sun, that sudden chill. Mr. Sands's skinny fingers had been drumming on the steering wheel as he listened attentively. None of them had been sure of what they had seen. Or *if* they had seen. But all of the mysterious and strange things, they had shared together.

Linda sighed but kept exploring, leaving the past behind her and looking at some more recent notes about Dark Core, favorable flow, and some kind of portal.

The most recent notes that she found were dated from last week. Linda sniffed the air. Had he been here in this room as recently as a week ago?

She shivered at the thought of the possibility that he might show up again, even though it probably wasn't likely. It was conceivable, though. Clearly this was where Mr. Sands did most of his research.

Get out of here, her common sense whispered to her. *He could come back at any time.*

A sudden ruckus outside the window made Linda jump and she dropped the notebook. She rushed over to the window. Adrenaline surged through her whole body as she very carefully grasped the heavy velvet drape and barely pulled it aside. She had to be sure that she didn't pull it far enough that anyone would notice. A rushing sound flooded her ears. Her mouth was dry and sticky from the fear.

Through the small opening she saw men dressed in green slowly approaching Meteor as he stood innocently grazing on the lawn. He noticed them and tried to move away from the men, but his bridle was caught. Meteor let out a loud, panicked, pleading cry that cut straight to Linda's heart. He was pleading for help. He was pleading for her.

And now Linda was screaming, too. This couldn't happen! They couldn't take him, too!

But it was happening. It was happening right in front of her and there was nothing she could do. She was too far away. The men grabbed Meteor and pulled him toward the trailer as he brayed shrilly and desperately. He frantically chewed on his bit, and reared and kicked at the men. Linda panicked and started sobbing uncontrollably.

She had tied him up. It was her fault he was being captured now, that he couldn't run away.

You, who hate being alone. Oh, my beautiful, beloved Meteor, what have I done? It's all my fault!

Linda rushed out of the library with tears flowing down her cheeks. She tried to find her way back outside as quickly as she could. She finally made it to the front door when she heard a low growling sound. Suddenly, Sabine stood right in front of her, blocking the exit. Her back was resting provocatively against the half-open door. *This far, but no farther.* Linda jumped with a little yelp.

"And just where do you think you're going?" Sabine hissed. Her eyes looked like coal just before the embers have burned out.

The window, Linda thought, backing away. The window in the library just might work. She desperately ran back to the library, so fast that her chest hurt when she breathed. She locked the door behind her and said a grateful prayer for those extra seconds, the slight lead that had allowed her to make it in there—without Sabine. She made it to the window, but the men in green were still right outside. She couldn't go out there now.

She rushed over to the enormous, shadow-shrouded desk and hid underneath it. It was far from the perfect hiding place, but it would have to do. Her arm hurt when it touched the floor.

Everything spun. Thoughts furiously came to Linda, making her nauseous, like the worst loop of a roller coaster. Sabine. Mr. Sands. Garnok. Meteor. Oh, Meteor!

From her hiding place she typed out a short text to Alex and Lisa. *Pine Hill Mansion. Meteor! Help! Please come!!!*

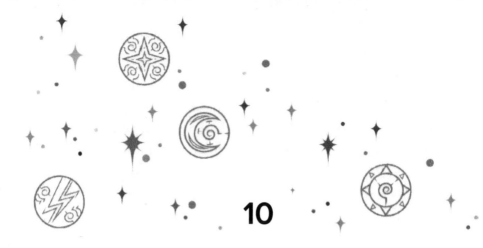

10

"We're finally here, Tin-Can!"

They were in the middle of the little village of Cape Point now, where a late breakfast and a small, much longed-for rest awaited. *Finally* was the key word. Alex could practically taste the piping hot toast dissolving on her tongue. Butter. Marmalade. Ice-cold juice. Scrambled eggs . . .

The little village was waking up around her. Shops' doors were opening, "open" signs being flipped around in the windows. The scent of freshly brewed coffee wafted out of restaurant doors as they opened. Her mouth was watering. She rode onto a cobblestone street and had almost reached the café she had been dreaming about when her cell phone chimed.

Alex sighed. Her mother? Again? She had said that they would discuss the money business when she got back home! What did she want now?

But it wasn't her mother. It was Linda, and the contents of the brief text made Alex immediately turn Tin-Can back toward the northeast.

Pine Hill Mansion. Meteor! Help! Please come!!!

Linda hated exclamation marks. As recently as last week she had gone on a long rant about how unnecessary and excessive they were. Three exclamation marks could only mean one thing. Linda and Meteor were in *real* danger.

Nor could Alex remember Linda ever having asked her for help before, not even once. It was usually the other way around. And maybe the most ominous of all: Meteor.

As she turned around on Tin-Can, she crashed into a fisherman walking up from the harbor with a tray full of fish. He yelled in indignation as half his catch tumbled to the ground from the collision.

"I'm sorry!" she called to him. "But I actually have a super good reason why I can't stick around to help pick up the fish!"

Tin-Can galloped down the streets. They just barely avoided a woman who was setting up tables and chairs in front of a restaurant.

"Sorry!" she yelled again and urged Tin-Can on.

The woman yelled something after her that Alex didn't hear.

A little farther on, after she was a safe distance from the people she had annoyed, she leaned back in her saddle and came to a halt. Then she turned her eyes back to her cell phone's lit display again with a sinking feeling in her stomach, but not from hunger this time.

Help! Meteor.

What could have possibly happened?

Alex dug down in her saddlebag and found an almost-empty packet of crackers. She shook out the final dry crackers and quickly chewed them up. They were dry in her mouth, so she washed them down with a few gulps of water.

"This is serious now, buddy," she said and patted Tin-Can, who looked attentively at Alex. "Linda needs us. Let's get to Pine Hill, pal, and step on it!"

Without her so much as moving in the saddle, Tin-Can set out in a gallop again. His hooves echoed on the street until she came back out onto a country road again. As they thundered up the hill outside the village, they almost rode straight into a girl out on an early morning ride. Tin-Can made a big leap to the side and Alex nearly fell off. The horse and rider stopped and Alex and Tin-Can galloped onward.

Alex shivered in the saddle.

"The temperature really dropped all of the sudden, Tin-Can," she said, wondering about the rider they had just seen. There had been something familiar about her, hadn't there?

Jessica could still feel the gust of wind from where Alex and Tin-Can had just galloped by.

That Soul Rider was truly prone to annoying her. She thought again about the last time she had encountered Alex. It had been near Jorvik Stables, when she was caught off guard. She remembered the lightning impacting her head and breaking up reality into sharp, angry shards. Her legs had given way beneath her. Her head had ached for several days afterward. It was tough to acknowledge, but Alex was more dangerous than one might think. Jessica clenched her jaw as she was reminded of Sabine's comment: "Try to stay on your feet this time."

"Believe me, Sabine, I'm planning to," she muttered angrily.

That was a narrow escape, she thought, and fixed her gaze on the horse and rider who were now disappearing over the hill. Alex's light brown hair was flying and Tin-Can's hooves drummed wildly against the ground. They would be out of sight soon if they kept up that pace.

Why was Alex riding back that direction? What was she up to?

Nothing was going according to plan, Jessica thought, and clenched her fist.

Using the power of her mind she had spent the whole night in Pandoria, going right into Anne's consciousness, whispering lies to her. Although—maybe not just lies. It was always much easier to make someone break down if you succeeded in weaving a few grains of truth in there, too ...

It had been so much harder than she had expected, trying to keep track of both Anne and Alex at the same time. She felt split, neither here nor there. Maybe if she had had more time ...

She allowed the irritation to consume her. What should she do? Finally, she decided. It couldn't happen any other way. She would let Alex ride off on her own and deal with her later. Right now she had to get to headquarters, and fast. And then, with the help of the Portal, back to Pandoria to have time to retrieve the horse before that spoiled horse girl Anne beat her to it.

Soon, the Soul Riders would get a taste of their own medicine. And it would be Jessica's turn to laugh when they were defeated ... and BOY would they be defeated! Not to mention Concorde and the others ... She started humming cheerfully and set out riding toward Dark Core's headquarters, which was just visible on the horizon like a menacing steel skeleton.

Suddenly, she was in the best of moods.

11

The corridors never seemed to end in this hulking industrial plant. Lisa ran down the long, dark hallways without any sense of where she was going. Maybe she had already been down this hallway before, maybe not.

The one thing she truly knew was that she had to keep exploring. Because Starshine might be in here somewhere.

And the one dressed in white—Katja? Was she here, too? Can she see me now?

Lisa shivered as she thought of those dead, milky-white eyes staring straight at her. It must have been a nightmare.

She finally spotted a massive green door. It stood wide open in the silent, empty corridor. Two voices inside her, both equally loud, battled with each other in her head.

Don't go in there. It's a trap.

Go in. You have to take chances. How else are you going to find Starshine?

In the end, Lisa snuck through the open doorway. Through the darkness, she could just barely make out the contours of the enormous room. An airplane hangar? Fresh, cold air streamed toward her, as if she were suddenly outside. She realized that the hangar must have a really high ceiling, maybe more than sixty feet

above her. The space was so vast that the sense of being inside a room was completely gone. And it was as cold as a winter's day. She pulled her hoodie closer and tighter around her neck as she kept exploring the enormous space. An immense concrete floor spread out before her. The room was so big that she couldn't see the whole thing, but what was that echoey, scraping sound coming from somewhere in the distance? It sounded like hooves scraping against metal . . .

Or one of those big, awful guys setting a trap for you. Come on, Lisa, don't be so naïve.

If I don't get to see Starshine and my father again, I don't care what happens.

As she thought about the two most important things in her life, she realized that it was true. If she wasn't able to find either one of them, she didn't care what happened to her.

She rushed across the vast floor, hearing her own footsteps echo throughout the massive space, bouncing off the walls and the ceiling way up above. However, she was following a different sound. Was it her imagination, or was the sound getting louder and louder?

She felt so small in that enormous space, so insignificant.

"Starshine!" she cried. Her words echoed off the concrete walls.

She had called out to him so many times since he had been taken away from her. Again and again she had yelled his name, calling out for the horse she longed for, the horse she loved, without really expecting any response.

Lisa moved along, across the concrete floor, farther into the enormous hangar, as she suddenly felt the air go out of her. She couldn't believe her eyes. There in front of her along one of the concrete walls was a row of several cramped metal cages, almost like stalls in a stable. They were separated by solid walls, but Lisa could see through the bars of the doors. There, in one of the cages, stood Starshine. He was tied in place with heavy chains and a shiny stainless steel halter.

He was barely standing. He looked tired, worn out, as if his legs might give way at any second. Lisa thought of all the horrific things that Starshine might have been subjected to since they had last seen each other. But the present moment was the most important. She was here now, with him. He didn't need to be alone any longer. And neither did she.

"I'm coming, Starshine!" Lisa called out and rushed toward the metal cages.

She threw herself at the door of the cage, but was repelled backwards by the powerful shock that zapped her body. She fell and landed hard on the concrete floor. It took her several seconds to understand what had just happened. She must have received an electric shock, the strongest she had ever felt. The whole cage was electrified! What kind of sick people could even think of something so cruel? That must be why Starshine looked so weak. How many shocks had he experienced as he had tried to break free from the chains or kick open the door to the cage? It hurt to think about it.

"Starshine," she said, her voice breaking. "Lovely, lovely Starshine. What have they done to you?"

She heard Starshine snort softly then, the way he usually did in his stall back home at Jorvik Stables when she groomed him and told him how her day had been. She would often just let her mouth run and her thoughts flow freely, even though she knew that he couldn't talk back. It was a quiet, tame snort, with no strength or mischief in it. But he had in fact snorted to her, to say hello. She was sure about that.

"Hey, pal!" she said to him, receiving a muffled whinny in response. Tears welled up in her eyes.

74

She got up, her legs shaky, and cautiously approached the cage again. She didn't dare touch the metal, but if she stood on her tiptoes she could carefully raise an arm over the electrified door and almost feel Starshine's warm breath on her hand.

"Hi," she said softly. "Hi, pretty boy."

Starshine angled his ears forward and eyed her attentively. His eyes were just as blue as she remembered, but the look in them broke something inside her. He looked like his wings had been clipped, small and pathetic despite his size. His coat, which used to be so glossy, was full of dirt and knots. Even his mane with its blue highlights had lost its luster.

But the twinkle in his eyes remained. He had not given up.

"Oh, buddy," she said quietly. "I wish I could bust you out right now, but I need to figure out how to turn off the power first."

He snorted again, nudging with his head to try to get closer to her. Starshine's motions made his chains rattle and Lisa held her breath. She was afraid that he might bump the metallic walls of the cage and get a shock. Starshine managed to get an inch or two closer to her and they could almost touch each other now. They breathed together, nostril to hand, breath by breath. Lisa closed her eyes. The drafty hangar suddenly felt much warmer now that she had found Starshine.

"We're going to fix this!" she said and leaned closer to her horse. "Somehow."

Then she couldn't help but reach out her hand to get a little closer to Starshine.

At the very instant she realized her mistake, she was hurled backward again by a shock.

Clap. Clap. Clap.

Lisa twitched from the electric shock as well as the sudden noise. She looked around groggily. The floodlights in the ceiling had been switched on, and the bright light stung her eyes as the sound of clapping hands echoed through the sparse, hangar-like space. A door on the far side had opened.

And there on the other side of the hangar stood Mr. Sands, applauding slowly and mockingly. He smiled a hollow, contorted smile that sent a cold shiver down Lisa's spine. Mr. Sands moved across the floor slowly, heading straight toward Lisa.

"Bravo!" he cried out. His words echoed in the chilly emptiness. "What a performance! You bit off a bit more than you could chew, I see. A little electricity probably did you good—always perks people up. I didn't think you'd actually go back for another taste of the electricity so quickly. How foolish of you!"

His grin had spread, extending all the way to his ears now. Lisa had never seen such a broad grin before. It reminded her of the wolf in Little Red Riding Hood. She instinctively backed away, toward the concrete wall behind her where the large cages were.

"Very good, little trespasser," Mr. Sands continued, rubbing his skinny, white hands together as he approached her. He sauntered along, slowly and unconcerned, as if he were out on a Sunday stroll and had all the time in the world. For some reason that frightened Lisa even more than if he had rushed at her like some wild animal. She kept backing away, her eyes wandering behind Mr. Sands. Metal and chilly surfaces everywhere, until she looked a little farther and shuddered. Because now she spotted Katja in the distance, and then she, too, started walking toward Lisa, at the same slow, dramatic pace. Lisa screamed.

Soon Mr. Sands and Katja stood before her. Mr. Sands kept smiling his wolfish grin while Katja regarded her with those dreadful white eyes. None of them said anything. The whole situation was so awful that Lisa was completely paralyzed—from horror and frustration. She really had let herself be led straight into a trap. Mr. Sands must have just stood there calmly waiting for his prey. How could she have been so foolish?

And how was she going to get out of here?

Should she just give up now?

Dad, she had time to think. *Are you here, too, somewhere?*

"Yes," Mr. Sands said, as if he could read her thoughts. Could he see the desperation in her eyes? Her longing, which had made her so careless?

"I suppose we'll have to see if this turns into a family reunion later," Mr. Sands continued, looking inappropriately cheerful. "But that will have to wait until later, because your father is not here."

"My father?" Lisa sobbed. "Where is he?"

"Yes, I suppose I might as well say it . . ." Mr. Sands began, but then he didn't continue. Instead he straightened his bow tie and merely smiled.

"Tell me!" Lisa hissed. But something black and ghastly welled up inside of her. Did she really want to know? What if they had done something to her father? What if . . . ?

No, you mustn't even think such a thing.

"Where. Is. My. Father?" Lisa's voice was growing steadier now. She had wiped away her tears and was staring at Mr. Sands, who was still sneering with amusement.

Her breath came in fits and starts, her body started to feel numb. She was afraid he would soon say it. Her father was . . .

"He's being held behind bars at headquarters in Cape Point," Mr. Sands said. "Your father is just as hopelessly nosy as you are. You two really ought to learn not to go prying into other people's business. Turns out he's not so clever with electricity either, even though he always does such a great job out on the oil platform!"

Lisa felt as if she had received another shock, straight through her heart. She needed to strike a bargain, she needed to plead, she needed to help her father.

"You don't need both of us," she whispered. "Keep me. Let him go."

His mocking laugh shook the bars on the metal cages. Lisa also shook when their eyes met. How could a person be so cold and yet burning full of fire at the same time?

She had been terribly afraid before when her mother had had a riding accident. Afraid for her life. But in her whole life, she had never experienced the level of fear she felt now, here with Mr. Sands and Katja standing before her. She sobbed.

"Take me to him!" she demanded as she lunged at Katja, who responded with a sharp motion with one hand. Lisa flew backwards and fell down.

Had she landed on the concrete floor? No, into one of the cages! With a bang that made the whole hangar rattle, Katja slammed the cage door shut. Mr. Sands pushed a button on a panel by the wall. There was a crackling hiss as the power started flowing through Lisa's cage.

She was trapped, surrounded by electrified metal walls just like Starshine.

Katja smiled over the door, a dazzling smile that made the whites of her eyes flash. Then she turned around and walked away. Lisa got to her feet. As she cautiously peeked over the door, only Mr. Sands remained in the hangar.

"Why so quiet, little trespasser?" Mr. Sands laughed. "Still sniveling inside your cage? There's plenty of room in there for a pathetic little thing like you. But it's best to avoid the metal . . . Well, I guess you already know that, eh? You'll have plenty of time in here . . ."

"You'll never get away with this!" Lisa spat through the cage door at Mr. Sands. The bars made a hissing sound, like when you fry an egg. "We know what you're doing. And I'm not the only one who's onto you."

"Who else?" Mr. Sands hissed back. "You . . . and your little pals? You don't stand a chance. Not now that I have three out of the four horses. Do you have any idea the great value you and your friends were messing around with over there at the riding school?"

"Three out of four . . . ?" Lisa stammered. Mr. Sands sneered.

"What, is math not your thing? Only one horse to go, then there's no going back! Once they're all together, the horses will help me liberate Garnok. And when that happens, then you can sit at home in your room and cry about how your beloved horsey died for a noble purpose! You would have done the same if you were in my position, but you don't understand that. Consider it an honor that you get to participate in this historic moment. Soon I will decide everything, and everyone will have to ask me for permission for everything. You'd better be grateful, little girl . . ."

Slowly Mr. Sands turned around and started walking away across the concrete floor. The echo of his footsteps was the only thing she could hear until a door at the end of the hangar area slammed shut. Soon Lisa and Starshine were alone again. She couldn't even see him behind the high cage walls, but she knew he was there, only a few feet away. If she really focused, maybe she could hear him breathing or moving, so that she could be reassured that she wasn't alone. But her cries of despair drowned out all other sounds, until finally that too subsided. Then it was as quiet as it could only be once all hope was lost.

Three out of four horses . . . Lisa thought as she lay huddled up on the cage floor. Yes, that's what Mr. Sands said. Starshine and Concorde she knew about, but another one? Was it Meteor or

Tin-Can? What had happened? She was on the verge of tears, thinking of Linda and Alex. And of Anne. She missed them. She needed them.

Then Lisa suddenly started to sing. She sang for herself and for Starshine, for her friends and their horses. She sang for her mother and her father, for everyone who had been or might come to be. She sang because it was the only thing she could do.

Then she heard the faint sound of chains rattling that gradually louder and louder. She realized that it must be the chains they had used to restrain Starshine. It felt as if Starshine were swaying along to her song. And even though she could not see him, she felt him growing stronger from her singing. So she continued.

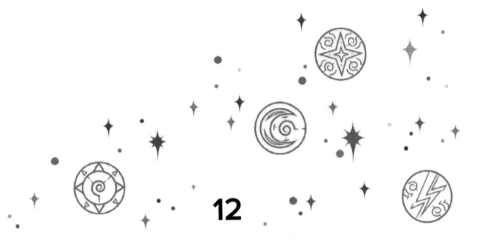

12

On the other side of the door, the footsteps out in the corridor grew closer and closer. They were so loud now, so excruciatingly close that they vibrated within Linda as she lay completely still under the desk, hoping for a miracle. A rift in time could make everything okay again; it could take Sabine away and bring Meteor back.

Another step. And then another. Sabine was taking her time, her pace almost exaggeratedly slow. Linda had a suspicion as to why. Sabine was so sure that she had Linda trapped in a little box that she felt like she could treat herself to toying with her a little.

It was quiet out on the lawn outside the window now. Linda had heard the van drive away just before Sabine's footsteps made everything else disappear. Even so, it was hard to focus on what was going on. Linda didn't want to be here; she wanted to be with Meteor.

Her heart was so heavy that it felt like it was sinking down into the ground. It was hard to breathe. Meteor. She had failed him. Her most loyal friend. Was this how she thanked him?

What if she never got to see him again? The thought was unbearable. To never scratch him under the chin in his scruffy little goatee, never get to lean into him, never sit astride him, never ever inhale his warm, horsey scent at the end of an unusually busy day. Sure, there were other horses, great horses, but none like Meteor. They shared a special bond between them that no other horse could replace. If Meteor didn't come back, then she would stop riding. She would never visit a stable again, never decorate a stall for Christmas with her friends, never sink down into the straw or sneak him a forbidden sugar cube.

The cut on her hand hurt. Linda focused on the pain, wallowed in it. She deserved this misery. She had deserted Meteor; she tied him up in enemy territory. Regardless of her best intentions, she had prevented him from being able to run away.

She heard Sabine out in the corridor. It was a long corridor, but Sabine was getting closer and closer still, almost here.

What if Sabine saw something outside or heard a sudden sound? Something—anything at all—that made her turn on her heels and walk away.

If there had been time, maybe she could have thought of a plan.

There was no time. That realization throbbed inside her in time with the throbbing in her aching arm. Sabine was right outside, and she would enter the room soon. It was only a matter of seconds.

The thin wooden door would not hold Sabine out for very long, even if the antique door lock worked. She should run over there and prop something heavy in front of the door. She should do it NOW, but she felt heavy and listless. Her head felt funny. Her body felt hot and weird; it would not cooperate. She just wanted to lie there on the thick Persian rug under the desk, eyes closed.

If you can't see it, it's not there.

Although it didn't really work that way, of course. If it did, Linda would have known. She would already have had a plan. That was the way Linda was, a girl with a plan. She had read so many books, visited so many worlds, and learned so much. There must be something from all that she could draw on to help her now. But all the stories she had ever read seemed the same now. They were about a girl being chased by the wolf.

"*Open the door and let me come in!*" *said the wolf.*

"*Not by the hair of my chinny, chin, chin!*"

"Here I come!" Sabine's husky voice sounded almost playful.

Linda got up and rushed toward the door. She was running on pure adrenaline, on the encompassing fear that was coursing through her. She spotted a velvet armchair in the corner. It looked heavy. That would do. She shoved it over to prop it against the closed door. She added her own weight, pushing the chair against the wooden door and resisting as best she could with her uninjured arm and shoulder. This was not a permanent solution to her problem, but it would allow her to gain a little time.

"*Then I'll huff, and I'll puff, and I'll blow your house in.*"

If only the others were here! They could have helped her keep Sabine out. She felt herself losing to the force of the door as Sabine kicked the wood.

"I know you're in there. You might as well just let me in." Sabine's voice was a muffled growl, *like an animal.*

She sounded so close, as if she were whispering into Linda's ear. Linda was breathing hard. She heard and saw how the door was beginning to give way. The armchair was being pushed toward Linda and splinters of wood floated down onto the floor as Sabine tried to force the door. She kept hitting, kicking, and scratching. Linda could hear her long fingernails scratching at the wood. She heard a snorting, puffing sound as well. Inhuman sounds. Howling. A squeaking hinge. Here came the wolf.

Linda shivered, but was sweating at the same time. She put her hand up to her cold, sweaty brow. She felt hot to the touch. The heavy armchair moved toward her alarmingly. She pushed against it, sweating and panting from her efforts. It was so heavy. She felt like she couldn't do it anymore.

But with her shoulder pressing against the cool wooden door, she made herself as strong and heavy as she possibly could again. She couldn't back down yet! The sounds Sabine was making made her think of something animalistic and primordially dark. This *something* had teeth and claws, and scratched reality to pieces as the door gave way.

Linda shivered. Even though she was swimming in sweat, she was freezing. Something didn't feel right.

The laceration on her arm was throbbing again.

The scratching and snorting grew and grew. Sabine shrieked, a battle roar that came from deep in her throat. Linda felt the armchair and herself sliding inexorably backward. She trembled through and through with adrenaline and fever.

Then a voice suddenly emerged within her. Was that her own voice?

It said: *Linda, the moon, let it guide you. Feel how the light flows, around you and within you. Think of the moon. Let everything else go. You can do this.*

She collapsed and could hardly keep her eyes open, but she thought of the moon's crescent. She thought of wide-open spaces, dark forest glades bathed in moonlight and birds that sing even though they are in cages. She thought about the stars surrounding the moon in the night sky. She thought about her friends, about the horses.

The Soul Riders and their confidants.

The moonlight flowed into her now and she disappeared into the shade on the far side of the moon. The moon has a back side, and that is a perfect hiding spot. Sabine could not reach her there.

It was so lovely to disappear and easier than she had anticipated.

Cool, she thought before she completely vanished.

Just then the door to the office broke open and the armchair slid, banging into the desk. Wood splinters flew through the room, kicking up dust and sheets of paper from the overfilled bookshelves. Sabine sniffed the air and furiously began flipping books and papers upside down, turning over pieces of furniture.

"Where *are* you?" Sabine growled. Linda felt Sabine's closeness like a dark cloud; she felt the movement of the air as Sabine moved around the room. She could smell Sabine. She smelled of horses, fire, and something rotten, slightly sweet. Linda held her breath, trying not to throw up.

The moon, stay there.

Maybe Sabine could smell Linda as well . . . but she couldn't see her. In the shadow of the moon, in a place where everything was quiet and tranquil, Linda held her breath and waited. Reality was turned inside out where she sat on the dark side of the moon, although still in Mr. Sands's study. She did not know how much longer she dared rely on the protective magic of the moon. The magic took a lot out of her. Her fever rose and with it, her fatigue.

Sabine ran over to the window and tried in vain to open it, although it had bars over it. She cursed and shook her long, thick hair, which swooped back and forth like a whip behind her back.

And then Linda heard Sabine race by, out the door again.

She could hear Sabine's footsteps from out in the corridor. There was a bang, rustling, and a crash as she started tearing apart the room next door. Linda knew that Sabine would not give up until she found her. But for the moment, for a little while longer, Linda was safe. For now, she could breathe. She could rest a little.

Her cell phone vibrating against the carpet roused her again. She was somewhere between sleep and wakefulness as she picked up her phone and read the message. It was from Alex, and in spite of everything she could not help laughing in relief.

On my way. Meanwhile, chill.

She typed a quick response.

I'm hiding from Sabine. Be careful!

Alex's response came right away:

I'm hurrying!

The singing of the birds was audible from out by the orangery. Their strange song made her feel sleepy again. But she kept herself awake, clinging to the knowledge that Alex was on her way. Alex was on her way and they would look for Meteor together. Maybe, just maybe, everything would work out.

As long as she didn't pass out.

13

The cage that Lisa had ended up in was big enough that she could stretch her arms out to the sides, stretch her arms straight up, do some basic exercises, curl up like a kitten on the floor, and then stand up again. Lisa knew because she had tried them all and more. Each time she moved she held her breath in concentration to keep from brushing the metal walls or losing her balance. The electric shocks she had already received still ached in her muscles. Plus, they also seemed to have fried her phone, which she couldn't get to turn on. She heard faint snoring sounds from Starshine, standing a few cages away. That made her smile. In spite of everything, she felt a sort of serenity now. At least they were together, her and Starshine.

You have a lot of time to think when you're locked in a cramped metal cage. So far Lisa had thought about the following things:

Her father.

Her mother.

Starshine.

Mr. Sands had mentioned a third horse, but she wondered which one.

How the other girls were doing.

What the right answer was for the question she had missed on her math test last week.

How to conjugate the Spanish verb *tener*.

Whether it was worth starting to sing the most annoying song in the world to get Mr. Sands to release her from this cage.

If so, which song would that be?

What had actually happened to her cat that had disappeared when she was little.

How long it had been since she had eaten anything.

This morning, right? A blueberry muffin and an apple.

Mmm, muffins.

She happened to think of Jorvik Stables and Herman. Why hadn't they told him about their plans? He could have helped them if they wound up in a pinch. Preferably *before* she ended up in an electrified horse cage.

Obviously because he would have stopped them. He would have taken them to the druids first. Truth. But she had been in too much of a hurry. She had needed to save Starshine. And now here they were—trapped.

And yet, shouldn't they have told some adult where they were going?

What if no one noticed she was gone? What a terrible thought.

How long could you survive without food or water?

Mr. Sands wouldn't let her starve to death, would he?

Lisa shivered. What was Mr. Sands planning to do, anyway? He seemed to need the horses to carry out his plan. Lisa had managed to grasp that much from his rambling talk earlier. But what was he planning to do with her? He could hardly just let her go, not after having locked her in an electrified horse cage. That was unlawful imprisonment, kidnapping, the kind of thing people go to jail for. Under normal circumstances, anyway . . .

Lisa suddenly remembered how uninterested the police had seemed to be in Starshine's kidnapping. Herman had hinted that Mr. Sands had friends high up in the police force. Could he get away with pretty much anything?

She almost wished that she and her father had never moved here, that they had stayed in Norway and she had never met Linda, Alex, or Anne. Everything that had happened—the horses being kidnapped and injured, the villains who seemed to have gotten out of hand and wanted a monster named Garnok for prime minister, the darkness creeping closer from every corner, her father who was in trouble—it had all happened after Lisa came to Jorvik. Did she do all this?

Was it all her fault?

She sank down onto the floor of the cage, careful not to bump any of the metal walls. She huddled in her mother's slightly too-big leather jacket with the fur collar, seeking a little comfort and warmth. All of the Mom-smell was long gone, of course. It smelled like horse and Lisa's perfume now.

But it still helped, at least a little. Starshine whinnied, a soft, muted sound that echoed in the big hangar.

Lisa stood up. Although she could not see Starshine, she knew that he wanted to tell her something.

Starshine whinnied again now, louder this time, and clopped his hooves on the floor. She looked around but saw only darkness in the massive room. But then at the very far edge, on the periphery, she saw something.

Above the cages, up in the darkness of the arched ceiling, there was an opening. Through that she could see the night sky and the stars. They twinkled and blinked at Lisa, where she sat imprisoned, dirty, tired, and desperate.

The stars had helped her before. Would they help her again?

Suddenly Lisa felt like she belonged here on Jorvik, among the stars. They had never shone as brightly as they did tonight, and they glowed for her and Starshine. Soon they would be galloping under the starry sky again. That had happened. She had to believe that it would happen again. Lisa planned to do everything, *everything in her power*, to make sure that it happened. There was no other option.

"We are where we are, and we can't see each other, pal," she said tenderly, in Starshine's direction. "But at least we're looking at the same stars."

14

In the library at Pine Hill Mansion, Linda was fighting uncon-sciousness. She had tried to keep herself occupied by thinking of all the odd journals and books she had found earlier. Mr. Sands seemed so certain that Garnok was in one of the bodies of water around Jorvik somewhere. Maybe in Pinta Bay or by Bay Ridge or over in Harvest Counties? Linda blinked and went over the maps in her head. The Great Reservoir? She tried to stand up, but her legs wouldn't support her anymore and she was forced to sit back down.

"I mustn't go to sleep," Linda mumbled. "I mustn't go to sleep."

Places and words, ripped out of context, kept spinning around in her head. *Favorable flow. Now is the time . . .*

"Don't go to sleep," she told herself. "Not yet." She had to stay on the back side of the moon, hidden in the shadows. She mustn't be visible to Sabine. That would ruin everything. Linda was tired and weak now, however Sabine was strong like a wild animal. The odds that she would be able to run away from Sabine were so low that she couldn't even bear to think about it. So she hid herself with the moon's help, but it was getting harder and harder to stay in the shadows.

She pulled out her cell phone and tried texting Alex one more time. It was hard to hit the right letters. She felt like her head was just spinning. Finally, she gave up and put her phone down again. Alex would hopefully be here soon. Really soon.

"Don't fall asleep . . ."

Unconsciousness was so close now, so comfortable and irresistible . . . She could almost feel it, how sleep was waiting for her on the other side of the moon.

In her feverish delirium, she heard Sabine rooting around in the empty rooms of the mansion like an angry wild boar. After a while—maybe it was minutes but possibly hours, Linda wasn't quite sure—the door to the library flung open once again. She felt Sabine sniffing around right above her head.

"Where did you go, little girl?" Sabine sang softly, as if everything was still just a game to her. "I'm going to find you sooner or later, so you might as well give yourself up now."

When Sabine exhaled, her breath was so close that it reminded Linda of old, rotting apples lying on the ground. Linda breathed through her mouth to avoid smelling the stench. Her whole body trembled with feverish chills.

She felt heavy and slow, sticky and red-hot. Her fever must be really high by now.

The cut on her hand must be infected by now and her body was fighting the infection. As she lay sprawled out on the carpet, her blood cells were fighting each other. And her thoughts wandered back to her school biology lessons, to the chapter in their biology textbook on disease.

Blood poisoning or septicemia happens quickly. What's taking you so long, Alex? Please, get here.

She was starting to have trouble breathing. She felt like she was at high elevation, atop a tall mountain with decreased oxygen and thinner air. Her cheeks glowed red. Her hair was wet and lank with sweat and her eyes hurt. The cut throbbed inside her makeshift bandage, which she probably should have changed a long time ago. Yellow pus and coagulated blood stains showed through the old torn-up T-shirt wrapped around her arm.

Something is wrong, Linda thought. *This is happening too fast. I shouldn't be this sick. Sabine,* she thought. *Sabine is causing me to fall apart like this. She is the plague.*

Then her wandering mind shifted, just as easily as a cloud drifting by in the sky, and was flung further into her feverish half-dreams. She flickered abruptly and violently between various locations, like disjointed film clips.

She could make out some sort of platform out in the ocean where an enormous rumbling engine hissed and bubbled like a maelstrom. A monotone voice droned: *I have seen the eye of Garnok.*

Notes, so many notes, spread out across a desk. The letters danced in front of Linda's eyes, sweeping on toward the big, red eye on the horizon.

Someone spoke to her through the texts. The jumbled words came from a cobweb of illegible, old-fashioned handwriting. She had to duck so they didn't crash into her face. She recognized the handwriting. It was Mr. Sands, and he was writing to her.

Soon, Linda, you, too, will get to see the eye of Garnok. Once we have gathered all four horses together, then it will be time. There is nothing you can do to stop it, so sleep on, young friend. Sweet dreams. Dream of a simpler time. Dream about your friends while there is still some use to dreaming.

Garnok will be here soon.

She managed to shake off the eerie, feverish vision, but was having more and more trouble keeping herself awake now. The room was dark and she could scarcely make out the pattern in the carpet she was lying on. She sat up, closed her eyes, opened her eyes, and closed them again. She clenched her hands into fists. She conjured up the strength she knew was there somewhere inside her, even as her fever made her feeble and weak.

In the dim light that existed between the two worlds, between dream and reality, she thought of Meteor. She thought of the others, of the burden they bore together, the responsibility they shouldered not because they wanted to, but because they were Soul Riders.

She was too weak to turn her head and look out the window. Even so, Linda knew that the moon was rising in the night sky. It must be beautiful out there now, the moonlight over the velvety black forest. That was what she was thinking about just before sleep washed over her and carried her away.

In her dream, Linda woke up on a rocky beach by a deserted, shipwrecked vessel. The beach was full of driftwood and she climbed over a pile of logs, moving a battered sign that said, "Welcome to Pinta Bay." The sign's giant, happy fish grinned at her with sharp teeth. Her clothes and shoes were drenched, but she got up and started walking. She walked until the scenery started to change and shift colors. What had once just been gray and black became pink, and the entire landscape was quickly flooded with pink light. Finally, the pink water rushed around her, pulling her down into the current. She was beneath the surface of the pink water now. Her lungs ached and her heart felt like it was going to explode.

Linda fought her way back up to the surface, guided by the brilliant, bright pink light. Everything was now completely pink. She swam to a new beach and staggered ashore.

Where was she? *When* was this? Was this the past or the future? She thought maybe she had been here before, in one of her visions. However, this time it felt more real. She could feel the pink light burning into her retinas.

This was a dream, but at the same time it seemed like so much more than just a dream.

On the beach, right by some strange, brightly colored plants that were slowly swaying back and forth at the water's edge, sat a girl looking out at the pink water.

"Anne!" Linda yelled her name, but it was as if Anne didn't see her. Anne kept staring out at the water. Linda walked over to her and saw that Anne was crying, calmly and silently.

"Concorde," Anne said. "I couldn't save you."

Linda grabbed hold of Anne, shook her shoulders, lifted her face so that she could look into her eyes. But Anne just stared blankly straight ahead, past Linda.

"It's too late," Anne said quietly. "They took him from me. Pandoria took him, and there wasn't anything I could do. Concorde is dead!"

"No!" screamed Linda, although Anne didn't seem to be able to hear her. "That's not true! It's *not* too late! Don't you understand? This hasn't happened yet! Listen to me, Anne! We can fix this, but we have to do it together. You have to find Concorde and bring him back to our world."

Anne sighed deeply and stared sadly at the ground. Then she stood up and started walking along the beach lined with pink rocks.

"Anne! Don't go!" Linda yelled.

In the dream she rushed after Anne. She grabbed her drooping shoulders and—yes!—finally Anne turned around. Her blue eyes opened wide in astonishment when she saw who was there with her. Linda's voice was clear as she put her hand on Anne's cheek and said:

"Anne, can you hear me? It's me, Linda."

15

"Hurry up, buddy! Linda needs us!"

Alex and Tin-Can galloped swiftly through Pine Hill Forest, and *how* they galloped! Twigs snapped, a flurry of pine needles swirled into the air as Alex had to lie down flat on her stomach in the saddle. She had to push away several big branches as they sped along the increasingly narrow trail. Steam rose off Tin-Can's golden-brown coat and the air was filled with the warm, sweet scent of horse. There was total silence apart from the sounds of hoofbeats and Alex's and Tin-Can's heavy breathing.

When the path grew so narrow that it was hardly discernable anymore, Tin-Can began to stumble. Alex dismounted right away.

"Poor guy," she said and gave him a little water. "You're so tired you're starting to trip. Are you okay, sweetie?"

She bent down and checked to make sure that his leg and hoof were all right. She scraped a small rock out of his right front hoof and ran her hands over Tin-Can's leg to feel for anything that seemed tender anywhere. Everything seemed okay. Tin-Can must have stumbled because he was tired. Alex knew the feeling. She was also exhausted from the pace they had been keeping. Tin-Can's neck was lathery and there was foam coming from the corners of his mouth. Alex's cheeks were red, and she could feel the throbbing in her temples developing into a headache.

"Okay," Alex said, patting her horse. "We'll keep going, but maybe a little slower, or . . . ? What do you say?"

They rode on, deeper into the woods. Now and then she dug her phone out of her pocket to check if she had service and if Linda had been in touch again. But her phone was quiet. Alex sighed and tried to keep her worry at bay.

No new texts. No missed calls. Alex had a sinking feeling in the pit of her stomach as she thought about what might have happened. The last time Linda texted, she wrote that Sabine was in the house and that she was hiding from her.

And then? What had happened after that? Alex didn't dare call Linda. What if she had forgotten to turn off her ringer and the call gave away her hiding place? Alex wouldn't be able to forgive herself if she flushed Linda out, straight into Sabine's hands, even if it was by mistake.

Sabine . . . They had suspected that she had something to do with Mr. Sands ever since they had seen her chatting with him in the school parking lot. The time when she had transformed, turning from an annoying teenage girl into something wild and bestial. Now Alex was sure.

"We can't be too late, Tin-Can! We have to find Linda before Sabine does," Alex said.

She talked to Tin-Can the whole time now as the Jorvegian countryside raced by them as if in a fog. The silence was too difficult otherwise. Alex hated silence. It made her uncomfortable. She was sure to start talking, jumping, laughing, joking, anything, just to avoid the silence. Sometimes she thought that perhaps she was afraid to find out what was hiding behind all the noise she filled her life with. It was easier to get lost in there, she thought, among the silence. So she continued to talk to Tin-Can in a low, intimate voice, as if he might answer her at any moment.

But of course he didn't answer her. Instead he shook his disheveled mane and trotted on. Alex could tell from his steps, which were less surefooted than usual, that he was increasingly becoming more tired.

"What a hero you are, dear friend," Alex said, petting his sweaty neck. An owl hooted high up in the trees before flying away.

At this point it was almost completely dark in the forest. Alex was going too fast to notice how chilly the air was. It was the type of cold that fills the late fall, after Halloween, when the last flame-colored leaves have fallen off the trees and all the students start drinking hot tea instead of soda during breaks. But Alex didn't feel the cold at all, just her hunger and tiredness, and the aching of her entire body. Her muscles screamed with exhaustion after all her hours on horseback. But Tin-Can galloped on. She felt lucky that she was riding the world's strongest horse.

Finally, the forest ended and Pine Hill Mansion's scary grounds loomed before her. She had arrived.

It all felt like something out of a wicked fairy tale, and Alex was riding right into it. She did so without hesitating. After all, she was desperately trying to help her friend.

In Alex's jacket pocket, her phone went black as its battery died. It was only her and Tin-Can now.

To get all the way out to Dark Core's headquarters, you had to cross the narrow bridge that led to the massive building. Finally, Jessica rode over it, just as poised and restrained as usual. Her big horse practically danced beneath her, as if they were at a dressage show. She reached the industrial complex in just a few minutes. And in the distance, behind the buildings, she could just make out the big portal, the portal that had been her goal. Hopefully she wasn't too late, she thought, and her dark eyes turned almost completely black. How had Anne managed to get to Pandoria so quickly, and only on her first try? It was absurd! Maybe they had underestimated the Soul Riders after all. She hoped that Concorde would be ready for transport back from Pandoria. Otherwise Jessica didn't know what to do. She couldn't bring him back until his full essence had materialized in Pandoria; then it would be time to bring him to the sacrificial table along with the other Starbreeds . . .

The perfect victim. So handsome, so pitiful. So . . . useful. Jessica grinned and clicked for her horse to move on. She was still smiling as she dismounted and led her horse through the enormous gate into HQ.

16

The enormous Norway maple had stood in the courtyard since Jon Jarl's glory days, when Jorvik Stables had served as the royal stables. Its thick branches and substantial root system had seen all sorts of things: lives kindled and extinguished, horses and riders who came and went. The tree's own seasons were capricious, impossible to predict. Some years the leaves were still on the tree well into December, but sometimes they fell when it got cold even before Halloween. No, you never knew when it would drop its leaves. It was as if the tree were living its own life, just like so many other things here in Jorvik. The moon, for example. The moon should not have been full yet, but it glowed, round and white, above the stable roof all the same.

When Herman opened the stable door, the big gravel courtyard was bathed in moonlight. The horses in their stalls had just been given their supper and were sleepily blinking their big, friendly eyes while they chewed their hay. Herman was about to return to his house across the courtyard where he had lived for many years and go to bed. Silence and an uncommon sort of peace prevailed over the stable.

It's so quiet here without Alex and the other girls, Herman thought, and smiled slightly. He was used to nonstop chatter, the sounds of teenagers coming and going. There was always someone who had forgotten their riding crop and had to rush out of the ring or a riding-school student who just had to hug his favorite horse one last time before his parents came to pick him up. Those early mornings and late evenings before and after, when everyone had a chance to rest, were a welcome break. Soon he would go to bed and sleep briefly but well, dreamlessly as always. But right now, for just a little longer, he was alone with his thoughts. He should have brought his evening tea with him out to the yard, he thought. It was a clear, beautiful night.

Then he stopped, looking at the view of the ocean and the fall foliage.

The big, red leaves came almost all the way up to the top of his boots. The fall wind that blew in after the last class must have brought them all down. Typical. He shook his head, fetched his rake and scooper, and got to work raking them all up. He didn't want to wait until morning.

It took time to rake leaves. Herman was busy scooping one of his many leaf piles into the wheelbarrow when he became aware of the sound of hooves.

Who could be out riding this late at night?

Turning away from the wheelbarrow, he looked behind him. A woman dressed in gray rode toward him on the back of a beautiful dappled gray horse.

Elizabeth.

He raised his hand in greeting. Elizabeth smiled and dismounted.

"Excellent," she said. "I was hoping you would still be up."

"You know me, Elizabeth. I haven't slept properly since Jon Jarl's day. Five hours is enough for me."

He laughed but then quickly stopped when he saw the look on Elizabeth's face. Her big, light-gray eyes were darker than usual as she twisted the thick, reddish-blond braid that hung over her shoulder.

Even her horse seemed focused, serious. Herman had seen many horses in his day: tiny little Falabella miniature horses and enormous Shire horses, black and white, fiery and calm, well-groomed and neglected. Elizabeth's mare Calliope, with her sleek, almost Arabian head and blended coat of silver-gray and dazzling white, was one of the most beautiful horses he had ever seen. In the bright moonlight her dappled coat was extra pronounced: every round spot, each variation in the light-gray string of pearls that were her markings, was bathed in the cold light. The mare's ears were cocked, and her velvety muzzle was tinged with pink.

Elizabeth had had mares for as long as Herman had known her, never stallions or geldings, and they had almost always been dapple-gray. It suited her, he thought.

"She looks great, Calliope does," Herman said and stroked the bridge of the horse's nose.

Elizabeth smiled and stroked her horse's neck. Still she said nothing.

"What's on your heart, Elizabeth?"

"The girls, Herman. Are they here?" Her voice sounded tenser than usual.

Herman's eyes were as blue as the sky. "No, Elizabeth. They're not here."

"And they're not with the druids either," Elizabeth sighed. "I need to get ahold of them. Have you heard from them? Do you know where they are?"

Herman scratched his big chin, trying to appear calmer than he felt.

"They were supposed to go to the Secret Stone Circle, I told them that. But I didn't think that they had set out yet. Fall break just started, you know?"

Elizabeth furrowed her brow.

"I thought they were still here. I was going to ride over here and gather them up so they could learn the Light Ceremony. It's time now, and fall break felt like a great time to do it. Oh, I . . ."

"Wait a second," Herman cut her short. "I'll try to call. You can usually always reach them by phone or text. I think Alex even sleeps with her phone under her pillow. We'll get ahold of them. Don't you worry, Elizabeth."

Herman, who was usually the personification of calm, felt something dark and uncertain flutter inside his checkered shirt. Did he fail at looking after the Soul Riders? Should he have kept a closer eye on them?

He started calling around. Alex first. *The subscriber you have dialed cannot be reached at this time.* Linda, no answer. Lisa, straight to voicemail. Anne's phone also seemed to be off. He sent a group text to all four of them.

Hi, girls! Please call me! I need to reach you.

He stared at his phone for a long time before putting it back in his pocket and shaking his head.

"None of them are answering right now, but I texted them. I'm sure they'll get back to me soon."

Elizabeth's eyes were still dark gray, but she did not look particularly mad, more sad. And disappointed. Herman had known Elizabeth for many years now, but he had never seen her angry. Elizabeth didn't get angry; she got disappointed. Somehow that was worse. Herman sighed deeply and tugged on his own gray hair.

"I'm sure they'll be in touch with you soon," he said. "It'll all work out, you'll see."

"We can hope so," Elizabeth said slowly. "We can certainly hope so."

"I'll be in touch as soon as I hear anything from the girls," Herman said. "Unlike the druids, I have a cell phone and I can be reached around the clock."

He caught a reluctant smile spread across Elizabeth's lips before she regained full control of her composure.

"Well," Elizabeth said as she mounted her horse, "if the world ends, it probably won't be due to cell phone problems. You know how to find me if you hear anything. Let me know as soon as you hear from the girls!"

Elizabeth urged her horse onward and called back, "I have to get to Fripp and the druids now! Maybe they've heard some news!" as she trotted away. Calliope's coat glowed against the red leaves in the darkness, silver, red, and black. Then they were gone. Herman stood and listened to the sound of the hoofbeats clip-clopping away, gradually ebbing into the night.

"Give him my regards," Herman said and picked his rake up again. He moved at a leisurely pace, just as always, but his mind was racing.

Why didn't the girls answer?

17

The water was gone, Concorde, too. Anne was standing inside a tall, Pandorian, church-like building with statues and strange inscriptions. Her dizziness had returned, that wobbly carousel feeling. She grabbed ahold of a marble statue of a girl on horseback. There was something familiar about the girl, but Anne's mind was so sluggish, she couldn't process what she was seeing. Why did she recognize this rider?

There was something important here, something she had forgotten. She kept exploring the space, running her hands over rough runestones and smooth marble. The space was trying to tell her something, but what?

Fripp, she thought, Fripp knows, but the statue of Fripp isn't here. Where had she seen it?

Had she seen it? She was so sure she had. Now she wasn't so sure any longer.

How did I end up here? she thought tiredly, looking around.

I dove. I dove down into the pool, toward Concorde. He called to me, and I jumped in after him. My mother was there, too. Where did I end up? And where's Concorde?

Concorde. The thought of him made her stand up taller, move farther into the temple-like building. She had to find Concorde.

She came upon more rooms filled with limestone, marble, tile with complicated patterns and inscriptions. One looked more like a dining room from another era, a time when life and movement had prevailed in the empty, echoing rooms.

The nasty voices had quieted. Maybe they couldn't reach her in here. Anne was alone with her vague, sluggish thoughts.

"Anne?"

She jumped. The voice came out of nowhere, from the deepest recesses of her brain, from hope and longing and despair. She recognized the voice immediately. But could it really be true . . . ?

"Anne?" the voice said again, quietly and patiently. "It's me, Linda."

Anne felt a light touch on her cheek, as if someone had cautiously run their hand over it. She shuddered because it was so unexpected. She looked around, her eyes roving, but she couldn't see anyone else there. But she felt her. It *was* Linda!

"Linda!" Anne gasped, her whole body feeling warm. "Is it really you? Promise me that it's you!"

"I promise," Linda's voice replied. "I can see you, but maybe you can't see me. Or can you? It doesn't matter. As long as you can hear me." It sounded as if she was smiling. Now Anne was smiling, too. Tears of joy welled up in her eyes. She had been so alone, so very unhappy. Was that possibly behind her now?

Did she dare believe it?

"I don't really know what's going on, or how I am in contact with you," Linda continued. "But I'm here now. Well, not *here*, if you get what I mean. I'm hiding from Sabine inside Pine Hill Mansion. I might be dreaming. Maybe I'm unconscious. Maybe I'm even . . . no, sorry Anne. I'm just thinking out loud. This place is just too muddled. Where are you, anyway?"

"It's hard to explain," Anne said slowly. "It's a kind of unreality. I think it's called Pandoria."

"Pandoria," Linda repeated thoughtfully. Should she recognize that name? She wasn't sure. "What does it look like there? Please tell me."

"Everything is pink," Anne responded. "Even the sun and the shadows. Do you remember that painting we saw at school a while ago? The clock that was kind of melting into a desert landscape? This is a little bit like that, only pink."

"Salvador Dalí," Linda's voice replied. "Yeah, I see. You mean, like, totally crooked? It feels really surreal where I am, too . . ."

"It's super hard to find," Anne continued. "I think everything is totally different here, even the air. Linda, I'm scared. What if I'm stuck here?"

Anne felt Linda squeeze her hand tight, a gesture that said, *You're going to be okay.* They were quiet for a moment.

"Why did you go off without us?" Linda wondered.

"I had to," Anne replied. "Concorde needed me."

"Did you find him?"

"I think so," Anne said. "Sometimes he's so close, but then it's like he slides away from me. And now it feels like I might never get out of here."

"Of course you'll get out of there!" Linda said. "And you'll have Concorde with you."

Anne smiled again, because Linda had painted such a reassuring picture. But her smile quickly faded when she thought of what Jessica and the creature pretending to be Alex had said—that she was worthless, she had no friends, she was no one.

Who could she trust?

They were quiet again. Everything was *too* quiet, Anne thought.

"Linda?" she said hesitantly. "Are you there?"

"Yes, I'm here."

I'm here. Two beautiful words that inspired hope. Anne decided to risk trusting Linda a little, trusting the warmth she felt when Linda spoke, the warmth that chased away the shadows and the doubt and filled her with purpose.

It was time for courage.

"It's time for you to continue," Linda said in a gentle voice. "I can't explain how I know this, but I know that Concorde is there, outside, that he's waiting for you. He misses you. Go out and find him. And do you know where you need to go after that?"

The words came out of Anne before she was aware that she had said them out loud.

"Yes, to the Secret Stone Circle."

"Yes." In another world, and yet here. Linda nodded, moving her thick, black bangs out of her eyes as the sea breeze caught her hair. "We'll be together soon, all four of us. Our horses, too. I just have to take care of a little . . . uh, thing first. I'll tell you more later, it's too complicated to go into now."

"I bet," Anne replied. "I've seen some pretty sick things myself."

Linda laughed. "Go, Anne, go now. I promise, you'll manage! I'm here if you need me again."

"Thank you," Anne whispered. Her eyes gleamed with tears of joy. She stood up straight as she walked out of the tall building, out into the unknown, out toward Concorde. He was out there somewhere, and she didn't plan to give up until she found him.

Inside Pine Hill, in another world, Linda smiled broadly to herself in her feverish sleep. "Exactly," she mumbled and nodded faintly. "We never give up."

The sky over Pandoria exploded in hundreds of shades of pink. Anne looked up and allowed herself to become absorbed in the colors, in the luminous, glowing sun. For the first time since she came here, she thought that Pandoria was actually a beautiful place.

"Thank you, Linda," she whispered.

Anne wished she was as brave as Alex, as smart as Linda, and as persistent as Lisa. But she was not like her friends, no matter how fond of them she was. In this life, her only life, she could only be herself. And thanks to Linda, she now knew that she had to find her own way to manage. That was the trick: to rely on who she was herself.

"Just so, my girl."

Anne jumped and turned quickly in the direction the voice had come from, but she couldn't see anything other than the enormous, blinding sun shining its strong, pink rays upon her.

"Mom?" she whispered.

The sun twinkled. With its warming rays on her back, Anne proceeded ahead, deeper into Pandoria's unreality.

18

Lisa didn't know how, but she had slept for a while. Through the opening in the roof, she saw the stars. She looked to the side, at Starshine's cage. In spite of everything, she was glad that he was there with her. She talked to him the whole time, babbling about whatever, childhood memories and birthdays, favorite foods and summer vacations. She told him how happy she was that they had met each other and how she had dreamed of him long before she came to Jorvik.

"I knew that you existed for real, Starshine."

He gave her a friendly snort from his cage.

So close, and yet so far.

Now she suddenly felt Starshine notice something. She peered over toward the door that Mr. Sands had come from earlier. What was that sound? A muffled, rumbling engine noise—and it definitely seemed to be coming closer . . . ?

"Do you hear it, too?" she whispered.

Starshine whinnied and scratched with his hooves. An enormous door opened and Katja came in, and behind her a large crane drove into the hangar. And at the end of the crane, suspended by two wide leather straps, hung a lifeless horse.

Lisa gasped. Her heart sank like a stone.

Meteor. Had they . . . killed him?

The crane with Meteor's lifeless body dangling from the end rolled slowly along. The tires crunched as they neared the metal horse cages. When the crane got closer, Lisa could tell that Meteor was weakly moving his tail. He was alive! But he was badly injured. At least one of his hind legs looked broken, and his skin was covered in deep sores. His big head and thick neck hung at a terrible angle from the sling straps. She heard Starshine's muted whinnies. Lisa felt a pang in her heart as she thought of what Meteor must have been through. And Linda. Where was she? Had they caught her, too?

The man driving the crane brought it up to the cage beside Lisa's and slowly lowered the horse's body. Meteor landed heavily on the floor, and Lisa heard his big body pushing against the cramped cage walls. The man operating the crane got out and started walking toward Meteor's cage to turn on the electricity, but he was stopped by Katja, who nodded knowingly at Meteor.

Katja and the crane driver left and a sleepy silence took over the hangar once more. Outside the window opening to the roof, the stars were visible far away in the universe.

"It just gets worse and worse," Lisa told herself, and buried her face deep in her hands.

19

Late that night, the stars gleamed with peculiar clarity all over Jorvik. They shone the clearest of all above the Secret Stone Circle, although it was quiet and calm up there. The druids who lived there went to bed early and missed the Big Dipper, Ursa Major, and Orion's Belt. When they drew their curtains and crawled into bed, they missed the other constellations in the sky, too. The ones that aren't in the astronomy books. Up on top of the Secret Stone Circle, right by a little hole in the rock face where only someone who is very small could live, stood the one who could see all the stars. He pushed open his little wooden door and peered outside.

Someone had lit a fire in the fire pit, where he often sat and contemplated things. In the gleam of the fire he could see who it was. Her golden hair looked almost red in the glow of the flames. She wore gray, as always, and she looked serious as she sat huddled on a large stone with her horse grazing beside her.

"Elizabeth," Fripp said, striding over to the fire pit. "I've been expecting you."

"Imagine, Fripp, that I almost sensed that," Elizabeth said, watching the little being with a slight smile. He reminded her of a squirrel, if you can imagine a blue, slightly overgrown squirrel. Once, a long time ago, Elizabeth had made the mistake of calling him that. A squirrel, that is. She wouldn't make that mistake again. When all was said and done, he was no squirrel. He was a cosmic being. She should have known that, if anyone did.

Fripp sat down on one of the runestones close to the campfire, letting his paws rest over the glimmering pink inscriptions. He raised his head and looked up at the stars in the clear night sky.

"When the stars change direction, a new era can begin," he mumbled.

"What do you mean by that, Fripp?" Elizabeth asked.

"Surely you must know this, Elizabeth?" Fripp grunted. "The Soul Riders and their guiding stars, the sisterhood of the last Soul Riders," he added in a dreamy voice. His eyes were fixed so intently on the fire that Elizabeth wondered if he could see something there that she couldn't see. All she saw were embers glowing red, and at the top of the log fire, a bit of brush being swallowed by the reddish-yellow flame.

"Yes, Fripp," Elizabeth replied. "I know. I was there, wasn't I?"

It was the stars that had united the four Soul Riders before they could even understand it themselves. The morning that Lisa arrived in Jorvik, they had all seen strange things in the sky. Lisa had seen a star, Anne a sun, Alex a lightning bolt, and Linda a moon. While Jorvik slept, the four girls had been awake looking at the same sky, but at different constellations. That was when things had been set in motion. Elizabeth herself had received a firsthand view of it.

She nodded thoughtfully now. "Yes, we're entering a new phase now."

"And it's certainly about time," Fripp said. His eyes were focused on the runes now, as if he were speaking to them. He did that sometimes, talked to runes. Nothing unusual about that.

"Although," Fripp continued, "I hadn't counted on your coming alone tonight. According to my calculations they should already be here by now, all four of them. Along with their horses. It's important that they get started on their training as soon as possible."

"Believe me, Fripp, I know," Elizabeth said, and then sighed gently. "Calliope and I have been out searching, but no sign of them yet. Herman didn't know anything either. But they *must* be on their way back here, right?"

Fripp got up off the runestone and started to wander around. He stopped by the fire, which was beginning to die down into muted, dark red embers. He picked up a stick, poked at the fire, and watched the flames kick up. If only it were as easy to speed up the Soul Riders, he thought. He said out loud, "You know that I can't read humans as easily as I can read runes. But that Anne, she was actually here."

"Here? What are you saying? Alone? Where is she now?"

"So many questions at once," Fripp sighed. "I helped her get to Pandoria. I know maybe I shouldn't have done that, but trust me, it was the right thing to do. She also wouldn't have taken 'no' for an answer. And she learned the magic of the sun's circle faster than anyone I've ever seen before. Trust me, Elizabeth, she'll be back soon. Although after the fact, I can now see that maybe it was a little foolish. She shouldn't have wound up in Pandoria all on her own so early on, but I sent her there because I knew that she could handle it."

An angry wrinkle had appeared between Elizabeth's eyebrows. Fripp spoke more quickly now.

"And then—when Anne comes back—the other three won't be far behind. I see that in the stars."

Elizabeth looked up at the starry sky with her furrowed brow. "How exactly do you do that, if I might ask?"

Fripp grunted and started blathering on about ancient stars, the heavens, and the cosmic balance. Elizabeth raised one hand in a gesture to stop him.

"You know what? Forget about it. It doesn't matter. We can sit here and talk ourselves silly about runes, stars, and the cosmos, but it won't help us. The only thing we need right now is those four girls, together, right here. They have to come here and learn the Light Ceremony book. It's time they learn how to influence the flow between Jorvik's reality and Pandoria's unreality."

"Yes!" Fripp exclaimed, waving one paw. "Then they can make cracks and sustain the vital balance between reality and unreality, everyday life and magic."

"Precisely," Elizabeth nodded.

"And the book?" Fripp asked. "Is it true what the druid Avalon said, that you have to ride all the way to Cauldron Swamp to get it from Pi? Won't the copies that we have here do? If you have to go, that will give us even less time later when . . ."

"We have to ride there," Elizabeth said, her voice firm. "It cannot be helped. We need to perform the ceremony in its strongest form. The copies of the book that the druids have aren't even close to being powerful enough. If you had read a little more and looked up at the stars a little less over the last few centuries, you would have known that. The journey to the Light Ceremony book can be both difficult and long, I am well aware of that. That's why it's so important that the girls get here soon."

"So, you will leave for Cauldron Swamp as soon as possible," Fripp said. "As soon as they have come here and gotten to rest a little. Yes. So be it." He looked up at her. "Have you given any thought to possible precautionary measures?"

Elizabeth's voice sounded bewildered. "You mean . . . the apple? Fripp, there's no need for that! We don't have time to ride to Scarecrow Hill and pick it beforehand, you know that. The time may come when we need it, but that time is not yet upon us. And things aren't so bad off with Pi. She's just gotten a little eccentric from being alone there in the Swamp for so long. She's not a . . ."

"Not a witch?" Fripp said suggestively.

A cold wind swept in over the fire and made the flames flicker before they flared up, burning stronger than before. Elizabeth pulled her gray cloak tighter around herself. "Exactly," she replied. "She is one of the druids. She will give us the book!"

"I see nothing about this in either the stars or the runes," Fripp said. "Well, surely you're right. As I'm right about the girls. They'll be here soon," he said confidently and then gazed back up at the stars.

"We can hope so, Fripp," Elizabeth said and looked dolefully up at the sky, searching for the Big Dipper. For a second, she felt like a little girl out on a big grassy hillside, her grandmother pointing out the constellations to her. Then she located the Big Dipper and continued, "Yes, we can hope that the stars will guide the girls true, back to each other."

Each other—Elizabeth used that expression often. *Together* was another typical Elizabeth word, Fripp thought. Fripp had noticed that humans were very much in favor of doing things in groups. A strange way of dealing with problems, if you asked him, but it seemed popular. And where the Soul Riders were concerned, it was the only way. He stood up.

"Well, goodnight then."

"Goodnight, Fripp. We'll hope for good news tomorrow."

"Yes."

With a deep sigh that made his tail tremble, Fripp entered his little burrow and shut the door. He settled down in his sleeping spot and planned for the following day. He didn't know what would happen in the morning when he woke up, and that bothered him. Usually his days were carefully planned out. Not anymore. *Humans*, he thought and then sighed deeply, *are fickle*. You can never predict what they will do next. They say one thing and do something else. The stars, on the other hand . . . The stars might be blind, but you can rely on them.

Outside Fripp's burrow, a star twinkled and fell from the sky. Elizabeth saw the shooting star and leaned against Calliope's long, snow-white mane, and smiled. "I know what my wish is, my love," she mumbled and closed her eyes. Calliope nudged her with her nose in response.

Many, many miles away, a girl looked up at the same sky.

"Did you see that, Tin-Can?" Alex said, patting her horse. "When you see a shooting star, you get to make a wish."

She pressed herself against her horse's warm body, closed her eyes, and whispered her wish.

20

When Lisa was little she had devoured books about horses. She took extra delight in stories in which the girl—because it was almost always a girl—and the horse had an extremely special bond, something inexplicable and vaguely mystical. The horse understood the girl in a way no one else did. Alone in the stall, it was like the horse could read her mind.

In Jorvik she had really been able to live out her horse-girl dreams, ever since she had met Starshine for the first time. And everything wonderful that had happened since she had arrived in Jorvik seemed to somehow be connected to Starshine. When she was near him, she felt like everything that was sick and broken could truly heal. The song, the beams of light, the stars only came in Starshine's presence.

Now Lisa was sitting in her cage and wishing that she could feel that bond, if only for a brief moment! That mystical, inexplicable something.

But the magic wouldn't come to her. She had tried singing, stretching her hands in Starshine's direction in the hope of feeling what she had been so close to being able to touch earlier. But he was just too far away from her. Lisa looked around in her jail of iron and steel and sighed. Hadn't Linda mentioned at some point that people used to use iron as a weapon against those poor women accused of being witches in the witch trials? The old superstitions said that magic couldn't get out or in if you enclosed it in iron.

They burned women at the stake, Lisa thought with a shiver. If they didn't manage to drown them first.

She was shaken from her dark thoughts when she heard Starshine start tugging on the chains he was tied up with. The big, heavy horse pulled and yanked. He brayed, a loud and shrill neigh, and then Lisa heard a sharp bang that made her ears ring.

"Starshine, what are you doing?" she screamed. "Are you trying to kick apart the cage? You're going to get zapped!"

Starshine snorted in response, as if he were trying to tell her something. Or maybe tell Meteor something?

"You're trying to kick apart the cage, aren't you? But that won't work. It's electrified!"

Starshine neighed again and then Lisa heard another loud bang that rattled the glass in the skylights.

"Stop it!" Lisa yelled. "You're going to hurt yourself!"

She heard Starshine breathing hard. The electricity must have really knocked the strength out of his muscles. Oh, if only she could shut off the power to Starshine's cage! He would have kicked the cage apart in no time.

Then it suddenly hit her. Meteor's cage didn't have any power! Katja hadn't turned the power on to his. It was as if she were on the verge of something important, an idea. Was Starshine thinking the same thing in his own horsey way?

"Think, Lisa, think!" she urged herself. "Think, think, *think*."

And then it was as if a shock raced through her, but this time it wasn't actually made of electricity. She suddenly realized something that clarified the whole situation. She realized that if Meteor were healthy and strong, he could kick open the door to his cage without any problem. And healing injuries was exactly what Lisa had the ability to do! She stood right by the door to her cage, so close that she could almost feel Meteor on the other side.

"Meteor, Starshine, I'm sorry I'm so slow, you know? But I'm only human."

She smiled and then she started to sing. She sang about loving horses; her friendship with Alex, Linda, and Anne; missing her father; and her mother. The song rose from her chest, out through the bars.

Behind the notes of the music, she started to hear faint scratching sounds coming from Meteor's cage. It sounded as if the big horse was slowly coming to, attempting a few motions as a cautious test. After another little bit, she heard rattling coming from Meteor's cage. He must have stood up. His legs were holding him!

Lisa stopped singing and felt full of happiness. She was still able to heal. Her singing really *was* magic.

She stood in silence and listened to Meteor's bewildered snorts. Starshine seemed to answer him. They snorted, sighed, and whickered, as if they were having a genuine conversation. Lisa almost laughed. It was so sweet when the two horses chatted with each other, like old friends.

Then, as if out of nowhere, Meteor made a loud whinny, and over the metal wall of the cage, Lisa saw him toss his mane high into the air. A second later there was a bang so loud that it temporarily deafened Lisa, and the whole metal cage shook. When the ringing in her ears finally stopped, she had to look over the cage door before she could believe what she was hearing. It sounded like hooves galloping over concrete. And sure enough, she saw Meteor race out into the darkened hangar, as if he were riding in the biggest riding hall in the world. Jorvik Stables's ring was like a toy compared to this, and Meteor seemed—in spite of everything—to be enjoying being able to gallop freely around the enormous floor.

Then it was as if something suddenly occurred to him. He came to an abrupt stop and walked back over to Starshine and Lisa, who were still trapped in their metal cages.

With a whinny that really sounded more like a laugh, Meteor walked over to the electrical panel on the wall next to the cages, where Mr. Sands had turned on the power to Lisa's cage.

"Uh, Meteor, you're not planning to . . . ?" Lisa stammered.

She saw Meteor turn around so his flanks were facing the electrical panel and then he raised his hind legs in a powerful kick. There was a crash, followed by sparks and crackling sounds. The sparks made Lisa drop to the floor. Everything went black.

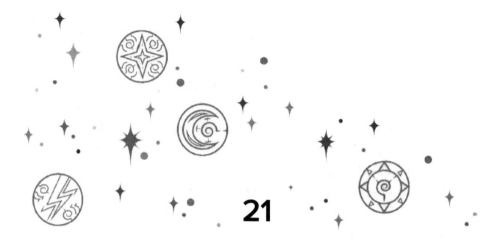

21

Darkness and night had fallen over Pine Hill Mansion and Jorvik as Alex and Tin-Can rode into the extensive courtyard. The mansion's big, unlit windows stared gloomily at them. The whole place seemed abandoned, Alex thought. If it weren't for Linda's text message, she would have bet it was deserted, too. She knew better, though. So, she dismounted and led Tin-Can along behind her as she started looking around. One of the light bulbs in the outdoor lamps in front of the mansion had burned out, so most of the front of the mansion was shrouded in darkness. Even though Alex had a flashlight in her backpack, she didn't dare use it. She didn't want anyone to know she was here. If she was going to help Linda, she was going to have to sneak in undiscovered. Sabine was surely still in there. Hopefully she hadn't found Linda yet . . .

A gloomy, heavy mood saturated the air. It made the hairs on her upper arms stand up, even inside all her layers of clothing she was wearing. The moon had crawled behind a big cloud, as if it wanted to hide.

Was this what evil felt like?

She thought of the old photograph they had found, where Mr. Sands was standing outside Pine Hill Mansion. That was another time, at least one world war removed, perhaps even two. The car he had been standing next to in the picture looked really old. But then again, he was, too.

She shivered, both from the cold, clammy, raw evening air and also from her own thoughts. With her hands stuffed into her jacket pockets, she continued her exploration.

"You stay here and stand guard, okay?" she told her horse. For a second, she considered tying him, but decided not to. "You'll stay put even if I don't tie you, right?"

Tin-Can responded with a muffled little whinny and stretched a smidge, seeming proud of his assignment. She smiled—Tin-Can always made her smile—and felt her way along in the darkness.

It wasn't just the air that was quivering with evil. The house itself and the rundown, somehow off-kilter grounds around it also made Alex feel uneasy. There was something dark and menacing about this whole place. And what was the deal with the birds everywhere? Why did they want to stay in such a creepy place? That in itself was downright creepy.

Although actually, she was glad about the birds. At least they provided some kind of company on this raw, chilly night. She could also hear Tin-Can munching on the apple she had given him. The sound of his chewing somehow always made her feel calm.

Wait. Was there another noise, too? A snorting, sniffing sound? A dog, maybe? As long as it wasn't an angry guard dog, she thought. She stopped and looked around to try and decide where the sound was coming from.

That was when she saw him. Big, wicked, and coal-black, definitely on his guard—yup. Only he wasn't a dog, but a horse. He stood stomping beside the stairs with his long ears cocked attentively. But luckily he hadn't noticed her yet. The whites of his eyes were exposed as his dull, black eyes scanned back and forth, back and forth. He was so close that Alex could see his muscles tensing under his glossy black coat. His entire body was covered in serious scars.

Khaan. So Sabine was still in the house.

Alex walked toward the big horse and watched as he puffed out his nostrils and stretched back his ears. His teeth, which were showing now, looked sharper than Tin-Can's and more predatory. *That horse eats something besides hay,* she thought, and shuddered. Then she collected her thoughts. With her back straight, her eyes wide, she summoned the lightning from within. *Please let it come this time!* An electric hum spread through her. It grew louder and louder, tuning her like an instrument.

Yes, she was ready now.

She looked back at Tin-Can and then she raised her hand toward Khaan. She let a bolt of lightning flash out of her and land near him. He whinnied and his black eyes almost rolled into his head. Then he galloped into the woods, away from the pink lightning bolts that kept shooting out of Alex's hand.

"Yes!" she exclaimed to Tin-Can and high-fived the fading lighting, which crackled as she touched it.

One less thing to worry about.

She heard Khaan disappearing into the trees and hurried up the beautifully appointed stone stairway. Then she saw that the front door was ajar. She turned around and looked down at Tin-Can. He looked back with his safe, brown eyes. Alex eyed the main entrance and the half-open door. She knew what she had to do.

"Can you handle this, buddy?" she said, her voice slightly unsteady. She thought of her friends' horses, of Starshine who had been kidnapped from Jorvik Stables, of Concorde who . . . disappeared, just sort of faded away. Of Meteor . . . If anything were to happen to Tin-Can while she was looking for Linda . . .

No. That was unthinkable. It was too unbearable.

She looked into Tin-Can's eyes one last time. She hesitated a second before stepping inside and allowing the darkness inside Pine Hill Mansion to engulf her.

A sound seemed to be coming closer and closer, a dull thudding. Something was being moved or pushed—furniture? She hoped so. The alternative was more frightening.

Thump. Thump. Thump.

She ran toward the thudding sound, deeper into the darkness.

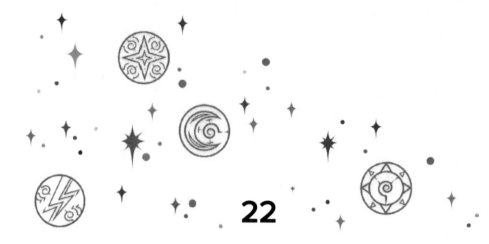

22

No one else was here in Pandoria right now, no *humans* at least. Even so, she didn't feel lonely, not anymore. As Anne made her way over those small pink, islands that surrounded her—one jump at a time—she carried Linda and her comforting words inside her. She felt the warmth of the strange sun on her back, heard her mother's voice telling her to keep going, to listen to herself.

The fact was that she was starting to feel strangely at home in this bizarre environment. The air was easier to breathe and the unusual gravity no longer made her fall as easily. Even her eyes had started to adjust to the garish, pink-saturated hues.

Leap, leap, leap. Over cherry-colored, babbling water and on toward solid ground again. Anne kind of felt like she was in a video game, invincible and bouncy, one move at a time.

She was now following a long, winding path made of pink bricks. Altogether, the irregular patterns formed an odd sort of mosaic that made her think of foreign cultures and times gone by.

Leap.

There was a bridge that looked half finished. Or maybe it was just very, very old? Enormous pillars that had once held up . . . well, what? Anne tried to make sense of the fragments that stood before her, piece by piece. But unfortunately this was no use; there was no pattern to follow. Maybe there had been a logic to it at some point, a rhyme or a reason to the architecture. Now it was all pink, broken up into pieces.

Was there something out there? Farther out by the water again?

The shadows followed, silent and docile.

With the shadows came the doubt. Another voice found its way into her consciousness, impudent and uninvited like a thief.

Jessica. It was so hard to defend yourself, so hard to feel warm when you were shivering and trembling. If Linda was warmth, then Jessica was for sure cold. Anne tried to hold on tight to Linda's words, Linda's warmth. Maybe she could try to establish contact with Linda again?

Jessica's words crawled down her spine like ice water, one drop at a time.

"You didn't believe what Linda said, did you? She was just faking. If you only knew what she says about you to the others when you're not there. Linda looks nice, but she's the worst of the bunch. I promise you. *Don't trust her!*"

Those words chilled Anne to the bone, but they didn't have the exact effect Jessica had hoped for. Instead of slumping or collapsing, Anne held her head up higher. She looked straight ahead, out at her pink surroundings. Her gaze was unwavering, stern.

"*You're* lying!" she hissed to her invisible tormentor. "YOU are the one who's faking. And do you know what? You don't really exist, not here anyway. Your words cannot reach me, not if I decide not to permit it. If anyone is a nobody, you are, Jessica. I have something you don't have—friends who would do anything for me. Do you even know how that feels?"

Silence. Dark pink shadows. They crept closer as Jessica's voice died away. Soon Jessica was just a weak echo over the stones.

You . . . have . . . no . . . real . . . friends.
You're . . . fooling . . . yourself . . . Anne.
Keep . . . pretending.
The . . . truth . . . always . . . prevails.
All those awards you have back home, do you really think they mean
anything? What are you trying to prove?

The words made Anne falter. Was Jessica right? It sort of *felt*
like she was. Anne had trouble breathing; her lungs suddenly
seemed like punctured soccer balls powerlessly hissing air.

And yet. Somewhere deep within here there was another truth,
her truth, the one that would defeat Jessica. Her body trembled
as she braced herself and knocked Jessica out. She had to get her
out of her head! Out of Pandoria! She summoned her sisters from
within. Linda. Alex. Lisa. Together they were strong. Together they
dared. She carried them within her as she looked Jessica in the eyes
and refused to back down.

"GO AWAY!" Anne shouted. "Nothing you say is true!"

Anne straightened up. Suddenly it was so quiet. She looked
around and listened for echoes of the words that had left her so out
of sorts. Nothing. Jessica was gone. A warm breeze off the water
caught Anne's hair and slowly warmed her again.

She had succeeded. As long as she didn't let Jessica's words into
her heart, they wouldn't hurt her. It was so simple, yet so hard.

Anne grinned and proceeded ahead. Now she knew that she
had to only pay attention to what she knew to be true if she
was going to find her way to Concorde. She could sense that he
was close.

Soon, she would get to see him again! When she thought
about her beloved horse it was as if her heart lifted her out of her
body to float on air. They had been through so much together, she
and Concorde.

But what condition would he be in? And how was she going to rescue him? Was coming here, to another dimension, enough? She didn't think she could do much more than that. Would he stand up when he saw her? Shake himself like a big puppy and give her a nose kiss?

Or would it take more than that? Would it require Lisa with her ability to heal him?

What if love wasn't enough?

Everything was still so new, so unfamiliar, but at the same time marvelously grand. She was a Soul Rider—she knew that much. With the help of the sun sign she could build portals and move through time and space. But then what? What happened then?

Anne felt the deep pink shadows creeping closer. She drove them away using her full concentration. She focused on Concorde, on the closeness that she sensed. She couldn't doubt it now.

Yes, he was here.

So close now.

Suddenly she became aware of how the pink landscape had changed color. Something big and gleaming gray lay at her feet. Her heart raced. *Concorde!* There he was!

She flung herself down on the ground and embraced the lifeless horse lying at the water's edge.

"Concorde! Oh, sweetie, you can wake up now. I'm here and I'm going to take you back to Jorvik and the real world if it's the last thing I do." She closed her eyes and kissed his forehead. Her eyes were still half closed as she noticed puffs of warm, horsey air softly blowing on her face. She would recognize that scent anywhere.

The scent of life, the scent of Concorde. Her love for him made the sun shine right into Concorde, all the way to his soul. His soul was her soul now. She was intensely aware of the warmth of how he felt under her hands. The sun's blinding rays guided her and helped her to erase all the pink.

Then she heard her mom's voice again. It was coming from the sunbeams. *The sun, darling, it's yours. Take it and do what you need to do.*

And Anne reached out her hands and took the sun and moved it even deeper into Concorde's slumbering soul. It was hers to take. She knew that now. It was hot, but it didn't burn. Nothing could hurt her as long as she had the sun on her side.

Red light, yellow light, white light, white heat—the sun's rays grew inside her until it felt like she was super tall. She was hot. She was strong.

She opened her eyes and inhaled as she saw Concorde's eyelids flutter and then open. The sun flickered and then withdrew. The cool breeze from the water gently swayed her clothing.

Anne hugged her horse again and again and again. His eyes were keen and alert as they gazed at her with what she swore was a look of gratitude.

"And now?" she said. "What happens now, Concorde?"

His roached mane flew back and forth like the tendril-like plants in the pink water as he got up and shook his entire body. He snorted playfully and stomped in place, puffed himself up and made a show of himself in the way only Concorde, the finest horse in the world, could. Anne laughed in delight.

"You really *are* back!"

Then, without hesitation, she swung herself up onto his back.

As Concorde started walking, it was as if all the awful things— Jessica in Concorde's stall, Concorde in a coma, Anne's desperate journey through time and space to a horrendous, pink world—had never happened. The colors that she remembered as home followed

Concorde's footsteps, spreading out into airy, ethereal veils. They changed from green to gray until pink eventually won out again.

They flowed and soared together, she and Concorde. It genuinely warmed Anne to the center of her heart to get to ride her wonderful, exquisite, and most beloved horse once again.

"We're riding home now, you and me," Anne said and hugged Concorde's warm neck. Even though she had no idea how that was going to happen, she knew it was true.

They had hardly made it around the first bend on their way back to the mainland when Concorde came to an abrupt stop and reared.

"What is it?" Anne wondered a bit worriedly. But she knew very well what it was. She had also started to hear the voice again, Jessica's voice.

"Fake," Jessica whispered with a honey-smooth voice. "You're just a big fake."

Anne jumped, but then she sternly settled herself. *No need to worry,* she thought. *I have chased her away before and I can do it again. Plus, I have Concorde now. We're even stronger together.*

"You think so, do you?" Jessica snapped back, lightning fast. "I did say that Concorde would die here. Didn't you believe me?"

Concorde whinnied, a prolonged and tormented sound. Anne looked up, straight into Jessica's jet-black eyes as she sat perfectly still on her big, black horse. She was there, this time for real. And her horse was much bigger than Anne remembered.

Then came the shadows. They coiled their way around her like a wreath. She realized that the shadow creatures had arms, legs, and big heads that slowly swayed back and forth as they took everything from her that made her who she was. Red, glowing eyes; a piercing, nasty sound reminiscent of drills, rusty chains, and barbed wire. They were everywhere. She was surrounded and had no chance of escape. So she just sat there motionless on Concorde's back and waited, waited for the end. Was Jessica right after all? Her eyes were a slick black and seemed filled with amusement as they bore into Anne's. There wasn't a single strand of hair out of place in her tight bun, not even when the breeze blew in off the water. Jessica sat stiff and straight on her black horse, cool and calculating. She didn't need to do anything. She was in control now. Every time she made a small, carefully calculated movement, the shadow beings would close in farther around Anne and Concorde. It seemed as if Jessica controlled them through her terrible, twitchy dance.

"What did I say?" Jessica sneered. Anne sobbed and hid herself in Concorde's soft, fragrant mane. There was nowhere else to go. Not now that Jessica and the shadows had found her.

She thought about Linda, about Alex and Lisa, about everything that had barely had a chance to begin. Maybe Linda could still hear her? She didn't want to give up hope, but hope was so fragile and so fleeting. She could feel it slipping out of her hands with each spiteful word from Jessica.

"Do you know, Anne," Jessica said slowly, almost playfully, "maybe I should take this opportunity to admit something. I was actually a little worried that you would manage to run off with the horse. Between the two of us, I arrived just in the nick of time. You were so close, Anne, so awfully close. How does it feel knowing that? Losing your horse twice, as it were? That can't be easy."

The shadows moved ominously closer. They were everywhere now. They seemed to be multiplying, like malignant cells. And now they were upon her, a whole army of growing, menacing shadows. They tugged at her legs now, groping at Concorde, who desperately tried to rear up and get free . . .

132

At least we'll die together, Concorde and me, Anne thought as she disappeared into the shadows.

23

When the echo from the explosion finally subsided, Lisa thought she could still see sparks from the electrical panel. After a few seconds—that felt like an eternity—she started to regain her vision and hearing. And what she heard, what she saw then . . .

Her cage door was wide open, with two deep dents in the metal. *As if made from hooves.* And what was taking place in the hangar was an even more beautiful sight. Meteor and Starshine were galloping side by side in long, wide arcs across the enormous floor.

"You did it, guys! Oh, you're the best!" Lisa rushed out of her cage and Starshine came over to her. He snorted, sighed, and rested his muzzle in her hands. Lisa nuzzled, pushing herself into his strong neck, and stood there just inhaling the scent of him for a long time. Meteor finally came over to see if he was going to get some attention, too.

"Yeah, yeah," Lisa laughed, flung her arms around Meteor's neck, and rested her head against his shoulder with a contented sigh. "You too, Meteor, of course! After all, we have you to thank, even if Starshine was maybe the brains behind the plan," she said with a furtive glance at her beautiful horse. It was almost as if Starshine nodded back at her. *Oh, you.* And of course without Lisa's healing song, Meteor would never have woken up.

"All right, you guys. Now we need to get out of here. Follow me!" she called to the horses, moving swiftly toward the door and, hopefully, toward freedom.

I never want to see this place again, Lisa thought as she ran across the concrete floor with the horses in tow, *not as long as I live.*

Meteor galloped ahead to the door and opened it with one well-aimed kick.

"Thank you, buddy. You're starting to get good at that, huh?" Lisa said and swung herself up onto Starshine. "Come on, guys! Gallop faster than the wind!"

Just as they thundered out the wide doors, the alarm went off. The world became a wailing, flashing inferno. A world filled with steel, copper, and blinding searchlights. A world with sharp and hungry teeth that had Starshine, Meteor, and her caught in its mouth.

Fight or flight?

Flight sounded good, Lisa thought, and urged Starshine on while the sirens wailed and lights flashed around them.

And they were on their way. They flew over lumber and copper pipes with green-clad Dark Core workers racing on their heels. The grounds behind the industrial complex were sizeable and full of dead ends. There were obstacles everywhere: first it was a burned-out van, then a squat, smoking chimney. Lisa rode on instinct with Meteor right beside her. He galloped just as fast as Starshine did, so close that she could smell the scent of him.

"You won't get away!" she heard the men in green yelling.

Soon Lisa also heard the sound of rumbling, roaring motors. She looked over her shoulder and saw big vans and motorcycles rumbling menacingly around the industrial space, like a massive thunderstorm. The kind of storm that bowls over buildings, flattens fields, topples towers, and sets everything ablaze. They were racing toward her and the horses now at top speed. Lisa and the horses zigzagged between tall buildings made of brick and steel, dodging parked cars and loading areas. At the same time, the sirens and flashing lights around them continued to blare. Meteor tossed his head anxiously. Starshine's ears flipped forward and back. Their eyes were wide and frightened. Starshine jumped to the side as their pursuers closed in.

"There, there," Lisa soothed. "They're not here, not yet anyway. Let's go!"

Lisa just wanted to close her eyes, shut it all out, but she had to keep her eyes open wide now. And she and the horses had one secret weapon that the enormous vehicles didn't have.

They could jump.

She steered Starshine toward a big, meandering pipe and leaned forward. It was no more difficult than jumping over an oxer, she thought. Okay, she had never jumped over an obstacle on Starshine before, but it would probably work. It *had* to work!

Her eyes teared up from the wind as Starshine sped toward the pipe. Lisa tried to flow along with his lightning-fast motions, although it was hard without a saddle. She only had her balance and Starshine's mane and withers to cling to. But they jumped and it worked! The fence coming up right in front of them would be tougher, but both Starshine and Meteor were true jumping horses. It *should* work. Lisa took aim with her eyes and leaned forward. Her hands were shaking so much that she could hardly hold onto his mane. There were no reins, no stirrups, nothing aside from her brave, beautiful horse.

Jumping was literally their only choice now. They *had* to jump. Otherwise they would be captured. Again.

The hooves thundered feverishly against the asphalt. If they slowed down, they wouldn't have a chance. If anything, they needed to gallop even faster. Lisa didn't dare turn around but she could tell that her pursuers were closer than ever.

"Get them, now!" someone with a deep voice yelled. A bright light blinded Lisa. She closed her eyes to block it out.

"Now!" she cried to Starshine.

The whole world swayed as they raced for the fence. This was going to be a crazy jump. Lisa was on the verge of losing her balance as they landed with a thud on the far side of the fence, but she managed to stay on the horse's back. With her legs still shaking and her breath jittery, she was able to take a steadier hold of Starshine. Without a saddle, he was as slippery as soap. And she could feel him working up a lather from panic.

"Good boy," she whispered. "What a good, good horse."

For a split second, she allowed herself to feel a sense of relief. She looked around, cast a glance back at the industrial area that they had now left.

"Onward to freedom, guys!" she said with a smile.

Then she heard the whirring, rattling sound of helicopters among the clouds. She looked up and saw how they were being surrounded as the cars' headlights blinded her. And then she realized that they were driving on both sides of the fence! And—oh no—*through* the fence. The men in green were waiting for her, blocking the path that was supposed to lead her to freedom.

She, Lisa Peterson, was doomed, and it was too late. She and the horses were surrounded.

There was nowhere left to run.

24

The front hall inside Pine Hill Mansion was immersed in darkness, but when Alex snuck in the half-open door she saw that a light was on by the stairway that led upstairs.

Then she connected the sound that she had been hearing—*thump, thump, thump*—with a visual. What she saw made her dart right up the old, ornate staircase. The lightning ignited within her again, flying out of her like bolts of anger. The anger blasted and boomed like thunder as she saw Sabine dragging Linda down the stairs, one step at a time. Linda was unresponsive as Sabine roughly yanked her by the legs. She looked like a big, loosely jointed rag doll.

"Linda!" Alex screamed. And then in a much rougher voice: "Don't you touch her!"

Sabine looked up and smirked. In the dark her glossy black eyes shone almost red.

"Or else . . . ? Yes, what *were* you planning to do, little Soul Rider? Call your mommy?"

Alex didn't answer, just raised her hand up. She felt the lightning shooting out of her. Her rage fed it, throbbing in pace with her heartbeat. The lightning bolts were accompanied by a rumbling noise and a sharp flash of light. She let the lightning fill her and guide her. It encompassed her field of vision, crackling pinkish-white in the darkness.

"Here you go!" she screamed at Sabine, her hand still raised. Sabine snickered.

The lightning hit Sabine but bounced off her like a rubber ball. Sabine shook herself and then laughed again.

"Is there a fly in here or something?" she said. "I don't know if you've noticed, but I'm the strongest general. You can't touch me. But, please, do be my guest. Go ahead and try!"

Alex responded by pushing out new lightning bolts aimed at Sabine. Longer and clearer this time, with long, ornate tails that glittered pink as they burst against Sabine's midriff.

Sabine pushed back. Alex kept pushing. She felt her lightning bolts losing their strength as they neared Sabine. Sweat poured off of Alex. The lightning flashes made her white-hot. She felt the burning at the base of her throat where the necklace pendant rested.

She grabbed the pendant as her pulse raced wildly.

Sabine was incredibly strong, but so was Alex. She would never back down, not on her life! She saw Linda lying on the landing, unconscious, and thought about how much she cared about her, how important Linda was. Her comforting friend who always had something smart and funny to say, who always listened and cheered people up. It was for Linda's sake that Alex's wild rage kept feeding the lightning. Linda needed her, and she needed Linda. *Now.*

Sabine lifted Linda up by her long, thick braid and spun her around in the air, grinning. Her teeth were white and sharp against the black shadows. "I'm going to smash her to pieces," Sabine said, spinning Linda. "First her, then you. Four Eyes is going to be almost *too* easy. I mean, look at her. But you, that'll really be a really fun match, a worthy match. Oh, I do love fighting!"

Sabine's words made Alex seethe with rage. She felt so hot, almost as if she were boiling over. She put her hand on the lightning bolt around her neck, which was crackling with heat.

The next flash of lightning seemed to come straight out of Alex's heart. She gasped for breath as she felt the shock in her chest.

This heart lightning coming from her chest was bright red and sparkled in the air like fireworks. It contained everything that Alex believed and was fighting for—friends, family, and Tin-Can. Everything was contained within this lightning flash, and Alex felt that it was the last lightning bolt she could produce.

"We have something in common, Sabine," she said, guiding her heart lightning to its destination. "I like to fight, too."

Sabine sneered again, but the lightning extinguished her smile as she faltered and seemed to freeze. Then she fell, over the stair railing. Alex heard Sabine curse angrily before she hit the floor with a hard thump, then silence. Alex couldn't help smiling.

I haven't lost it. The power is still there.

Now she needed to save her friend. Linda looked so pathetic lying there on the stairs that it pained Alex. Her heart was pounding. She rushed to Linda and bent down next to her.

"Linda, can you hear me? It's me, Alex."

A faint mumble came in response. Finally! Alex patted Linda on the cheeks and felt how hot they were.

"Linda?" she tried again. "We have to go now, before Sabine comes to. I don't know how long she'll lie down there."

Silence. Alex stroked Linda's brow, sweaty with fever. She felt the panic throbbing in her chest. What if she was too late? Then she reached for the water bottle in her backpack and poured the water over Linda's head.

Finally, a sign of life. Linda shook her now soaking-wet head and blurted out, "What the . . ."

Then she spotted Alex and smiled weakly.

"You came! Oh, Alex, you came! I prayed you would come, and you did!"

Alex hugged Linda and wiped a stubborn tear from one eye. She hadn't realized until now how worried she had been.

"Yes, I'm here now. But Linda, we really have to hurry." Alex suddenly recoiled as she saw the big dark wound on Linda's arm. "And you need to get to Meander Village, where they can take care of that, right away. Do you think you can stand up if you lean on me?"

All the color drained from Linda's face. She went from tan to pale gray. She had dark circles under her eyes and a big bruise on one cheek. Linda feebly raised her head and then let it flop back down again. She made a face. "Ouch. Bump. Head."

Alex's heart was full with worry for her friend. "You look like you're in bad shape, Linda. What happened? I mean, aside from Sabine?"

Linda slurred incoherently, but in the end Alex understood that Linda had cut herself on something. After that Linda said everything was foggy.

"Meteor!" she exclaimed. "Where is he?" She tried to stand up but slumped back against Alex.

"We're going to find him. And we'll take care of that wound once we get somewhere safe." Alex suddenly stopped, thinking she heard a sound from the darkness down where Sabine had landed. Was she coming to already? "Lean on me, okay?"

Linda forced herself up with all the strength she had left, supporting her weight on Alex. Every move was a monumental effort. Alex heard Linda's rasping, ragged breaths in her ear, and also recognized the rank odor of infection. It seemed to surround Linda. Alex should have ridden here sooner. And she shouldn't have come alone. They should have come together, all three of them—her, Lisa, and Anne. They should have stuck together. That realization cut into her, hacking away at her. It hurt.

"Come on, Linda!" she urged in a whisper. "You can do this. You're the strongest person I know!"

Linda's eyes were mostly glazed over, but even so they twinkled a bit in response.

"I guess we'll see about that," she replied and took a few staggering steps.

Finally, they managed to make it outside. Tin-Can was still standing outside the house, stomping nervously. Alex saw a pair of glowing red eyes just before she closed the heavy door.

They heard growling from inside the mansion. The sound of nails—claws?—on solid oak. The door flew open and Sabine dragged herself toward them. Her eyes were filled with coal and fire, and they were getting closer.

Alex faltered under Linda's weight and desperately tried to lift her up onto Tin-Can from the stone stairs.

Do not drop her. Do not . . .

Her hands were still sweaty and hot from the lightning inferno. She could feel her hold on Linda slipping. Those predatory eyes were getting closer, accompanied by a shuffling sound.

"I . . . will . . . crush . . . you."

Sabine struggled toward them with difficulty as Alex finally got a better hold of Linda. Tin-Can stood extremely still to make it easier for Alex as she pushed Linda into place on Tin-Can's back. In a snakelike motion, she slid into place in front of Linda and let Linda lean against her back.

"Put your arms around my waist," she told Linda. "Don't let go, okay?"

Even in the daylight there was something murky and impenetrable about Pine Hill Forest. At night, the darkness was so dense that you had to grope your way along through tangled branches and thick roots. If you stretched your hand out in front of you, you could maybe—*maybe*—make out its outline. Otherwise everything was oppressive darkness, a nothingness that was easy to lose oneself in. A number of Jorvik's scariest ghost stories, the ones people told around campfires at harvest festivals and on overnight field trips, took place here. On a night like this it wasn't hard to see why. The fall air was crisp and cold, and the altitude was high enough that if you didn't arrive strong and rested, it was hard to breathe.

The night's three visitors to the forest were anything but rested. They were exhausted, injured, and they were alone. They should have ridden together, all four of them. That was so clear to Alex as Tin-Can's hooves broke the ghostly silence. She wanted the others with her. The burden of this night was so heavy to bear alone. She knew she was staggering under its weight.

By this time of night, a heavy silence rested over Pine Hill Forest. No wind whispered through the branches, no birds twittered, no animals moved among the underbrush. This was not a good place to be during the dark hours, but Alex and Linda had no choice. At least the moon was out tonight: suspended over the treetops, its bright light guided them through the cold, damp night. Alex sat in front on Tin-Can. Linda slumped behind her, clinging to her shoulders. They moved purposefully out of the forest's depths toward its southern edge.

They were tired now. Linda, who was still half-unconscious, clung convulsively to Alex while Tin-Can walked along, slower than before. The girls were not heavy, but they had been on the go for a long time now, and it had been an eventful evening, to put it mildly. How long could Tin-Can keep this up?

Linda mumbled into Alex's shoulder, "He's going to die!"

"Meteor?" Alex said, her brow furrowed. "Don't worry. We'll find him."

"Not Meteor," Linda whispered weakly. "Concorde. He's going to die in Pandoria."

"Shh," Alex shushed, not understanding what Linda was saying in her delirium. Surely it was Linda's fever making her confused. "Rest now."

Alex noticed her faithful horse slowing down. She leaned forward over his withers and patted him affectionately.

"I know, Tin-Can. Even a warrior like you needs to rest a bit now and then. We're super tired, too, and Linda is sick, but we have to keep going a little longer. What if Sabine is following us? Plus, Linda needs to see a doctor right away."

"Meteor," Linda mumbled from somewhere between dream and reality. "We have to find him!"

Alex hadn't succeeded in determining any concrete details about what had happened to Meteor, but she understood that it wasn't good news. Linda kept going on about tentacle monsters, pink rocks, and a dam bursting. Her fever was obviously continuing to rise. *Because it was the fever making her say these things, wasn't it?*

"Pinta Bay!" Linda exclaimed. "Don't you see the tentacles? *The tentacles, Alex!*"

"Uh, no offense, but I think you need to get some sleep, Linda," Alex said worriedly. "I don't understand anything you're saying."

But Alex's voice sounded far away to Linda, as if she were on the other side of a mile-long tunnel—faint echoes, barely more than that. Linda saw Tin-Can moving underneath her, past roots, stones, and onto ever-narrower paths. She was vaguely aware of the intense darkness and the silence of the forest. And yet it was like she was somewhere else. The woods were raw and damp.

A cold fog engulfed them like an uninvited guest. Linda was shivering. Alex stopped and turned around to look at her friend, who was flopped over against her back like a rag doll.

"How are you doing, Linda? Should we take a look at your arm? Are you in pain?"

Linda could barely shake her head. Tin-Can snorted while Linda struggled to wake up. She heard them calling her, the voices, so many voices. It was hard to separate them.

There was something else, too, something so faint that Linda couldn't really put words on it yet. As soon as she closed her eyes, she was flooded with images of a big dam bursting, enormous amounts of water gushing toward the houses down below.

Maybe the images were nightmares, but Linda thought it was something else.

Thought? Actually, she *knew*. Even now, in her hazy condition, she carried an awareness of this. She knew that she could have visions and through them shape her own destiny, their destiny, and Jorvik's destiny. Maybe that was why she felt a sense of calm at this moment in spite of everything. She had not seen any visions of her own death. Wouldn't she have seen or sensed something if there was a risk the infection would endanger her life?

"Oh my God, Linda," Alex said. Her voice was shaking with concern as she saw how her friend was barely able to hold on. "We really need to get you to a doctor. Like, now!"

Linda grunted before dozing off again. Alex rode on. In the twilight it was hard to see, but she thought she could make something out by the distant mountain peaks, actually nothing more than a faint, faint mirage between the trees. There was some source of light up there, lit up in the darkness. Was that lightning?

Where was the light coming from? Wasn't that where the dam was? Alex kept staring eastward toward the mountains as if hypnotized. Eventually she could no longer see the light. She urged Tin-Can along.

"Maybe you're right, Linda. As usual. Something is going on. Come on, buddy, we've got to get a move on!"

Tin-Can whinnied and started walking. They quickly emerged from the forest and proceeded into a flood of moonlight, moving up into the mountains where the air was even thinner. It was still quite a ways to Meander Village over in Winter Valley. That was where the nearest doctor was. Then, hopefully they would be able to continue onward, and soon . . . as soon as Linda started to feel better. Because Alex knew Linda was right. Something was about to happen . . .

25

It was like having the flu. Here in Pandoria, something sticky and slippery had gotten into her and muffled everything: the pace, the clarity, even her ability to think. She felt the crazy sounds, the vibrations, boring their way into her. The sounds of the shadows. Every shadow creature that approached her—a whole army of them, in fact, as blatantly intrusive as black flies on a hot summer night—made her resistance dwindle.

The dark shadows that surrounded her and Concorde were starting to block out the sun, like storm clouds, but Anne didn't plan on letting the clouds cover her for long.

They wanted her away from the sun—weak, drained, and broken.

She had no intention of giving them that satisfaction, never, not on her life. She wasn't about to let the strength seep out of her. After all, she had the sun, Linda, Alex, and Lisa on her side. And Concorde.

"Concorde," she whispered. "Sweet boy, calm. Stay calm, we can handle this." But it was clear from her voice that even she didn't believe what she was saying, and Concorde's eyes looked more and more panicked.

"Give him to me," Jessica ordered. Her eyes were black and deep as wells.

Anne didn't respond; she just stared resolutely straight ahead. Suddenly, she had an idea. It glowed within her like the sun's rays, which warmed her skin. The clouds were much smaller now, heading away into the purple-colored sky. She felt warm and strong, inside and out.

Jessica took a step back.

Anne raised her chin and stretched her arms out toward the sun's warming light. She had been right: Jessica *was* afraid of the sun. The brighter its light, the more Jessica backed away and the more Anne's doubts faded. The shadow creatures shuffled after Jessica, away from the sun's blinding rays.

It had worked as she had hoped. The light that Anne herself had created from the sun streamed around her and Concorde. It started as a blue, nondescript shape on the ground. When it was reflected, it looked like a sun inscribed in a circle. From Anne's side the glow increased, and the shadow creatures paled in the light, dwindling away with a feeble whimper.

"No, it's not over yet," Anne said, eyeing Jessica and smiling.

She took in everything around her: the shimmering pink rocks, the burning, dazzling white sun, so much bigger and brighter than the sun she was used to.

The shadow people, crouching down, withdrew farther still from the sun's circle. Jessica attempted to make new attacks, pressing forward, but was forced back as the sun's circle burned her.

"Ow!" Jessica yelped, grabbing her hand. Anne just smiled.

She took everything in and did her part. She took control of the sun, of the clear pink water, of the slowly swaying vines that had made her dizzy before. It all became hers. The ground and the air, and the strange statues that whispered that the world was bigger and more amazing than she could ever have suspected. She felt Pandoria flowing into her and saw Jessica backing away even farther, along with the shadow creatures. It felt as if their contours grew hazier as everything else became clearer. They felt less real.

Jessica said nothing, just crouched down and protected her face from the heat. Good. Everything was going according to plan.

With her hand on Concorde's withers, she tried to conjure up a place. She pictured it: the green hills, the immense stone cairns high up in the mountains, the battered stone bridge. She stepped in the heart of the light. Soon she saw the portal that she had created was just as she had hoped. The light formed a rotating spiral. The movement of the swirling spiral was hypnotic. She could already feel herself being sucked in.

She knew what she had to do.

"Come on," she told Concorde, who was eyeing her curiously. "It's time for us to go home, buddy."

An instant later, everything disappeared among a reddish-pink tornado.

26

Concorde was with her and the world had returned to its normal colors again. That was the first thing Anne noticed when she opened her eyes and saw that she was lying on rough, yellowy-green fall grass. She blinked and took in the various hues of nature that surrounded her—black, dark green, orange, brown, gray, and especially Concorde's grayish-white coat. A dark stripe of navy blue was just visible through the thick nighttime clouds across the sky. The world was muffled, quiet, and nocturnal, lit up only by a few stars in the sky. *White*, she thought. Nothing pink in sight; how beautiful.

How long had they lain here, her and Concorde? How had they gotten here? She couldn't remember. The last thing she remembered was that she had sort of shoved Jessica and the shadow creatures away with her mind, with the energy of the sun. She had built the portal and come here.

Now she was back home in Jorvik. Not home-home, but finally back where everything began to make sense again, back at the Secret Stone Circle. She had traveled through time and space, away from the saturated pink nightmare, away from the nagging, awful thoughts that had almost—but only almost—succeeded in carrying her and Concorde into something so horrible that she scarcely dared think about it. She had escaped. She had done it.

And yet it felt as if she had somehow failed. Only she and Concorde were here. Where were the others? This was where they were supposed to meet, wasn't it? Wasn't that what Herman and Fripp had said?

The sound of approaching footsteps made her stand up. She rubbed her temples. Her head was sore and her skin felt like it was being stretched. Everything felt tight and unfamiliar, so frustrating. But at least the air here was easier to breathe, and she had Concorde with her. He stood up beside her and did a little dance in the fall grass. Maybe everything would be okay after all . . . maybe.

She saw that the footsteps approaching her belonged to Elizabeth and Fripp. Elizabeth flung her arms out and rushed to meet Anne where she was standing by the stone formations. Her face was beaming with relief, but it was also filled with something else, something harder to interpret.

"Anne, you're back! Finally! Oh, if only you knew how worried we've been!"

"Some have been more worried than others," Fripp added.

Elizabeth looked at him sternly. "How could you leave her to fend for herself, Fripp? You should have known better."

Fripp's blue fur shone in the sultry nighttime light as he rushed over to them. "Yes, yes, well she's back now, isn't she? And she succeeded in bringing Concorde with her, too."

"She's back," Elizabeth conceded with a big smile. "And she must be starved!" She pulled something out of her bag and poured it into a bowl for Anne. "Here's a bit of hot soup for you. It will help to counteract the effects of portal travel."

Anne gratefully accepted the soup and found it lovely to have someone take care of her a little. She was so exhausted. And yes, for the first time in ages she felt hungry.

"How long was I gone for?" she asked as Elizabeth wrapped a warm blanket around her shoulders. "I don't really understand how it works with time and that sort of thing over there," she added a little shyly.

"No one does," Elizabeth responded. "Not really. And the one who should know," she cast a knowing glance at Fripp, "well, he's not so concerned with all that time and space business."

"What is time?" Fripp said. "It's not always so important. *Whether* something happens can be more important than the order it happens in."

Anne rolled her eyes and peeked at her watch, which showed that it was half an hour to midnight. But which night? How many nights had she been away for? It was true that time felt different in Pandoria. Everything there moved in slow motion, just like the sticky pink plants by the edge of the water. She could have been gone for a year or only an hour; it was hard to tell.

She was back in Jorvik now, and she had rescued Concorde. But where were the others? She turned to look at Elizabeth, who seemed to be thinking the same thing.

"The other girls, Anne," Elizabeth said. "You don't know where they are?"

Anne shook her head. "They were in school when I took off. I have no idea where they are now. Or, well, I did talk to Linda. I think. She didn't say anything specific, but I'm afraid that she's in danger. It's hard to explain. We have a bond, she and I. I noticed that when I was there, in Pandoria. She was able to reach me somehow."

"The sun and the moon are strongly allied." Elizabeth nodded seriously. "And you know, right now we are actually two suns existing at once."

"Two suns?" Anne looked puzzled. Elizabeth quickly explained.

"Yes, two suns. And two Soul Riders. One old and one new." Elizabeth smiled as she saw Anne's look of astonishment.

"Two Soul Riders?" Anne repeated. "You mean ... but then, what are you now? If you're not a Soul Rider anymore, I mean?"

"Now," Elizabeth said, running her hand quickly over Anne's hair, "it's my job to help you. Just like the sun helped you in Pandoria."

Anne thought about the hot, burning sun that broiled over Pandoria, about how, even though everything felt so weird and wrong, she had managed to make it her own. And then she remembered back to how curious the sky had looked that morning on her way to the stable. Before Lisa arrived at school on her first day and everything changed. She remembered that ride in the woods when she teleported herself and Concorde away from danger. The squealing tires that just simply vanished.

Yes. She thought she kind of understood.

"It's been a long time since two strong suns stood in the Secret Stone Circle at the same time," Elizabeth said cautiously. "We should be able to utilize that. We can make use of the favorable conditions in the magic flow up here and try to build a portal together. For the other girls," she added by way of explanation. "Linda may very well be in danger. We can't get ahold of the others and that worries me as well. We have to try to get them here, and fast!"

"Wait, wait, wait." Now suddenly it was Fripp slowing things down. "You're talking about building a portal? Together, using the combined strength in the sun's circle? Elizabeth, you know very well that that hasn't been done in a very long time. And playing with such powerful magic can be lethal. You never know what the consequences will be. Don't do it! Do I need to remind you about that time when . . . ?"

"You don't need to remind me, Fripp," Elizabeth replied. "You're right that it can be dangerous if it's done the wrong way. It's always risky to unleash that type of powerful magic; it almost unfailingly affects the flow between our reality and Pandoria's unreality. But, Fripp, this time there's something in particular. Haven't you felt it, too? This generation of Soul Riders already has powers beyond the ordinary."

This generation of Soul Riders. Those words made the hair on Anne's arms stand up. It was almost inconceivable to think that Elizabeth was talking about *her*, her and her other stable friends.

"The stronger the magic, the bigger the side effects," Fripp warned. "Couldn't you just, I don't know, try calling them? After all, there is every indication that they're still in our reality, isn't there?"

"I didn't realize you were so into cell phones, Fripp," Elizabeth retorted with a wry smile. "But, sure, we could try that first. Anne, is your phone working?"

Her phone! Anne hadn't thought about it. She could actually just *call* her friends! A giggle bubbled up inside her as she realized how absurd her last twenty-four hours had been.

Or forty-eight hours, she realized, looking at her phone. *Two days?!* It had felt like years that she had been gone. She wouldn't be surprised if she had gray hair now.

A line from a play she had read at school recently popped into her head. *The time is out of joint.* She shook her head.

She kept scrolling and saw that she had several missed calls and unread messages. Her brow furrowed. "Herman tried to reach all of us," she said. "But no one seems to have seen it. Poor Herman, he must be super worried! I'll call him right now."

Herman answered on the first ring. "Anne?" His voice sounded hoarse.

"Yes," she replied. "I'm at the Secret Stone Circle now. Just wanted to let you know that."

Herman's sigh of relief carried out across her phone to Elizabeth, who was standing very close to her. Elizabeth smiled, and Anne smiled, too.

"I think everything is okay. But I have to make some other calls. We'll be in touch."

She hung up the call with Herman. "And now Linda," she said. Her smile faded as it went straight to voicemail. "Her phone seems to be turned off or the battery is dead," she finally said with a sigh.

Same for Lisa and Alex. The worry line between Elizabeth's eyebrows deepened. She regarded Fripp with a steady look. Neither of them said anything. They just stared deeply into each other's eyes, hers light gray and his black. Who would back down first? Finally, Fripp nodded, almost imperceptibly.

"Okay," he muttered. "Fine, we'll take a chance. Let's hope the odds are on our side." He looked anything but satisfied. "Elizabeth," he said then, "go get the portal sickness brew. If the girls were too far away, they might be in really bad shape. We have to be ready when they arrive."

"I made a whole pot of the elixir yesterday," Elizabeth replied. "That should be enough for all four of them. The horses, too, if necessary."

Elizabeth took Anne's hand. "Before we start, I want you to understand a little more about what we're going to try to do. I know that Fripp has already taught you quite a bit about energy flow and portals. What we're going to do now is actually the same thing, the difference being that you're not going to be teleporting yourself or your horse anywhere. This time we're going to teleport someone— several someones—here. We have to start by finding the place."

"Places," Anne corrected her. "When Linda found me . . . I'm not positive, but I had the sense that she was alone, too. And scared. I don't know why, but I think they're in several different locations."

"The Soul Riders separated," Fripp mumbled. "Even though that's the most dangerous thing they could possibly do."

"You're stronger together, girls," Elizabeth said. "You know that, too, don't you, Anne?"

Anne nodded. They had to be together. She knew that for certain now.

"Okay," Elizabeth said, and then inhaled. "Hold onto my hand hard now. Don't let go. I'm going to try to guide you."

In the dark night, a strange light suddenly lit up the sky. It almost looked as if the sun had decided to defy all the laws of nature and appeared in the middle of the night. The residents of Jorvik were asleep in their beds, completely unaware of the extraordinary happenings up in the mountains, at a place most of them didn't know existed. Anne squeezed Elizabeth's hand tightly and felt the light and heat from the sun flowing into her. Right above the light source in the sky, she saw something spinning. It was a pale pink rotating disk that was spreading a spiral-shaped light. She recognized it from Fripp's lessons. With Elizabeth at her side, with the magic pulsing in her body, Anne raised her free hand and made the disk follow her own movements. She saw the disk widen to form a sort of opening. Elizabeth looked at her encouragingly.

"Like so. Position yourself in front of it and wait."

"You want me to . . . ?" Anne wondered, feeling fidgety. "Wouldn't it be better if you . . . ?"

"It has to be you," Elizabeth said, shaking her head.

And then, with the magic like a warming force inside her, Anne walked toward the portal. She saw what awaited on the other side—and yes, they *were* pressed for time. There was only a matter of seconds, if that. Would she be able to make it?

Lisa knew that there was no point, that it was too late. She felt rough arms grabbing for her and Starshine, carrying chains and ropes. She saw the awful, gleaming steel halter nearby, far too close. Both Starshine and Meteor reared. Lisa fell forward, draped like a rag doll over Starshine's mane.

Would the man with the scary halter get them? Or Katja? She who extinguished life and light. Her white eyes shone in front of Lisa now. It would be fitting in some way, because there was no hope anymore. Lisa knew that. It was time to give up. They were surrounded. It was too late. She allowed her tears to fall onto Starshine's mane as she felt how he trembled beneath her.

Then she spotted a hovering, pink spiral shape floating along in the air. It was coming right toward her.

"What in the . . . ?" she mumbled. Starshine whinnied and sped up; he struggled free of the men in green, who shuffled after him, cursing. They galloped toward the disk of light, so fast that the wind whistled in her hair.

"Come on now, buddy!" Lisa yelled. "In you go!"

She had no idea what she was galloping into, but it was her only chance.

Time and space seemed to fold up and then unfurl as Lisa and the two horses vanished into the portal.

Neither Linda nor Alex knew anymore whether they were awake or asleep, whether it was night or day. The exhaustion felt more like a final destination than a temporary condition. Their heads lolled and they could barely keep their eyes open.

Tin-Can was tired, too, but he refused to stop. He had never yet failed to live up to his rider's expectations. And if Tin-Can had any say, that never would happen. He planned to carry her and her friend through thick and thin. So he kept going, but without any of the usual verve in his step. His big, light-brown eyes were glossed over and he was having a hard time holding his head up after the long journey.

They had traveled so far now.

"Soon, dear heart," Alex whispered sleepily. "Soon we'll get to rest."

But she was afraid that that wasn't true. Had they really chosen the right path? It was as if the forest was getting denser and denser when it should have been thinning out.

"It's so dark," she mumbled. "You can hardly see the moon."

Linda moved abruptly when she heard Alex mention the moon.

"We can't lose the moon!" she barely blurted out, her eyelids almost shut. "It's guiding us!"

Then she started talking about tentacles and water again. Alex just shook her head.

Should they stop here, deep in the forest, and sleep for a few hours? She was afraid that Linda wouldn't be able to get back up again if she lay down. Worry gnawed at her heart. They had to get to Meander Village.

"Maybe we should have said to heck with it," Alex said, more to herself than to Linda. "Two Soul Riders in the stable is bound to be better than two Soul Riders lost in the woods."

Although deep down inside she knew that wasn't true. She knew that what was happening now, the paralyzing exhaustion she was experiencing, Linda's injury and fever, Tin-Can bravely walking on even though he could hardly carry them anymore, all of this in some way was the point. This was their destiny. But was there any way to fast-forward past this horrible destiny, and if so, how?

She leaned her head against Tin-Can's mane and felt herself slowly drifting off. Linda leaned heavily against her back.

Then Alex spotted it, a pink disk with rotating spiral arms floating in the air, coming closer and closer. She halted Tin-Can and looked around, puzzled. What *was* that?

Then she saw Anne waving on the other side of the pink, spinning disk of light. Alex exhaled and grinned and rode straight toward the pink light. She took a running start and jumped in.

27

One by one they tumbled into the Secret Stone Circle with their horses. It was anything but a smooth or graceful entrance. They flopped onto the ground, smashing knees, landing on their heads, scraping elbows, and tearing their riding pants. First came Lisa, Starshine, and Meteor, and then finally Alex, Linda, and Tin-Can. They toppled onto the wet grass with a thump and a chorus of astonished cries.

Everyone was screaming, groaning, and making noises. Except for one.

"Uh . . . what?" Alex said when she opened her eyes. Her heart was pounding like a whole orchestra of drums, and her legs were wobbly. The adrenaline coursed and sang through her so much so that she felt dizzy. Then she saw Tin-Can and something eased.

"Oh my God," Anne said, looking around at the others. She felt like she had completely failed at what she was trying to do. What was that again, anyway . . . ? Her head felt empty. She put her hands on her head, as if she could just physically pull out the memories that she seemed to be missing at the moment.

Lisa felt sick and she could barely stand up, but she paled even more when she spotted Linda lying on the ground a short distance from her. Lisa had longed to be able to show her Meteor, but Linda seemed unconscious. She lay ominously still in the darkness, her breathing spasmodic, a filthy bandage draped loosely around her arm.

"Linda!" Lisa blurted out, crawling closer to her. "Are you okay?"

Elizabeth came hurrying over to them and dropped down onto her knees in front of Linda. She gasped when she saw how bad of a condition Linda was in. Then, the others looked her direction, too. Alex jumped up from the ground and rushed over to Linda. Anne seemed to almost wake up from a nightmare; suddenly her glazed-over eyes became clearer. She hurried over to her unconscious friend.

"She's super sick," Alex said, running her hand over Linda's red-hot forehead. "Some kind of infection, I think. Blood poisoning, maybe? She was totally out of it by the time I reached Pine Hill. Lisa, please, help!"

"Yes, Lisa, you have to do something!" Elizabeth repeated, her eyes fixed on Linda. Linda's one eyelid twitched.

Lisa fought against the nausea growing within her like a disgusting, soggy, gray mushroom. She gulped and nodded.

"Of course I will," she said. Then she put her fingers between her lips and whistled.

"Come here, buddy!" she yelled to Starshine, who had already started galloping toward her. His blue mane billowed in the night air. Alex held Linda's hand tightly and gave Lisa an encouraging look.

"You trained him really well, you know?" she said with a small smile as Starshine stopped right beside Lisa, his muzzle in her outstretched hand.

Lisa smiled shakily in return and stroked Starshine's soft muzzle. Then she squatted down in front of Linda and removed the bloody bandage. It smelled of infected pus and the nauseating, metallic smell of dried blood. She gulped again to avoid being sick and put one hand over Linda's wounded arm and the other over Starshine's warm withers. She pushed fairly hard on Linda's arm and started to sing. The melody came to her naturally, without her needing to search for it. She felt it almost right away, how the song and the hot, flowing light, everything that she had searched for so desperately but had not been quite able to find during her captivity, guided her. Starshine stood right close by, completely still. Finally, she was home again. Home in the magic, in the healing power that was her absolutely special gift.

And she had the others around her, Alex, Anne, and Elizabeth. They followed her every move with their eyes, holding each other's hands as they knelt around in a small circle. Lisa felt their body heat, heard them singing along with the melody, their voices breaking. The song rose over the Secret Stone Circle, over to the sleeping druids. The air was filled with a pink light with ornate blue bands of light that swirled up into the sky. There was a flash and they were blinded by a sudden, sharp light that made them all look up.

Lightning, Alex thought.

The moon, Linda thought in her delirium.

The sun, Anne thought.

The stars, Lisa thought, and sang about stars that could dazzle, but also guide.

Linda whimpered. Lisa kept singing. *Take me away to the stars.* After a few minutes, Linda opened her eyes and reached to touch her injured arm. It looked completely normal again.

"What the . . . ?" Linda said, looking around. Then her whole face broke into an enormous smile as she saw all the girls and their horses. Her friends flung themselves over her, all of them hugging her at once.

Lisa saw Linda's eyes gleam, not from fever but from joy. She felt Linda's forehead just to be sure. It was cool again now.

"Yup," Lisa said contentedly, kissing Starshine on the nose. "Still great."

They lounged in the grass with their horses beside them, dead tired, slightly delirious, sick to their stomachs—but together. Meteor gently nudged Linda's now-healed arm with his muzzle. Tin-Can curiously nosed Starshine and nickered cheerfully.

"Oh, do you see that? They missed each other!" Alex said, and the others joined in with a chorus of oohs and aahs. Elizabeth had gotten a warm fire going and was checking to make sure none of the others had anything broken or injured that needed to be looked at or healed by Lisa.

"You seem to have managed pretty well, given the circumstances," Elizabeth finally pronounced, relieved. "Traveling from one place to another the way you all just did is not without its risks, and you must never forget this: all magic comes at a price. In this one case, though, the price was probably worth it. Just know that I was so scared!"

Us, too, Lisa thought.

"Hmm," said Fripp, who had come out of his burrow to check what all the fuss was about. Then he walked a little distance away and continued gazing up at the stars.

Alex stared after Fripp and mimed "*A squirrel?*" to Anne.

"He doesn't like to be called that," Anne replied with a smile. "He's . . . a timeless being."

"Okay," Alex said, looking skeptical.

Lisa didn't say anything, just held her hands to her stomach. Her face had a greenish tint to it.

"I know," Elizabeth said. "You're feeling super sick, right?"

Lisa nodded, breathing in quick gasps.

"I'll get you something for that," Elizabeth said and got up quickly.

Together they looked around, taking in the strange runes and the place which breathed of magic and ancient worlds. They took in everything new with wide eyes as they fought to control their nausea. They watched how familiar the horses seemed, moving around in the Secret Stone Circle. Against the old stone formations, they all looked even bigger and more regal than usual, even more like timeless, legendary beings. Linda lay leaning against one of the runestones and gasped when she touched the runes. They lit up in pink as she touched the ancient text.

"Wow!" Anne said. "They weren't this bright when I was here alone. It was kind of more like a dim glow then, not like this at all."

"You know what that means, right?" Alex said, winking at her.

"That Linda has a way with ancient writings?" Anne replied with a feeble smile.

"Mm, obviously, but the most important thing is probably something else," Alex said. "That we're all here together. Don't you feel that, too?"

The others thought about everything they had witnessed, the fear and the icy cold. And then in the middle of it all: that resounding certainty of *why* it had gone so wrong. They should have stuck together. They should have been together. They all nodded.

"Can we just agree on one thing right now?" Linda said, followed by a big yawn. "That we will never split up again, unless we have an EXTREMELY good reason to do so?"

"Yes!" the others all yelled over each other, gazing into the fire. Everyone was so tired that they could have fallen asleep on the spot, but they didn't want to, not yet. Not now, when they were finally here with each other and their four horses.

They were safe now. They really were. They were weary and battered, but they were safe. And, most important of all: they were together.

"You need to take this for the portal sickness now," Elizabeth told them as she hurried back over with a container of something dark and sludgy looking. "Drink every drop!" she continued. "Don't let any go to waste. This is very precious stuff. You need to know that."

It looked like coffee grounds, or maybe a long-stagnant mud puddle.

"Hmmm," Lisa said.

"Yeah. 'Hmmm' for real," Alex added. "Are you sure about this, Elizabeth?"

"Yes, I'm sure," Elizabeth said. "Here, Alex, you go first. It's extremely important that you all get this into you."

"Ugh, it's so gross." Alex's face contorted after she drank her share in a few gulps. "What's in it, dead toads?"

"I will never reveal my secret ingredient," Elizabeth replied. "Here, Linda, your turn."

Linda was still a little dazed where she sat leaning up against the glowing runestone. Elizabeth poured a few drops into her mouth and Linda spat it out when she tasted it.

"Eh-eh-eh! Don't spit it out," Elizabeth reminded her and gave Linda an extra dose. "There, like so."

When it was Lisa's turn to drink, Elizabeth's special brew almost came back up again. All four of them could see the panic in Elizabeth's eyes.

"The dose has to be extremely precise," she said. "I can't make more than is necessary. Please, Lisa, try not to throw it up!"

Lisa's face was completely green, but in the end she managed to swallow the drink. Anne was the last one to have the container passed to her. She took a deep breath, pinched her nose, and swallowed quickly.

"Good job, Anne!" Alex cheered.

Anne shrugged. "I had so many ear infections when I was little," she explained. "I've taken so much disgusting medicine that I've learned to just drink it quickly."

"You'll feel dizzy for a little while longer before the medicine begins to work," Elizabeth said. "Disoriented, nauseated, and you'll have trouble balancing. Portal sickness is a bit like extreme dizziness. Like after you ride a carousel or spin around and around for too long. Or maybe like a nasty bout of motion sickness."

"Anyone want to neutralize that disgusting flavor with something sweet?" Linda asked, waving Herman's cookie jar around.

"Thank you, Herman," Lisa said, helping herself to a cookie. Her nausea was almost completely gone. "And thank you, magic," she added.

The taste of sugar made her think about the kitchen back home in Jarlaheim where she usually sat with her dad in the evening and had a cup of tea. She felt a pang. Her eyes filled with tears and she had a hard time swallowing her cookie.

"My dad," she whispered. "Mr. Sands said he's locked up somewhere in the Dark Core complex at Cape Point. Did you ever get there, Alex?"

Of course she didn't, said a cold, hard voice inside Lisa. *Do you see your dad anywhere here? Well?*

Alex shook her head. "I had to ride away the other direction, to get to Linda. But don't worry, Lisa. We'll help your dad. Soon."

"Yes, of course!" Linda interjected. "You saved Starshine and Meteor. The least we can do is save your dad. But we need to prepare super carefully and the time needs to be right. We can't leave anything to chance. When I was in the library at Pine Hill, I discovered some really messed up stuff about Mr. Sands." She looked up at her friends and said somberly, "Number one: he *is* actually several hundred years old and it *is* him in all those pictures I showed you before. He stopped aging in the late 1700s."

They all shivered around the crackling fire. They looked at each other wide-eyed and felt the reality they had always taken for granted crumbling and falling apart, ripping like a piece of thin fabric.

"Number two," Linda continued in a steady voice. "He is planning to liberate Garnok using magical energy, and he is planning to do it soon. Three: Sabine is helping him. And I think Jessica is, too, although I didn't see her."

"Jessica is," Anne confirmed without saying any more than that.

"There's a girl named Katja, too," Lisa added. "I know it's hard to believe, but she is actually *even* scarier than both Sabine and Jessica."

"I won't believe that until I see her," Alex muttered.

"Trust me," Lisa replied. "You don't want to see her. Those three girls seem to be more dangerous than we thought."

"Is this really happening?" Anne said, sounding timid. In her mind she was back in Pandoria among the shadow whisperers. The shadows and Jessica had blown away everything that was warm inside her. She shivered and reached her hands out toward the campfire.

"I know," Lisa said and squeezed Anne's hand. "Everything is sort of warped. Did it even happen?"

"I understand exactly what you mean," said Anne, who was still surprised that the night sky was deep blue instead of dark pink. "The things I saw . . . I can't even explain them. I can hardly talk about it. Not yet, anyway."

The others looked at her and nodded.

"But when you're ready to talk about it, you have us," Alex said. "And we have each other." The four girls looked at each other and smiled.

"You've all been through a lot," Elizabeth said. "I need to take you over to the druids' houses right away. It'll be nice to be able to sleep in proper beds again, won't it?"

"Yes," Lisa sighed, and the others nodded eagerly.

"Ah, to sleep in a bed," Linda said, her eyes radiant. "Sweet music to my ears. What else did you guys miss?"

"Hot breakfast," Alex said dreamily. "Piping hot toast with tons of butter."

"Oh, yeah," Linda said. "Preferably a whole loaf."

"Coffee and milk," Lisa said. Coffee made her feel closer to her father. She gulped and smiled at her friends.

"A long, hot bubble bath," Anne said. "And, I'm sorry to say it, but clean underwear!"

"Yes!" all four of them agreed, giggling together.

"We'll arrange for all of that," Elizabeth said. "Aside from maybe the bubble bath. My friends the druids live a purely spartan lifestyle, I'm afraid. Oh, by the way, you should call your parents," Elizabeth added. The glow of the campfire made her face look like an old religious painting. There was something timeless about Elizabeth, so it felt strange to hear her talking about cell phones and bubble baths. The girls had told their families that they would be out riding for a few days, but they didn't want them getting worried.

For those who have parents to call, Lisa thought, feeling a long shadow sink down over what had just been a cozy campfire mood. She would probably make a call tomorrow, but it wouldn't be to her father. Linda glanced anxiously in her direction as she stood up and walked off into the night's deep shadows.

"Time for bed!" Elizabeth announced once everyone had called home—everyone except Lisa. "I'm sure your horses are asleep already." She pointed knowingly to a snoring Tin-Can, who stood leaning on three legs against a tree a little way from them. "I'll make sure they're moved to the yard below the druids' houses and given food and water a little later. Now, get a move on, Soul Riders! School starts tomorrow and you'll need to be thoroughly rested."

"School?" Alex said, confused. "I thought we were on fall break?"

"A different sort of school," Elizabeth explained. "Now that you're all gathered here together, it is high time you learn more about your new, magical world. But now, sleep. You're going to need your rest."

"Is it okay if we just sleep until next week?" yawned Lisa, who had come back and was standing next to Linda.

They cast one last glance at their sleeping horses. Then they turned around and walked toward the druids' houses, which were just visible like small, lopsided sugar cubes on the rock ledge below the Secret Stone Circle.

Together, at last.

28

The morning sun had been shining through the sheer curtains for several hours by the time the girls finally woke up. Linda was the first one up. She yawned and opened the door a crack to peer out at the hypnotically beautiful landscape. Her eyes roamed over the funny, crooked roofs of the druids' houses. She saw the horses grazing in the meadow below the cliffs. Everything was peaceful and beautiful, like in a painting. The morning air felt fresh and new. Linda felt renewed, too, in some way. The sticky, dark panic she had felt inside Pine Hill suddenly seemed far away, like a feverish dream. But just like waking up from a bad dream, vague traces of fear still lingered within her, although, she only really noticed them if she let herself. She glanced down at her arm and shuddered. It was completely healed now, her skin soft and intact. She remembered how it felt to have the life slowly draining out of her, to be so sick that she could hardly breathe. But she tried to stop thinking about what had happened and instead what might happen next. She wanted to linger here in the sunshine, in a safe place, even if just for a little while.

They would find themselves in the darkness again soon enough, Linda was sure of that. For now, she wanted to stay in the light for as long as possible.

Through the open door she smelled the homey aroma of coffee coming from the kitchen with its old woodstove. She hoped the others would wake up soon. But while they were asleep, she made sure to call her aunt. She hadn't answered her phone yesterday, which wasn't so strange since Linda had called in the middle of the night. She was probably asleep, just like Linda had been the second she lay down on the soft druid bed. As sleep had wrapped her in soft cotton wool, she realized that of all the things she had experienced in the last twenty-four hours, sleep had not been one of them. And even here, it was like something else. It was like her body had turned off.

Her aunt answered on the second ring.

"Hi, Aunt Amal."

"Oh, Linda, it's you! So nice to hear from you! Is everything all right?"

"Everything's fine. How are you guys doing at home? How's Misty?"

"Misty misses you," Aunt Amal said, sounding cheerful.

Linda heard a growling sound and smiled as well when thinking of her little black cat who could purr so loudly that it was audible over the phone. She could picture Misty's gleaming green eyes, her one damaged ear, her paws that felt like little kitten feet when she jumped into Linda's lap and made herself comfortable.

"I miss her too," she said. "We're going to do more riding today, all four of us, Anne, Lisa, Alex, and me. We'll probably be gone at least a few more days, but everything's going great. I just wanted to say hi."

They chatted a little while longer. Then Linda hung up and went back into the house. She waved to Lisa, who was also talking on the phone. She wondered who Lisa was talking to. Lisa seemed upset and was pacing back and forth on the squeaky wooden floor, gesticulating wildly.

"What do you mean there's no oil platform off of Cape Point? We know there is! Why aren't you DOING anything? My dad is being held prisoner there. You have to help him!"

Lisa listened quietly with a furrowed brow.

"Thanks for nothing!" she hissed and threw her phone on the bed.

Linda walked over to Lisa and put a comforting arm around her shoulder.

"That didn't sound like it went very well!" Linda said. "Were you talking to the police?"

Lisa nodded and wiped away the tears that were running down her cheeks.

"I called to report it, the fact that my dad is being held prisoner on Dark Core's oil platform off of Cape Point. I *know* he's there! But the officer I talked to claimed there was no such platform."

"No way," said Alex, walking in from the kitchen with a sandwich in one hand and her phone in the other.

"We have to make them understand!" Lisa exclaimed, looking more angry now than sad. "I don't get how they can just lie to me."

"Something tells me that they are under pressure from a totally different direction," Linda mumbled. "Mr. Sands has a lot of power over a lot of people. It's warped but true. I don't think I would trust the police in this situation."

"Well, in that case we're going to have to ride over there ourselves!" Lisa said. "Today, right now. Well, after breakfast."

"Lisa," Linda said softly. "I get that you want to help your dad, but to be totally honest, what's going on right now is probably not resolvable in any normal way. We're going to have to rely on magic, powerful magic, and in order for it to work we need to listen to Elizabeth and Fripp."

"Precisely, girls," Elizabeth said, coming in from the kitchen. "And I recommend that we meet up at the Secret Stone Circle in a little bit. There's quite a bit that we need to discuss. But first, breakfast. And by the way, where's Anne? Have you seen her?"

Everyone looked around the cramped little cottage. A reflection from the sun danced across the floorboards. Uncertainty hung in the air like a big question mark.

"Yeah, where is Anne?" Lisa said.

"She's not still asleep, at any rate," Linda said and pointed to Anne's unmade bed. "She must have snuck out before I woke up."

They left the peculiar little house and walked along the steep, rocky path that took them to a grove of trees and down to the meadow where their horses were grazing. Although it was fall, the meadow was lush and green and full of beautiful wildflowers; a lovely, peaceful place. Timeless, like its inhabitants. But below that idyllic meadow, at the cliff's edge, there was a steep, abrupt drop-off. Lisa had a dizzying tingle in her belly when she looked down there.

In the middle of the meadow, surrounded by autumn roses, stood Anne with her arms around Concorde's neck. There was a distant look in her eyes.

"There you are!" exclaimed Alex, rushing over to her. "Couldn't you sleep?"

"Oh yes," Anne replied, her eyes focused on the mountain peaks. "I slept really well, actually. I just needed to spend a little time alone with Concorde. And then I called my parents again. They wanted me to come home right away."

"Is that what you want?" Lisa wondered hesitantly.

"I don't know," Anne shrugged. "I feel like I don't know anything right now. This has been such a weird time lately. It's hard to put it into words. I woke up this morning and was astonished that the sky was blue and not pink. How long am I going to feel like this?"

"It can take time," Elizabeth said cautiously. "Pandoria's unreality has seeped into you. That's not something that just goes away overnight, but the good magic, the magic of light, can help you. Even if it doesn't feel like it now, you will eventually be yourself again. Anyhow, come to the Secret Stone Circle with us now. We have a lot to discuss."

"Yes, do!" Alex exclaimed. "Please, Anne? We have to be together now!"

"Yes, come with us!" echoed Lisa and Linda at the same time as they scratched their horses behind the ears. Starshine had put his big, heavy head in Lisa's hands and looked like he was about to fall asleep.

Anne happened to think of that day at the stable when they were getting their horses ready for the Light Ride. She had felt so lonely then, like she was in the way of all the other merry riders moving through the aisles in the stable and giggling. She had always felt like the odd one out at the stable, the one who didn't fit in. Her clothes were wrong (too expensive), she talked wrong (too snobby, the way they do in the exclusive neighborhoods in Jorvik City), competing in dressage while the other riders raced each other in the woods (too pretentious). Anne had thought that maybe it was best if she kept to herself, best if she actively chose to be alone rather than waiting to be left out. But then Lisa, Alex, and Linda came over to her in the stable and encouraged Anne to join them, to not be alone.

Ride with us, Anne!

Anne nodded. "Okay," she said. "I'll go with you."

Alex high-fived her in what might have been the most awkward high-five of all time. Linda gave her a hug while Lisa just watched her, blinking a little. Anne exhaled and patted Concorde.

A druid they had greeted before brought sandwiches, fruit, and drinks to the meadow. His cloak flapped in the gentle breeze as he set down the food. Everyone dug in; they were famished. The horses munched on grass and oats. For a while, only the sound of enthusiastic chewing could be heard. It was a pleasant quietness, a quietness to rest in. The girls all took another sandwich, and then another. Above them the sky was as intensely blue as it could only be in the fall. Anne lay down on her back and gazed up at the sky. The airy cirrostratus clouds were reflected in her blue eyes.

"Blue," she whispered to herself. "Blue, blue, blue."

"Is she okay?" Linda whispered to Elizabeth.

"She will be soon," Elizabeth replied. "You all will, but now it's high time that Fripp and I told you more about your assignment. I understand that you have a lot of questions. Come with me!"

29

"You're together," Fripp said. "For the first time in a long time, all four Soul Riders and their four Guardians are united here in the Secret Stone Circle."

The girls looked at each other with solemn faces. They held hands and formed a circle together.

"You have such tremendous potential," Fripp continued. "I don't believe you even realize how much. The druids have waited a long time for this day."

"We have," Elizabeth nodded. "And you still have a lot to learn, but you have already shown that the magic is strong in you. As the four members of the last sisterhood . . ."

"*Last?*" Alex cut her off. "As in THE END, or . . . ?"

Elizabeth nodded. Her face was impossible to read, both open and inscrutable at the same time. *Like the Mona Lisa,* Linda thought.

"As members of the last sisterhood," Elizabeth continued mildly and yet firmly, "you are even stronger than the Soul Riders who came before you. You have all felt and been able to use your special powers. Now you have to learn to cultivate and hone them."

"How is that actually going to work?" Alex wondered, squirming a little. "I mean, sure, I've already figured out that I have the lightning as a . . . I don't know, a sort of guide or something? A lodestar, you might say?"

"That's right," Fripp confirmed. "Your power, Alex, is the lightning's, your path that of the warrior. You are strong and unafraid and you persevere. And you, Lisa," he continued, "you find your magic in the star's circle, in the beauty of the natural world, and in taking care of others. That is the path of healing and nature."

Lisa thought of Starshine's broken leg and Linda's injured arm. She nodded somberly. "I know."

"Anne, as you know, the sun is your domain," Elizabeth said and gave her a sly wink.

Anne winked back and hoped that she didn't look like she was having a stroke or something. Should she mention to the others that Elizabeth was a former Soul Rider? She liked that she and Elizabeth shared this secret. She stood up a bit taller and smiled at Elizabeth in anticipation.

Elizabeth continued, "That means that you are the master of the portals' secrets. The druids believe that the sun is the strongest power and she who rules over the sun is a leader."

"A leader? Me?" Anne said, looking astonished, to put it mildly. "I didn't think that."

"I did," Linda said, giving her a nudge.

"Now we come to the moon," Fripp said. "Linda, as the moon's ally, you are the master of visions, mystery, and knowledge."

"It's not exactly like that last one is anything new," Alex said in a fake whisper. Linda rolled her eyes but couldn't help laughing. This all felt nerve-wracking and ceremonial, like getting your report card or walking up on stage to accept your diploma from the principal.

Only bigger, so much bigger.

"What are we actually supposed to do?" Lisa asked. "As Soul Riders, I mean?"

"Yes, please tell us!" Anne interjected. "This all feels really fuzzy so far."

"It's actually all very simple," Fripp replied. "The Soul Riders' role is to fight darkness and make sure the flow of Pandoric energy—you know what that is now, don't you, Anne—is just right. This is done by closing cracks between our world and Pandoria via a special ceremony."

"You say that the flow needs to be just right and that we need to help with that," Linda said. "But Pandoria is an evil place, isn't it? Anne felt so awful there. I saw and heard that myself . . ."

"Pandoria is not an evil place," Fripp corrected her. "But nor is it good. It's all about balance. Here in Jorvik we need the energy from Pandoria so that everything that's here on the island—the magic, the magnificent natural splendor with all the incredible plants, our Starbreeds—can remain and flourish. But it's important that there not be too much."

"What happens then?" Alex asked.

Fripp's eyes were darker than usual, even more inscrutable.

"Then," he said slowly, "it encourages Garnok. The darkness could become so strong that Garnok is released. Garnok is all that is evil. He comes from a place where chaos reigns, and he wants to return there. But before he returns, that chaos and destruction would also be spread throughout our world."

"Is that what Dark Core wants, too?" Lisa wondered, thinking of Mr. Sands's wolfish grin. She turned to Fripp. How quickly you forget how strange it is to have a small, bright-blue creature as a teacher, Lisa thought. It felt almost normal now.

Fripp nodded. "Yes, at least Dark Core's leader, Mr. Sands. He thinks he will get to control the havoc once Garnok is liberated."

Linda thought about her awful visions, the black water rising and drowning out all the screams, Garnok's eye, Mr. Sands's diary. She shivered.

"I think Mr. Sands wants revenge," Linda whispered.

Fripp shook his head. "Revenge? Whom against and why? No one has harmed him. On the other hand, thousands of innocent lives will be affected if Mr. Sands manages to release Garnok."

For a moment, Linda considered telling them about the diary entries. Rosalinda. How she could almost understand how Mr. Sands felt as the love of his life wasted away and died after having been tossed into the icy water. But Linda didn't say anything, just looked down at the ground.

"It's getting darker," Elizabeth said, "but those of us who believe in the light still have a good chance of winning. This is where the Light Ceremony book comes in. We need that so we can teach you the necessary rituals. And we need the original text, not the copies that the druids have divided up among themselves. That's why we need to ride, just as soon as we've had a little to eat."

"Ride? Again? Where?" the girls asked in a chorus.

"To Cauldron Swamp to pick up the original book from an old druid who has protected it for a long time. Her name is Pi and she lives in a cottage beyond Goldenhills Valley."

"Hold on," Alex said. "I want to make sure I've got this right. You're saying that we need to ride our horses to some old druid who lives in a swamp to pick up a book? Why can't we just call her and ask her to bring it to us?"

Elizabeth burst out laughing but then stopped abruptly when she saw Alex's face.

"I'm sorry. I didn't mean to laugh at you, but it does sound pretty ridiculous when you put it that way. Pi has protected the Light Ceremony book in her home in Cauldron Swamp for many years now. She lives a little beyond the bounds of civilization, even compared to other druids. Well, you'll see for yourselves ..."

She was quiet for a moment, letting her gaze rove over each of the stone formations and then the clear blue sky. Then she continued.

"To be completely honest, it's been a long time since I last saw Pi or even heard anything from her. I don't really know what awaits us."

Something protective, almost worried, had crept into Elizabeth's voice. She looked serious when she continued, "You have to ride there and I will accompany you. I can't let you go on your own, not there."

"So, everything hinges on a book?" Linda said. She liked the thought of that, traveling day and night for the sake of a book. Totally reasonable, she thought.

Elizabeth nodded. "The book is actually the only thing lacking now before we can perform the powerful magical ritual of the Light Ceremony. We're so close to the goal now, my friends!"

"But what about my dad?" Lisa objected. "Shouldn't we help him?"

"We're going to help your father, Lisa. You have my word. But right now, it's quite simply too risky," Elizabeth said. "Jessica, Sabine, and Katja seem to have gathered on the platform, and we need the book if we're going to be strong enough to resist them. We need to bide our time. Only once we have the book and you have gained access to the magic that it contains ... only then can we pursue the Dark Riders and free your father."

"Elizabeth is right," Linda said. "If we're going to be able to help your father, we need to know what we're rescuing him from. It's dangerous to go there too soon, unprepared."

They got up and Fripp returned to his burrow. The girls felt exhilarated, but their legs were like overcooked spaghetti. So much information, both new and the sort that they knew already or suspected. And now they had to go out riding again even though they had just gotten here.

But they knew one thing, even though their heads were spinning. They needed to ride together this time, as Soul Riders. One by one they stepped toward the largest of the runestones in the Secret Stone Circle. They put their hands on the runes and felt the text waken to life, vibrating a warm pink under their fingers.

"Check this out," Alex said, squinting and pointing to one of the runes that looked like roughly sketched letters. "Four horses, four riders. Is that, uh, *us*?"

The runes blinked. Elizabeth gave them an almost unconscious nod and took the lead, walking back to the druids' houses.

"All right. Now we'll have a little lunch, and then we head out. Next stop: Goldenhills Valley and Cauldron Swamp!"

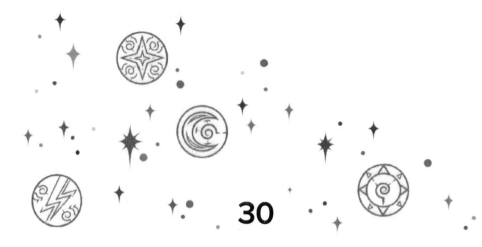

30

"Are we there yet?"

Alex asked the question with an annoyed smile. She knew perfectly well that they still had many hours of riding ahead of them. They had left the druids' houses a little while ago and had a long day's journey into night ahead of them still. They didn't know yet exactly where they were going to spend the night. Elizabeth said it was a surprise. Alex didn't know how the others felt, but she was downright sick of surprises at the moment. But she rode on, happy not to be alone in spite of everything and not to have an unconscious Linda slumped against her back.

The sun was at its zenith over the mountain peaks. The sky matched the brightly colored leaves in the trees and the air was cool. Elizabeth gave Alex a patient smile and shook her head. "Don't you see how happy Tin-Can is to trot?"

Tin-Can shook his head and snorted. Behind him, Starshine whinnied and sped up. The horses' coats gleamed brown, gold, and silver in the autumn sun.

As they rode they chatted about everything they had learned at the Secret Stone Circle. They were excited, thinking about what they were. How they could use their unique powers to make the world a safer place together. It all felt a bit woozy sometimes, but it was starting to seem more possible. The four of them, the Soul Riders. Of course that's how it was.

Linda thought about the dark sense of foreboding that lingered urgently just below the surface, somewhere between dream and wakefulness. Crying horses, muddy water, a dense, bubbling darkness that devoured you alive. She shivered and squeezed her legs into her galloping mount. Best to get everything over and done with as soon as possible. Too late to turn around now.

The whole gang kept up their rapid pace. Elizabeth rode in the lead on her beautiful silver-gray mare, Calliope, with Alex and Tin-Can hard on her heels. Then came Anne on Concorde, Lisa on Starshine, and finally Linda on Meteor. It was nice to focus on the ride, become one with the horse's movements. Lisa tried to get a little singalong going but didn't get much of a response from the others, so she gave it up. Alternating between a trot, canter, and gallop, they rode into the twilight until they saw houses spread out below them, on the far side of the mountains and the woods. Down there in the big valley, the forest's mossy green color scale and the yellow, red, and orange hues of the leaves got some competition from the white mother-of-pearl tones and fresh green grape vines.

"Look! A vineyard!" Lisa exclaimed, pointing. "And a castle! Wow, that's beautiful!"

"That's Silverglade Manor," Elizabeth said, gesturing with her hand at the magnificent light gray-castle with more towers and pinnacles than they could even count from this distance. "That's where we're staying tonight."

"You're kidding, right?!" Alex said and broke into an enormous smile.

Elizabeth shook her head, smiling. "The baroness and I are old friends. I've been invited to overnight there as often as I'd like when I'm out on long rides. Calliope, too, of course. Well, I suppose you'd like a tour of the stables now?"

Everyone looked down and saw the enormous stables gleaming white with reddish-brown roofs and black wood details. Beyond the stable buildings there were several enclosed pastures, paddocks, and jumping courses. They also saw several smaller stable structures in the area, spread out like a little village in the valley.

Linda exhaled quickly. "Wowza! I forgot how huge this place is!"

"Silverglade is Jorvik's largest and most lavishly appointed equestrian center," Elizabeth said. "They run riding camps here nonstop, all seasons of the year. Many international competitions in dressage and jumping are held here, too."

"Yeah," Alex said. "I came here once to watch. Dusty from Jorvik Stables came in second in the 1.30m class. It would be so epically cool to compete here sometime."

Anne took a breath and eagerly asked, "Is it true that the baroness has Lipizzaner horses in the stables?"

Elizabeth nodded with a laugh. "Does she ever! You'll see for yourself in a minute. Now do you understand why I wanted to surprise you?"

"Yeah, yeah," Alex said, acting blasé. "What's so great about a night in a castle with Lipizzaner horses?"

The others laughed. With Elizabeth and Calliope in the lead, they walked down the sloping hillside that led onto the grounds of Silverglade Manor. Once they came down from the hill, they trotted and rode at a leisurely pace across the last stretch to Silverglade, feeling happy and bubbly. They saw several horses being ridden out in the paddock. A chalky-white dapple-gray, a gleaming chestnut horse, and a coal-black Thoroughbred. It was just like a painting.

Maybe we needed this right now, Linda thought, enjoying watching the skilled riders in the paddock: a smooth, supple transition into a canter, the invisible helpers, the harmony, the elegance. *Maybe this is the calm before the storm.*

Or after the storm?

Before and *after the storm is probably more like it.*

She watched her friends for a long time, laughing and joking around as they rode ahead of her. It felt like they had stumbled upon a masquerade ball where they were expected to play different roles, happy roles. And yet they were tired and still shaken up from everything that had happened. Was that why their laughter seemed so shrill, a little *too* shrill, and their conversation was so loud, a little *too* loud?

Maybe it was all a masquerade, a play that no one had the script for. But if so, Linda planned to play her role, too. She told Meteor to giddy up and rode to catch up with the others, who had reached the paddock already.

Elizabeth shocked them by whistling to one of the riders, the one riding the chestnut horse. The woman, whose age was hard to pinpoint—about Elizabeth's age or older, maybe—looked up in surprise but broke into a laugh when she saw Calliope lean her sleek head over the paddock fence.

"Elizabeth!" she exclaimed. "It's been ages! You arrived just in time for the evening feeding, what luck!"

The women greeted each other warmly before Elizabeth turned to the girls. "This is the Baroness of Silverglade, who has been so kind as to let us spend the night here. Baroness, allow me to introduce Alex, Anne, Lisa, and Linda."

The baroness, a tall, slightly angular woman with silvery-gray hair that she wore in a bun below her riding helmet, gave them a friendly nod.

"We just finished the last dressage ride of the day here. I'm just going to cool down my horse for a few minutes and then I'll meet you in the stables. Elizabeth, you know the way, don't you? I thought your horses could stay in the aisle where my Lucky has her stall." She stroked her horse's neck and the girls saw the muscles playing inside horse's glossy coat. Lucky's mane was a light sandy color done in button braids.

Lucky, Lisa thought. Yes, that was probably a good name for a horse who had the good fortune to live in a place like this.

"With the Lipizzaner horses?!" Anne exclaimed, her eyes aglow.

The baroness laughed. "They're across the aisle. You can't miss them, I promise."

They walked along behind Elizabeth with their reins loose, heading for the stable where the horses would each get their own clean, spacious, sawdust-scented stall. Soon they would also get hay and molasses, and fresh, cold water. The girls currycombed them, cleaned out their hooves, and combed their tangled manes, which were full of pine needles and leaves. Anne got to pet the fantastic white Lipizzaner horses. She walked back over to Concorde's stall as if she were on little clouds.

"Although of course you're handsomer, Concorde," she explained to her horse, grooming him in long, steady strokes.

"Do you think Tin-Can would look good with button braids like Lucky is wearing?" Alex hollered across the stable aisle.

Lisa tried to picture the sturdy little horse, more of an overgrown pony than an elegant dressage horse, with his mane done in button braids. She utterly failed and started laughing. "I think he rocks the natural look, honestly."

Alex nodded, pushed aside Tin-Can's long, straggly bangs and kissed him on the bridge of his nose. "Yup, he's a real hippie horse, this kid."

"Does anyone have a sponge handy?" Anne called. "I want to make sure I wash and dry Concorde's snaffle properly since we have access to a real stable and all for once. His snaffle is kind of fifty shades of gray right now. So gross."

The others looked around and shook their heads.

"Maybe check with Elizabeth or the baroness?" Linda suggested. "I saw them over by the tack room a minute ago."

Even from the doorway, the tack room smelled of soap and new leather. Anne was on her way in but stopped when she heard voices whispering. Elizabeth and the baroness? She leaned forward as far as she dared without being seen.

"... years since anyone was there. And you know how people talk. I'd stay away from there if I were you, Elizabeth, for the girls' sake. It's too dangerous."

Elizabeth's voice rose from a whisper to what was almost a yell, barely under her breath.

"I'm doing all this for their sake and you know it! I've heard the rumors about Pi, too. But we have to go there. It can't be helped! If there was some other way, well, no one would be happier than me. Believe me. But I've thought about it long and hard and it can't be done any other way. I ..."

Anne tripped, bumped the doorframe, and tumbled into the tack room with a loud crash. The women looked up from where they sat cleaning their stirrup straps and looked as if they had been caught off guard. And so they had, Anne thought. Why was the baroness so worried? What hadn't Elizabeth told them about Pi? Anne's stomach felt like it was full of little knots, but she gave Elizabeth and the baroness a big smile and they smiled even more broadly back at her. A little more and they might crack the corners of their mouths.

"Sorry, Anne! We were just chatting about how it was time to get going on dinner. There are freshly baked scones in the kitchen and strawberry jam. You like that, right?"

"Definitely," Anne nodded. "Are there any sponges here in the stable? I was thinking of following your example and cleaning up Concorde's saddle and snaffle."

The baroness pointed to an enormous rack of grooming supplies. "Help yourself. Supper will be served in the kitchen in, shall we say, about half an hour? Do you think you can be done with your horses and saddles and everything by then? Or do you maybe need more time?"

"A half-hour should be fine," Elizabeth said. "Although it would be great if one of you girls could help me get Calliope ready for the night."

"I'm sure we can handle that," Anne said, thinking that all four of them would be happy to take care of Calliope. She took the sponge and hurried back to the others, her heart pounding.

"You guys!" she hissed. "Get this. I heard Elizabeth and the baroness talking about Pi just now. It seemed like the baroness didn't want us to ride there. Too dangerous, apparently."

Linda's brow furrowed, and she lifted Meteor's cleaned saddle and put it on the saddle holder next to his stall.

"Dangerous? But . . ."

"Ssh!" Alex made a show of whispering. "She's coming!"

Everyone suddenly became engrossed in finishing up their tasks. A little while later they followed Elizabeth to Calliope's stall to get her ready for the night. While Linda and Alex groomed her sides, Lisa cleaned Calliope's hooves, and Anne, who had already brushed Calliope's mane and tail, stood stroking the mare's beautiful muzzle. It was smooth as silk and slightly pink.

"You're so pretty, Calliope," she said and kissed her on the muzzle. Calliope snorted and looked at her with her dark, soulful eyes. Her ears were tilted forward in curiosity and her head cocked to the side.

"And clever, too," laughed Elizabeth, who was standing next to her, looking on. "You have no idea how many times she's saved me from difficult situations. I'll tell you more over tea later."

They said goodbye to Calliope, who nickered gently back at them as they walked down the aisle toward the wide, gilded double doors.

They ate tons of freshly baked scones with butter and strawberry jam for dinner and washed it all down with tea and freshly squeezed orange juice. They ate until their stomachs were sticking out and they could hardly move. When was the last time they had truly eaten their fill? Several days ago, at least. In the Secret Stone Circle they had still been slightly sick to their stomachs from the portal sickness, so the druids' nice breakfast had been served in vain.

"I'd better take one more," Alex said, reaching for the plate of scones. "Cauldron Swamp probably isn't known for its great food, right?"

"What *is* Cauldron Swamp known for?" Anne turned her innocent face toward Elizabeth.

Elizabeth sipped her tea and slowly set her cup back down on her saucer. Finally, she spoke.

"Yes, well, it's a unique place, to put it mildly. Pi, who's an old druid, has lived there on her own for many years now. Cauldron Swamp is totally different from Silverglade, I'll tell you that much." She laughed and raised her teacup to her lips again.

The baroness, who was sitting at the other end of the table, raised one slender eyebrow but said nothing. The silence that followed was uncomfortable. Everyone fiddled with their porcelain cups or their silverware and looked out the window.

The baroness's kitchen had floor-to-ceiling windows and looked out over the vineyards, horse pastures, and paddocks. Alex sighed happily and patted her belly.

"This is the life, I tell you! It should always be like this. Just imagine if we could all start working here after we finish school!" Her golden-brown eyes sparkled. Then she looked at the baroness a little shyly and realized that maybe she should have checked with her before saying such a thing.

"You'd be welcome," the baroness nodded. "I always need good horse people here. But I'm going to bow out now and say good-night. Sleep well, everyone."

"Goodnight!" they all replied.

"I don't believe it for a second," Lisa told Alex once the baroness's footsteps had receded down the hallway. "That you would work here. You would die of boredom if you just sat around eating scones and grooming horses all day. Admit it, you love being a Soul Rider. Even when things look hopeless."

The moment Lisa said that, she realized it was just as true for her.

"Yeah, you've got a point," Alex said. "But hold onto that idea, would you? All four of us here at Silverglade Manor—can you imagine how great that would be?"

190

Linda had no difficulty at all holding onto that idea. To the contrary, she had already been picturing it herself. Ever since she had regained consciousness, she hadn't been able to stop thinking about the future, about her plans, or more accurately her lack of plans at the moment. Linda always had to have a plan. It was driving her crazy now to know so little about the future. Would she be able to stay in school and be a Soul Rider at the same time? Should she plan for a life on her own, a life outside the sisterhood? How long was this battle between good and evil going to last? Did evil have a season? If so, were they in the middle of it right now?

She thought of Mr. Sands, who had given up his humanity for Garnok because he believed he could bring the woman he loved back to life. Or at least get revenge for what people had subjected Rosalinda to. How far was she herself prepared to go for what she believed in? How dark was this all going to get?

"You're so quiet, Linda," Anne said, looking at her with her friendly blue eyes. "What's on your mind?"

"Yeah, well, what am I *not* thinking about?" Linda said with a laugh. "I'm thinking about the darkness, I guess. And the light. And how they basically both have to exist. Before, when I only had to worry about homework, the stable, and those kinds of things, everything was so simple, so black and white. I thought I knew exactly how a good person behaved and how to spot a bad person. But now I don't really know. How do I know that what we're doing is the right thing? Do you know what I mean?"

"I think so," Alex replied. "There's sort of different shades of black in the darkness. We have Garnok, who's the evilest of all. A kind of primal evil, like mythical monsters. And then we have Mr. Sands, who turned to evil because he stood to gain from that. Or maybe because he didn't have anything to lose. And then we're supposed to represent some sort of light on the other side. It's really hard to take it all in; *we're* supposed to do all that."

Everyone was quiet for a bit. Elizabeth's eyes shone in the light of the candles in the candelabras.

"My mom said something once," Anne said, looking thoughtful. "She said that Jorvik is a place that brings out the best and the worst in people. And those who become greedy and want more and more of the island's resources don't stop. It's like a poison. That's why she stopped cooperating with corporations that were like that. She couldn't carry on knowing that our house was built with dirty money. So now she works with other people for a greener Jorvik. She lost some customers at the bank, but she won over many new ones."

"Your mom is brave," Linda said. "More people should be like her."

Suddenly Anne missed her mother. And her father and little brother. She missed her soft bed, and her TV shows, and the bathroom where she loved to take bubble baths that went on for hours. She missed everything that she usually took for granted. She felt a pang of homesickness and looked away from the others.

"It's probably time for us to go to bed, huh?" Alex said with a yawn. The others nodded and started standing up.

"Sleep well, girls," Elizabeth said with a warm smile. "We have a tough ride ahead of us tomorrow."

31

Elizabeth was right—it was a long and grueling ride through increasingly muddy and rocky terrain. They had to stop several times to drink water, give their horses water, and check to make sure they didn't have any rocks stuck in their hooves. No one said very much. Everyone was focused on the ride, on avoiding branches and boulders, on maintaining a decent pace. When they finally rode through the wrought iron gates into Goldenhills Valley the next afternoon, the silence between the five riders had changed from comfortable to slightly oppressive. Maybe it had to do with the place. The air seemed to get colder as the fall colors of the leaves became increasingly intense. The trees glittered in vivid shades of yellow and red.

"Is it just me, or did the temperature just drop ten degrees?" Anne said, shivering.

"It's not just you," replied Lisa, who had ridden up alongside Anne. She loosened her grip on the reins and let Starshine properly stretch out his head. Anne followed her example and both of the horses snorted and tossed their heads. The horses' bodies were steaming and the steam rose up into the leaves, which burned vivid gold and blood-red everywhere around them. The scents of fall—cold, crisp air, leaves, and woodfires—blended with the sweet, heady scent of horses. The girls shivered, grateful for the warmth from their horses. Everyone was moving slower now. This happened without them really thinking about it. However, they did it for the same reason: it didn't feel good being here. Somehow they felt as if they were breaking in when they rode through the gates. The same feeling took root in all four of them: *Nature doesn't want us to be here.* It grew colder and colder with every minute that passed. They broke into a trot to warm up.

"I've never been here before," Alex said, looking around.

"Me either," Linda said.

"Me either," Anne said.

"Considering that I only arrived in Jorvik about five minutes ago, me either, obviously," Lisa said.

"Goldenhills Valley is a strange place," Elizabeth said. "Even by Jorvik standards. Have you ever heard people say that the valley is kept locked in the winter?"

"I think so," Linda responded. "That was mentioned in a book about Jorvegian folklore that I read. Wasn't it because of some old superstition? They didn't want to let the winter spirits out or something like that?"

"Exactly," Elizabeth said. "The fact is that the mayor still locks the gates during the winter. They do that to keep the winter's horrors contained, away from Jorvik's other residents."

Goldenhills Valley was a very strange place for sure. Inside the iron gates, the leaves continued to burn in gold and flame colors long after the first snow had blanketed the rest of the island with a thick layer of white. Farther away toward the immense ridge, there were rumors that scarecrows came to life while shadow witches, the most light-shy sort of witch you can imagine, scared away all life and light.

Superstition or truth? It was hard to say. Did the island itself even know? There was a primordial force here. Everyone who had ever ridden through the gate knew that, and so, too, did the girls on this crisp autumn day.

"This Pi," Lisa said thoughtfully. "Just how long has she lived here?"

"Many years now," Elizabeth replied. "Ever since she was entrusted with the Light Ceremony book. It's said that she's more than a hundred years old, but no one really knows for sure."

Elizabeth looked different when she spoke about Pi, Linda had noticed. Her brow was furrowed with deep wrinkles, and it was as if the friendly smile that so often played over the corners of Elizabeth's mouth disappeared. Why would the baroness advise Elizabeth against taking them to see Pi?

Who actually was Pi? Linda wanted to get to Cauldron Swamp and find out for herself. But the last leg of the ride was going to be long. Her muscles were already sore, and that would worsen. She thought that she wouldn't turn down the bubble bath now that Anne had been talking about yesterday. Linda urged Meteor on, riding up alongside Anne. Lisa was on her far side. Linda didn't want to ride alone anymore. She didn't want to carry all her strange thoughts on her own.

Anne didn't say much. Was she always this quiet, or was it the events in Pandoria that were still weighing on her? Linda decided to ask.

"How are you doing, Anne?" she said quietly.

"I don't know," Anne replied with a half-smile. "Just as I think I'm starting to feel like myself again, I think about what happened to me there, and then everything becomes sort of slippery and weird again. It's like somehow Pandoria has gotten inside me."

"I know what you mean," Linda said, thinking about the long, dark shadows of Pine Hill Mansion, Sabine scratching on the door, and the feeling that everything would be blown to pieces.

Lisa thought of Katja's white eyes, of everything hidden within them. She thought that she would probably never understand evil, but that she still had to try and confront it. Because somewhere in the darkness was the key to the light, to her father, who *had* to be freed. She felt the icy chill seeping down her spine like cold water. Suddenly she pictured both Katja and Mr. Sands in front of her. She heard his uncomfortable, creaky voice. *Why so quiet, little trespasser?*

"I met Mr. Sands at Dark Core," she said. "There is something really, really creepy about him. Something . . . I don't know, a kind of evil and timelessness, almost like a vampire."

Anne pulled her jacket around her tighter, as if a cold draft had surrounded her. Lisa did the same with a quick, instinctive motion.

"Well, he's no vampire," Linda said. "Those only exist in horror movies. But he probably did make some kind of supernatural deal with Garnok, and that's equally as creepy. I read about it in Mr. Sands's diaries. If Garnok is real, anyway, which Mr. Sands seems to be convinced he is. The druids, too, right?"

She caught Elizabeth's eye, as if seeking confirmation. Elizabeth nodded in silence and snuck a peek at Linda.

"What was the supernatural deal you read about?"

Linda felt her cheeks grow hot. Suddenly she felt unsure. Should she tell them everything she had read about Rosalinda? Or would the others think she was nuts to think that Mr. Sands had emotions, or had been in love?

"I don't really know," Linda said, a little cautiously, and urged Meteor on, "but it seemed like Mr. Sands wanted to get revenge against, well, everyone. And he seemed to know where Garnok was imprisoned. But one thing is for sure: Mr. Sands means business. We have to—*have to*—stop him!"

"One thing at a time," Elizabeth said as she gave Linda a troubled look. "Otherwise it'll be too much. First we'll get the book, then we'll discuss our options further. A lot of things will fall into place for you as soon as you have been initiated into the Light Ceremony. That's why it's so important that we get the book from Pi. This is the first time in a long time that we have strong enough Soul Riders who can conduct the ceremony. I'm sorry to put more pressure on you. That's actually the last thing you need, but there's no getting around it. You appear to be our only hope right now."

"Oh," Alex mumbled. "Is that all?"

They lapsed back into silence again. They alternated between walking, trotting, cantering, and galloping, depending on the surface they were riding over. The horses were alert and curious, snorting and nodding their heads. Finally, Elizabeth pointed to a black dot that was just barely visible on the horizon.

"Do you see that up there? That's Cauldron Swamp."

The girls saw it together, but their responses were completely different.

Linda was filled with intense anticipation. Soon she would get to see the book!

Lisa was struck by a sort of low-level panic. Was she really doing the right thing, going along? Why wasn't she at Dark Core and trying to help her father escape instead? Could this really be right, doing this . . . ?

Alex was pulled along by the adventure of it all and by Elizabeth's words about the Light Ceremony book. She longed to learn more. She was made for this!

And Anne? Anne had slowed down and was riding a fair distance behind the others. She didn't want to reach Cauldron Swamp.

Mostly she just wanted to turn around and ride back home, back to her family and safety. She felt small and afraid, like a little insect drowning in a big glass of water. The pressure in her chest made it hard to breathe.

Do it. Turn around. It's not too late yet.

She shook off her thoughts and cast a grim look at the swamp that awaited them. Then she trotted after her friends, closer and closer to the darkness that was spreading all over the entire landscape, an unfamiliar terrain that it was easy to slip into. What would it do to you, living out here alone in a swamp year after year?

They were about to find out.

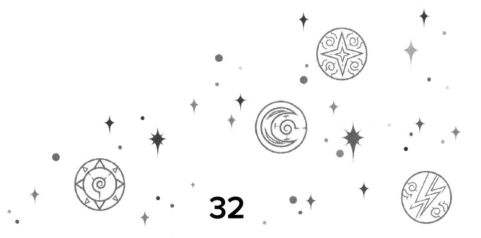

32

At one point in time, Cauldron Swamp had been a pleasant forest with a deep, sparkling mountain lake. It was said that the water there was so crystal clear that you could see all the way to the bottom. A stone's throw from the water, majestically framed by tall mountains, lay what had at one time been a beautiful lodge. An idyllic spot, perfect for a fishing trip or maybe a dip in the clear, fresh water.

That was a long time ago now. Today the water was black and sludgy, bubbling with frogs, creepy crawlies, and other more ominous things. Anyone who happened upon Cauldron Swamp by surprise should make sure not to fall into that black water with the steam rising off of it. Farther out in the swamp, will-o'-the-wisps flew around in the dull gray light. Anyone the will-o'-the-wisps lured out into the swamp was at risk of sinking to the bottom and never coming back up . . .

They had slowed their pace now, carefully considering every step. The horses moved cautiously through the increasingly soggier terrain.

"You really weren't exaggerating, Elizabeth," Alex said. "We're not in Silverglade anymore." Everyone mildly laughed, but the laughter stuck in their throats. There was something about this place . . .

Linda had thought Pine Hill Mansion had a dark soul, but nothing compared to Cauldron Swamp.

Elizabeth also seemed affected by the ominous atmosphere in the place. She had stopped and was looking out over the marshy ground. Her face looked grim.

"How strange," she mumbled. "This really does look like a real cauldron now. I wonder what happened."

"Halloween is coming early this year, it seems," Alex said, grimacing at the foul, boggy stench coming off the swamp. "But at least she set up little lights. Look over there!"

Alex pointed to some kerosene lamps hanging here and there along the bridge that extended out in front of them. From this distance, the network of bridges looked a lot like part of a crooked, meandering labyrinth.

Some of the lamps were lit, they saw, but far from all of them. A timeless, dusky mood lingered over the swamp, which was shrouded in thick fog.

"Cozy," Lisa said and patted Starshine, who started tossing his head and whinnying. "What is it, buddy? Are you afraid of the bridge?"

"We have to be extremely careful now," Elizabeth urged, dismounting. "I knew the terrain here in Cauldron Swamp would be treacherous, and I've certainly heard the rumors, but I hadn't expected this. You know, this doesn't feel good at all . . ."

"Do you think we should ride back?" Anne blurted out, a little too quickly.

"No," Elizabeth replied just as rapidly. "But we have to be vigilant. We don't know what to expect. And whatever you do, don't get too close to the water! The will-o'-the-wisps are wily, you know. Keep your eyes straight ahead, and don't look out at the swamp for too long. That's where they hide."

200

"Got it," Linda said. With every step Meteor took along the bridge, she was filled with a nagging sense of discomfort. Around them the swamp bubbled and fizzed. A big, poison-green toad jumped onto a log just beside Lisa and sat there. The toad's eyes were black and penetrating, almost verging on human. Lisa couldn't help staring back.

"What do you want, little toad?"

"I would avoid kissing that if I were you," Alex said.

The toad continued to stare at Lisa. Did it want to tell her something? Finally, the toad croaked but remained still, its eyes shiny and black.

"Come on," Lisa told Starshine. "Let's go."

The boards creaked ominously under them as they slowly led their horses across the meandering wooden bridge with foot-bridges leading off in various directions. Lisa and Starshine picked up the rear. She was careful not to look around.

33

It came from the swamp, a whispering sort of chuckling sound, a human sound. Lisa didn't dare look in that direction. She just kept her eyes fixed down on the leaky wooden boards of the bridge that would lead them to the house where Pi lived. It creaked a little more than she really felt comfortable with, but Elizabeth was confident that the bridge would hold under the weight of the horses, so it would probably be fine. If they kept their eyes open.

But don't look out at the swamp. She *mustn't* look.

She heard it clearly now. Her friends were a little ways in front of her, leading their horses. Why weren't they reacting? Was Lisa the only one who heard it?

Isa . . . Isa . . .

Lisa stiffened. No one called her Isa anymore. That was her father's affectionate nickname for her when she was little. Her father's and . . .

There it was, that icy hand around her heart.

Mom. Mom always called me Isa.

Her frozen heart revved. She snuck a peek at a narrow side path leading off the main bridge. The voice seemed to be coming from there, from just below.

Elizabeth and the girls led their horses forward a bit, oblivious to the fact that Lisa had dropped behind.

She mustn't. She simply *mustn't*—but she did it anyway. Starshine whinnied, resisting when she tried to lead him onto the narrow footbridge. But eventually he came along. She got closer and closer to the black, bubbling swamp water.

She heard it again now, the whispering voice. It was coming from the swamp.

Isa, my dear Isa, come here. I miss you so. Come here, so I can give you a hug. It's so lonely down here, so cold . . .

Lisa stopped, transfixed by the voice. She recognized it. Her heart froze again.

Isa! Isa dear, come to Mommy!

Lisa couldn't resist and looked out at the water. A white light was dancing over the swamp. It expanded into a hovering ball of light. It made her think of the sparkler she had lit with her mother one Christmas Eve when she was little. Her face lit up with joy at the sparkling, festive light.

Then she heard it again, the summoning voice. It embraced her heart. She was bewitched by the flickering white flare of light out over the dark water. It was so beautiful, she thought, so peaceful, like swans gliding slowly on the water. How could she imagine that it had looked unpleasant before? This was a fairy-tale lake where sad princesses found their missing mothers. They were waiting down in the swamp, the mothers, and they had lit sparklers to help people find their way to them. You just had to be brave and look deep enough into the water.

They were down there.

Lisa took another step forward, hearing the gentle, familiar voice calling to her.

Come to Mommy.

It happened in a flash. It was instinctive. Lisa let go of Starshine's reins and he screamed. She didn't turn around to calm him down. She didn't have time. She had to get to her mother!

It's NOT your mother.

Yes, it IS my mother, my only mother. She needs me! And I need her.

And then she stepped down into the black, reeking swamp water as if it were a swimming hole on a warm summer's night. Slowly she waded farther out and felt the cold water waking up parts of her that had been dead for years. Three years, to be exact.

Starshine galloped after her and bit frantically at her clothes with his teeth. He got ahold of her jacket collar, but Lisa wriggled out of her jacket and kept moving farther into the swamp, toward her mother's voice, toward the curious sparkling lights. She was almost there, with her mother.

"Did you hear that?" Alex yelled, back on the bridge. "What was that?"

They heard Starshine's desperate shrieks and all blurted out "Lisa!" at the same time. Together they all rushed back and out to the little side bridge she had taken, following the splashing sounds.

"Nice and easy, Lisa! Don't panic!" Linda shouted, although she sounded panicked. They raced out to the end of the little side spur, reaching their arms out to Lisa. Alex managed to grab one of her legs, Anne an arm. They felt how strong the currents were in the swamp.

"Hold on tight!" Alex yelled to Anne. "Don't let go!"

"I'm trying!" Anne replied.

Alex shot lightning at the swamp, but the bolts rebounded, veering around in the air with the will-o'-the-wisps. Linda called on the moon but received no response. Anne flailed around in the air frantically. She wanted to summon the sun's power, but no sunforce came through. They tugged and pulled on Lisa's unwilling, kicking body. She was trying to get away from them, deeper into the swamp.

Anne made one last attempt to summon the sun's magic. Her forehead broke out into a cold sweat and tears of frustration rolled down her cheeks. Her hand trembled as she held it up. "Don't fail me now!" she whispered, feeling Alex move her arms around her, then also feeling Linda's arm. Anne could feel her friend's body heat and allowed it to spread.

Then a piercing sunlight rose over the night-blackened swamp and blinded Lisa.

"Help!" she screamed. "I have to get out! Help me, please!"

She heard her mother's voice fading into the swamp, growing fainter and fainter. Instead she heard another voice, a darker voice. It was her father's.

Time to get out, Isa.

Lisa felt the icy currents and the lights of the will-o'-the-wisps trying to pull her down to the bottom. Pond weeds clung around her legs, holding her. Finally, the others managed to pull Lisa up with one massive collective effort. They collapsed onto the bridge. A swift current of muddy swamp water flowed beneath them. They lay there for a bit, all partially on top of each other in a stinking heap. The only sound was their exhausted panting. Their hearts seemed to beat out of sync.

"Thank you," Lisa finally whispered.

"You know it," Alex replied feebly.

"I was so sure it was her," Lisa said after a while. "It was so real. And the light was so bright. I couldn't think on my own anymore. It was as if my brain were infected by that hovering light."

"I know," Elizabeth said, her voice gentle. "Will-o'-the-wisps can lead a person astray so easily. There are many different kinds of will-o'-the-wisps. Some are more like kind, fluttering butterflies in light form. They can guide you through the darkness. But this kind, the type they have here, live off the souls of the bodies that drown in the swamp. And then the will-o'-the-wisps use their energy to lure new souls down. They're almost impossible to resist, but they're not real. Your mother isn't here."

Lisa shook her head and wiped away her tears. Her mother had never been to Jorvik. She had died and was buried where they had lived before, on the ranch in Texas right by the Mexican border. Surrounded by horse paddocks and desert wildflowers, she slept her eternal sleep, and it was Grandma, not Lisa, who tended the grave and made sure there were always fresh flowers there. Thousands of miles from the dark, unrelenting swamp full of lost souls.

And yet. When the will-o'-the-wisps spread their tempting glow over the swamp, in that instant, she could have sworn that she saw desert wildflowers.

"It was stupid of me to stop," she said. "I mean, we're supposed to stick together, aren't we?"

"Well, but what about us?" Linda said. "We should have checked to make sure you were keeping up, and not just gone on ahead like that!"

They all nodded. Then they got up and walked back over to Elizabeth, who was waiting a few yards away with the horses. She peered out at the swamp with a troubled look on her face. It was starting to get dark now, but Pi was out there somewhere in the shadows. She knew it. The sound of Lisa splashing in the water must have been audible all over Cauldron Swamp.

Finally, they reached Pi's cabin, and Elizabeth realized that her worst forebodings were right. She could feel Pi's evil energy in the air, and the dark power grew stronger and stronger the closer they got to the cabin.

"Pi," Elizabeth whispered sadly. "What's become of you?"

· ⁙ ·

Suddenly Elizabeth yelled, "Come on! We need to get out of here right away."

"What?!" Linda exclaimed. "But what about the book? Weren't we supposed to get it?"

"We can't," Elizabeth said doggedly, her face looking chalky white in the shadows. She started leading her horse back again, away from the cabin. Her movements were jerky and she spoke quickly.

"It's witchcraft," she said and impatiently waved for the girls to follow suit. "I'm sure of it. Pi has switched sides. It was a mistake to come here. We need to get out of here before . . ."

She stopped, her eyes steely gray and determined.

"We need to get to Scarecrow Hill, to the big tree. The apple is ripe now, ready for picking. We need that apple!"

"The apple . . . ?" Alex repeated, looking confused. "You mean *the* apple, the one from the stories? Do you mean that it really exists?"

"It exists. And it's the only thing that is stronger than Pi," Elizabeth replied. "The apple's power will make her weaker, easier to convince. We need the book more than ever, but she'll never hand it over to us like this, not now that the darkness has taken her over. We need a weapon to use against Pi. We need the power of the apple. So now we ride to retrieve the apple so that we can get the book."

Elizabeth sighed loudly. "Oh, I should have listened to all the rumors! She's become what I feared . . ."

"A witch?" Linda suggested quietly. The shadows grew around them. The horses fidgeted.

Elizabeth didn't respond, just stared wide-eyed at Linda.

The horses reared in panic now. A crashing sound startled them all. The sound of rapid footsteps on wood. One of the oil lamps flickered and then they saw her.

She emerged from the darkness. The darkness sent her to them. All they could see was a figure shrouded in shadows, dressed in a dark cloak with something in front of its face. A wooden mask? The mask was glowing with pink, almost luminescent letters. Anne gasped as she felt the Pandoria sickness wash over her, sticky and pink.

She recognized those letters.

"Do you see that?" Anne whispered, but the others didn't seem to see or even hear her. The putrid stench of death and swamp was everywhere now. A cold laugh echoed across the swamp. They screamed and then they ran away quickly as Pi chased after them. She towered over them with her wooden mask and black cape.

She cackled, reaching out a bony hand toward Elizabeth. Calliope backed away shrieking in alarm.

"Hurry!" Elizabeth yelled, running away at the very back of the group with a firm grip on Calliope's reins. "Ride away from here!"

The night sky lit up with lightning, green and pink. One of the bolts hit Elizabeth, who collapsed and lay there on the bridge, unable to move. Calliope reared and neighed, moving farther and farther out on the rickety wooden bridge. The whites of the horse's eyes rolled back and forth. Calliope's beautifully arched nostrils flared.

"Calm down, pretty girl," Elizabeth soothed her. She tried to stand up but slumped back onto the hard wooden planks. "Calm."

But Pi had stretched out her frightful, gnarled hands toward the panic-stricken horse. She mumbled something in a language they didn't understand. Her words and motions caused Calliope to rear again. The wooden planks creaked dangerously beneath the horse.

"No!" Linda shrieked, lunging for Calliope as she realized what was happening.

Calliope staggered and backed up. She was champing foam and neighing in a panic. Linda walked toward her, trying to grab her reins, which dangled loose.

"There, there, sweetie. Come to me."

Pi took a step forward. Calliope shimmered grayish-white against the thick, sinister air surrounding the witch. Calliope's whole equine body trembled, taking a desperate leap away from Pi. The boards cracked under her weight and gave way.

"Come here, Calliope!" Linda screamed, her outstretched hand groping after the horse's flank in one last terrified gesture.

The sound of hooves slipping and falling filled the air, followed by another shriek and then it was all too late—the terrified horse plunged into the swamp.

"No! Calliope!"

They all screamed for Calliope now, for the beautiful, clever horse that was disappearing at a sickening pace down into the mire. Her white mane was black as tar. Her legs flailed in panic, creating big ripples in the water, and she screamed, screamed louder than they were screaming, pleading to be rescued.

Alex rushed toward the water. "We have to get her out!"

"Alex!" Linda wailed. "We can't get her out by ourselves. She's too heavy!"

Now Alex was crying, too. She sucked in sobbing breaths and threw her hands up into the air. She tried to shoot off lightning, a prayer, something—anything—that could stop this awful thing that was happening in front of her.

Nothing came of her efforts. Something was in the way; something dark and muddy had oozed in and was blocking the magical electricity.

"Work now!" Alex yelled in desperation. "You've got to work!"

They could only see Calliope's sleek head now above the water's surface. The same head they had been patting and combing just last night in the stable at Silverglade.

Elizabeth lay motionless on the wooden bridge, but sad tears streamed down her cheeks.

Lisa buried her face in Starshine's coat so she didn't have to look. The horses whinnied, stamped, and reared up.

"Not you, too, Tin-Can!" Alex cried as her horse tried to break free from her. "Please, sweetie, not you!" She pulled back on the reins, hard, and finally Tin-Can stopped. But he kept shrieking loudly and shrilly, his ears flattened back.

"We have to do something!" Alex yelled. "We have to!"

"If you jump into the water, you'll never come back out," Lisa warned, her sad eyes on Alex. "We can't lose you, too. Please."

A shriek and a horrifying, viscous bubbling sound rose from the water. The will-o'-the-wisps fluttered. In the gleam that arose, they saw Calliope's eyes, her beautiful, expressive eyes that somehow seemed to reflect her soul. They were vacant now. Calliope had given up. She sank and then vanished below the surface.

Then it became horribly quiet.

"She's gone!" Linda wailed, letting her tears fall onto Meteor's trembling neck. "Oh, Calliope!"

They could see air bubbles rising from where Calliope had sunk. They felt sick at the sight.

From Elizabeth's motionless form, they heard a sob. After that everything became a brilliant, hovering light.

Pi stood over on the bridge with her hands outstretched in a silent, wicked appeal in their direction. She crackled with pink energy and the magic spread straight from Pi toward the spot where Elizabeth lay.

"Elizabeth!" Alex screamed. The pink shimmer engulfed Elizabeth, gurgling around her. Her contours became blurry, eaten away by the pinkness. Linda reached out for Elizabeth, who shook her head.

"No! Save the apple! The apple!" she yelled. "Retrieve the apple and ride back here with it! That's our only hope!"

Elizabeth's voice sounded like it was floating, dispersing. Then she was gone. Where she had just been lying, only a weightless, vaguely pink, fluctuating light hovered.

"NO!" Linda screamed. She stood there on the wooden bridge as if paralyzed. At the same time, she saw Pi approaching. Her feet looked like rough tree roots.

The being changed the wooden mask over her face now. Linda stood frozen, staring at the ghastly face, a non-face, a chimera. What was hiding under that mask? Was it something . . . even worse?

New mask.

Angry mask, Linda thought mechanically.

Her claw-like hands moved with lightning speed as they swapped out the mask.

Happy mask. This was the nastiest of them all. It sniggered at her, sneering, bewilderingly like a skull.

She smelled rot, the swamp stench.

"Linda!" her friends yelled in warning. They were already on their horses, ready to gallop away. "Come on!"

But Linda was following the light with her eyes. She watched the will-o'-the-wisp—Elizabeth—slowly glide through the air, into the swamp's darkness.

Maybe she could do something. That pink glimmer brushed the tree branches over her.

Pi stopped in front of Linda and Meteor, close, way too close.

"The moon?" hissed the woman behind the mask, groping around in the gloom. Once again, Linda smelled a rotten puff of swamp air, like something old and diseased. She was startled. Her friends were yelling at her, praying and pleading for her to ride away with them. Now! There wasn't time!

"Come on, Linda!" Anne yelled. "We can't stay here!"

Linda dug with one hand in her saddlebag and pulled something out—Herman's glass cookie jar. Thank goodness for Herman.

She opened the lid and poured the cookies out into her hand and stuffed them in her jacket pocket. Then she yelled to Elizabeth.

Pi was coming toward them but was more hesitant now. Her tree roots clapped against the bridge as she moved. Then she stopped. From farther away, the friends watched her, wide-eyed.

"What's going on?" Alex whispered to Lisa.

The pink will-o'-the-wisp moved toward Linda.

"The moon," the creature that was Pi whispered again.

"Elizabeth!" Linda yelled again and smiled in relief as she saw the will-o'-the-wisp fly toward her and into the jar. Quickly, with her hands trembling, she closed the lid.

"I promise I'll ride carefully," she said as she climbed onto Meteor's back. She looked at Pi's monstrous wooden face one last time and then rode away at a gallop.

Phantom noises echoed within her. Calliope's shrieks of fear as the swamp swallowed her. Then, the awful chanting from the witch Pi. The sound followed her away from Cauldron Swamp and into the woods, where it became whispers and echoes.

In the end, finally, it faded away.

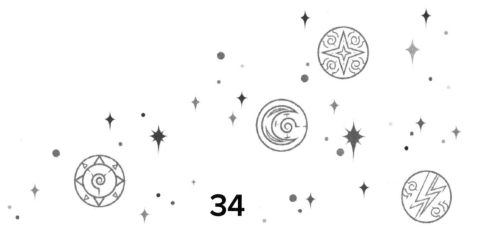

34

They rode as if there were an inferno raging behind them. They rode for their lives. They rode together, away from the swampy, marshy ground toward Goldenleaf Forest. They rode without looking back. They rode and thought about the terrible wooden masks and the rotten stench of the decaying bog. They rode with their heads bowed, remembering Calliope and how scared she was in the end. It had been too late and there wasn't anything they could do but look on and cry.

They cried now, too. Their sobs echoed along with the horses' hoofbeats.

They hadn't been able to rescue Calliope from drowning. How could they forgive themselves?

The girls were pale and trembling. None of them said anything. Maybe there were no words. Later, perhaps once they had set up camp, they would talk. Not now. They weren't ready yet. After the repulsive swamp, the air felt extra fresh. The smell of fall was everywhere here: leaves, apples, and burning wood. The horses' warm bodies were steaming when they slowed their pace.

Linda peered sadly into the glass jar. If she looked for a long time and carefully, she could just make out Elizabeth's face in the will-o'-the-wisp. She thought Elizabeth looked frightened.

"Don't worry," she said, carefully pulling her fingertips along the surface of the jar. "We'll find a way to break the spell."

Even so, she didn't dare believe her own words. There was no expression in her monotone voice.

She was tired and hungry and didn't want to run away anymore. She wanted Elizabeth to be here. The real Elizabeth, not a fluttering will-o'-the-wisp in a cookie jar. Only now that she was gone did the girls appreciate how important she was to the group. She was the one who had held them together, guided them though all the difficult things, the uncharted territory. And she had done everything with a smile, as if she harbored a secret that she was maybe—but only maybe—planning to share with them.

"Sorry, Elizabeth," Linda whispered to the glass jar. There was fluttering in there. For a millisecond, Linda thought she saw a trace of Elizabeth's sad face. Then she could only see the pinkish-white light again.

"All right, what was that that just happened?" Lisa said. "I can't really believe that's Elizabeth in the jar."

"I know," Linda replied with a sigh. "Everything from the swamp felt like a nightmare. But clearly this is our reality now."

"I don't know how you guys feel, but I would be happy to wake up any time now," Lisa said.

"Hmm, that would be nice," Alex replied. "But Linda is right. This is our life now. I don't like it any more than you do, but we have to keep going. We can't give up now!"

Lisa nodded and stroked Starshine's soft coat with her cool hands.

"We'll stop soon," Anne said. "I can't keep going. Concorde either."

"We could probably stop right here?" Lisa said.

The others nodded. Alex pointed to a fire pit in the distance. Some visitor to the forest must have stopped here to warm up or cook a meal over the fire. "This looks like a perfect campfire waiting to happen, doesn't it?"

Her friends agreed, and suddenly the witch Pi, the swamp, and the awful masks felt a little further away.

After a while, they had the fire going and had doled out the last cookies in sisterly fashion. Linda had taken out the glass jar with the will-o'-the-wisp in it and set it next to them. In the orange glow of the campfire, Elizabeth's face was clearly visible.

"Should we, you know, talk directly to her?" Alex wondered. "Can she hear what we're saying?"

"I think so," Linda said, patting the jar gently. "At any rate, it can't hurt to try, can it?"

"Probably not," Alex said. "And lately I *have* done weirder things than talk to a will-o'-the-wisp in a glass jar."

"I miss Elizabeth," Anne said. "Real Elizabeth."

"Me, too. We all do." Linda stood beside the crackling fire, dragging her feet back and forth. She chewed on her lower lip and her dark eyes looked even more thoughtful than usual. "I want to talk to you guys about something. Actually, I should be talking to Elizabeth, but that doesn't really seem to be an option right now, so . . ." She peered into the glass jar before continuing. "There's something I can't let go of, what Elizabeth said earlier at the Secret Stone Circle, the part about the last sisterhood. I didn't dare ask at the time, because . . . well, you know how you don't really want to know the answers to some questions, because it's nicer not knowing? But now I regret that I didn't say anything."

215

"I've been thinking about that, too. So much," Lisa admitted. "What does it actually mean?"

"Well," Alex said, pulling on another sweater. "The way I look at it, there are two possible outcomes."

"Which are?" Anne raised her right eyebrow.

Alex's honey-brown eyes were fixed firmly on her friends. "Right, as it's been said, we have two options. The first is that we're the last Soul Riders—the last sisterhood—because we're going to defeat evil once and for all."

The fire flared up, making their faces look ghostly white. Lisa inhaled before whispering:

"And the second?"

Don't say it, Linda thought, but Alex said it. Of course she said it. They were all thinking the same thing.

"We're the last," Alex enunciated slowly, tossing a stick into the flames, "because this is the end, because none of us will survive this. We're the last of the dinosaurs, the last Soul Riders."

Over where the horses were bedded, Starshine brayed. Lisa rushed over to him and caressed his shimmering blue mane.

"There, there, buddy," she said. "Easy now. You're okay."

Starshine rested his muzzle in her hand and they stood that way for a long time. Eventually, Lisa came back over to the campfire.

All four of them sat around the fire for a while longer, but no one said anything. Instead, the silence hung over them, heavy and dark.

And the truth, which was so hard to face.

Because what if it *was* true? What if no one, not even Jorvik itself, survived?

Everyone sighed and looked at the Elizabeth glowing in the glass jar. Were they imagining it, or was the glow fading now?

Suddenly Alex stood up. "Listen, forget about the end of the world for a while. We need a plan! We have to ride and get that apple, and bring it back. That was the last thing Elizabeth said: that we need that apple so that we can take the book."

"But," Anne said. "Aren't you forgetting something here? Or *someone*. There is someone we need more than the apple, someone who can help us explain everything. Maybe he can help us with Elizabeth, too." She eyed the others seriously. "I'm talking about Fripp, obviously," she continued. "We have to ride to the Secret Stone Circle first and ask for help!"

Alex put her hand on her forehead and sighed deeply. "What?! How can you go against Elizabeth's orders? We need that apple!"

"What we need even more than that darned apple," Anne said in a steady voice, "is instructions from someone who *gets it*. And I don't get any of this. Neither do you guys. Admit it! Do you even have any idea how to pick the apple?" She hid her frozen hands inside her sweater sleeves, clenching her hands into fists where no one could see. Then she said, "There's no shame in asking for help. Especially not in our hour of need." She peered sadly at Elizabeth who fluttered inside the glass jar. "This is an emergency."

Something clicked inside Lisa when she heard Anne's words. She thought of what Elizabeth had said about Anne in the Secret Stone Circle. *She who rules over the sun is a leader.*

"Anne's right," Lisa said. "We should check with Fripp before we do anything else."

Linda nodded. "Okay, Fripp first. The last thing we need right now is to squabble with each other. Right, Alex?"

Alex crossed her arms over her chest and sighed again. But finally she nodded slowly. "I appear to have been overruled, so okay: Fripp first. Surely he can help us. So, now that's decided, I NEED some sleep."

"Me, too," yawned Anne, who had already crawled into her sleeping bag.

"Hmm, same here," Lisa said.

Linda didn't say anything. She had already fallen asleep with the Elizabeth jar beside her. The flickering, elusive glow of the campfire made them drowsy.

"Hey, listen," Lisa said. "Shouldn't we take turns standing guard? It feels scary for us all to be asleep at the same time."

"I've heard there are wolves in these woods," Anne said. She had crawled into her sleeping bag with her mittens on. Every now and then, when the fire flared up, the dark circles under her eyes were visible.

"Uh, there's too much talking," Alex grumbled, brushing aside the concern.

Lisa saw Katja's eyes in the fire in front of her. "Wolves or not," she said, "I think we should take shifts of watch duty. I'll take the first shift. I'd just have nightmares anyway if I slept right now."

So it was decided. The others got comfy in their sleeping bags and slept, warmed by the fire that continued to crackle.

Soon it was Alex's turn to stand watch. *Too* soon, thought Alex, who would have liked to sleep for a couple more hours. But once she was up and out of her sleeping bag and had eaten a power bar that she had found in her saddle bag, she had a surprisingly easy time staying awake. The fire had died down and Alex was contemplating putting another log on when she heard noises farther off in the woods.

The sound of horse hooves. And then voices talking in rapid, irritable tones. Alex cautiously crept closer to the edge of the woods to get a better view.

Dark cloaks. Muscular, black horses. Three of them. Three riders in the night. They spoke in hushed voices. Alex couldn't make out what they were saying. She crept closer. She thought of her friends sleeping nearby, completely oblivious to the fact that these three riders dressed in black were just a few seconds away.

Should she have woken them up? She obviously should have. But she didn't dare move. Not now, when the three black-clad riders were so close that they would definitely hear it if a twig snapped. She would have to stay here and hope for the best. Alex did have a theory about who the riders might be. She had not met the third one before, but she recognized the other two, unfortunately.

They were approaching. She heard Sabine's voice clearly now.

"Are you sure they're here? I think we would have picked up their tracks . . ."

"Huh, what do you mean?" Jessica said. "The forest is big. I'm sure they're on their way to get the apple."

Then a third voice, even more hardened than the other two.

"I'm not so sure about that, actually. They probably slunk back home with their tails between their legs, crying for their mommies."

Then Sabine again: "As long as they didn't manage to pick the apple before they crawled home to mommy, because if they did, we have a problem."

"There's no way they could have made it there. We'll be there long before our little friends have reached the place," Jessica hissed. "That accursed apple needs to be destroyed."

As soon as the sound of the hoofbeats grew more distant, Alex raced back to camp and woke the other girls.

"I heard them in the woods! They're on their way to pick the apple!" she hissed.

"Who is?" Anne mumbled drowsily.

"Sabine, Jessica, and one other."

"Katja," Lisa whispered, looking pale. "Oh no."

"They're on their way there right now! We have to ride even faster if we want to get the apple before they do. Come on, you guys, get up!" Alex slipped Tin-Can some oats and then passed the bag around. Anne was quiet, her light hair sticking out every which way and her eyes blurry. But she was already on her way over to saddle Concorde. Alex and Anne exchanged glances and Alex mouthed, *Thank you.* Anne nodded briefly in return.

"But what about Fripp?" Linda said, still half asleep. "Weren't we going to go see him first?"

"Forget about Fripp for the moment," Alex said. She didn't actually like railroading other people this way, but there was no time to discuss this now.

"We need to hurry to Scarecrow Hill! Otherwise Sabine and her crew will beat us there. And that," Alex said, looking older and more serious than ever before, "simply cannot happen. If it does, they will destroy the apple and we won't have any hope of defeating Pi."

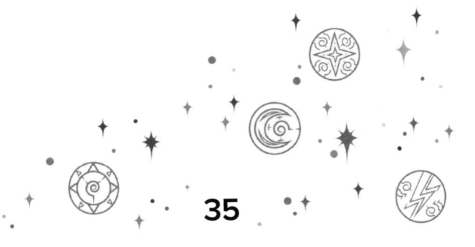

35

The very early morning was still dark and foggy, and the prospect of rain loomed like a vague threat in the chilly air. The recently awoken riders yawned as they left their campsite behind them on horseback and hurried onward toward Scarecrow Hill. Jessica's words echoed in Alex's mind. *That accursed apple needs to be destroyed...*

The apple, the only one that grew on the tall, knotty tree atop Scarecrow Hill. Only one grew each year. Everyone in Jorvik had heard of it, but few believed that it really existed. And now they were off to go pick it. She felt a funny, tingly feeling inside when she thought about it. She had read about the apple to her little siblings in some old book of legends and fairy tales without suspecting that it *was* magical—and that she would one day go pick it.

The legend awakens, she thought. Well, thanks to them it would. If they made it there in time.

"People say there is a magical apple," she told Lisa, who had never heard of this remarkable apple. "It cannot be picked by just any old person ... but that doesn't mean that plenty of people haven't tried. There was an old tradition to arrange a race to see who could reach the apple first. To many people it was a game. For others it was deadly serious."

"Didn't things get totally out of hand one year?" Anne wondered, addressing Linda, who was riding in the lead ahead of Lisa and Alex. "I think I remember hearing something about that."

"Yeah," Linda replied. "There was a terrible accident right by the tree. Several horses and riders were seriously injured, and one girl even died. It was total mayhem, people and horses all over the place, pure mass psychosis. After that they tried banning the apple race, but they never succeeded. It kept going and it's still going today. I had always thought that the apple was sort of symbolic, but it really exists."

"We *have* to pick that apple," Alex said, sounding just as determined as Sabine had in the woods. "One of the last things Elizabeth said was about the apple, that it would help us against Pi. The apple must be some kind of cure for Pi's witchcraft. That must be what Elizabeth meant! And we need to pick it ourselves. If Sabine, Jessica, or Katja get there first, we're definitely sunk."

"But what if they're already there?" Linda said. "What if it's already too late?"

Lisa pictured Katja's cold, white eyes again. She felt the chill creeping in despite her two sweaters. "We need to beat them there," she said, clicking her tongue to Starshine. "Come on, time to gallop now!"

"I think I know a shortcut," Alex said. "Tin-Can and I have ridden here several times on long rides in the past, and this way should be quicker. Right, buddy? You recognize where you are!"

Just then she remembered a half-destroyed stone bridge that she and Tin-Can had crossed with great difficulty the last time they had ridden out here. She decided not to mention the stone bridge to her companions. No point in scaring the others now when speed was of the essence.

She rode ahead and took the lead, where she picked up the pace. The coming dawn was just visible in the east, the vague promise of a new day.

As the four horses came to a gallop, they heard it. The sound of hooves at a mad gallop. It was coming closer . . . from in the woods.

Anne, who was picking up the rear, looked back over her shoulder and found herself looking straight into Sabine's furious eyes. She screamed, but Sabine just laughed in amusement. The girls farther ahead heard Anne's scream and turned around in their saddles. They paled, and then urged their horses to speed up.

"Faster!" Alex yelled.

The three riders and their coal-black steeds were getting closer. In the darkness the girls could see the horses' bodies lit up with glowing, rune-like patterns. Sabine's horse had red patterns in its coat, like coagulated blood. Jessica's horse had green, like the moss in the woods, and Katja's horse gleamed a bluish-white like her own eyes.

"They're gaining on us!" Linda yelled through all the chaos.

A collective shudder ran through them all. The woods felt even colder now. The wind whipped against their cheeks as they galloped wildly onward.

Linda leaned forward in the saddle to avoid taking a big branch to the face.

"Duck!" she cried. Her friends ducked. The horses' hooves thundered against the moss, pebbles, and pine needles. The riders' eyes teared up from the force of the wind as they raced along.

Lisa took a cross-country position and pushed onward. It felt as if Starshine was going to stumble, but he compensated and then jumped over a big tree root. His breathing was rapid and rhythmic.

"We need to hurry!" Alex yelled.

The Dark Riders were only a few yards behind them, trying to force them off the trail. Flames flickered on the moss where their hooves had trampled it.

"Don't let them get away!" Jessica screamed.

Katja raised an impossibly long, white arm into the air. The girls held their breath, riding faster and faster. How much faster could they ride? They kept needing to push even harder and harder as thundering hooves and whistling winds stifled the air.

Just then an enormous tree toppled onto the trail right beside them. The crash made Starshine neigh uneasily and gallop even more wildly.

"It's okay," Lisa said and tried to calmly stroke his heck. "It's okay." She felt Katja's eyes on her back like frozen fire. Until now she had never known that fire could be made of ice, that dead, icy-white eyes could burn you.

Now she knew. And she knew that she had to keep Katja away. If she let her in again, it was all over. The apple was lost.

Tin-Can's ears were cocked forward. In the morning mist, his thick coat was even shaggier than usual. He took a running start and flew over the fallen tree.

They heard Jessica mutter something behind them. An incantation? Her voice rose in the forest, over the mossy rocks and the ancient mountains. They heard cracking and crashing again. Alex nervously scanned around her but didn't slow down as Tin-Can continued galloping ahead, faster than ever. It was hard to keep their balance on the turns, they were riding so fast. She grabbed hold of Tin-Can's mane for extra stability. She felt the wind whistling and pulling around her in pace with the gallop.

"Watch out!" Linda screamed, pointing to a mound of stones ahead.

The boulders on the slope were rolling downhill, heading straight for them. They would be crushed if they didn't make it past them in time.

Anne, who was riding last, realized that they were not going to beat the sliding rocks. They were rolling way too fast and the muddy wooded trail was making the horses' hooves slip. When the first boulder was only a few seconds away from smashing into them, it exploded. She closed her eyes and screamed in fear, loudly, a scream that echoed throughout the entire forest. Seconds passed and Concorde kept galloping.

"Wow, what happened? Are you okay, Anne?"

Alex's voice made her cautiously open her eyes again. Suddenly they were at least 150 feet farther down the trail. The boulders had come to a rest far behind them. Anne's legs were shaking so much that she had to sit back down on her saddle. Her field of vision pulsed with pink light. Was that just from the exertion, or what?

Then they heard hoofbeats behind them again. Jessica and the others had also made it around the boulders and were now riding at a furious pace toward the girls, who urged their horses on. But by now they were all so tired and their pursuers were gaining on them.

A life and death race and all for the sake of an apple. Was this how it had felt in the past for the riders who fought over the apple when the race got out of hand?

Every shortcut through the woods bought them a little time. Every time they splashed through a waterway, every time they were led onto narrower trails, they came closer to Scarecrow Hill, closer to the apple, closer to everything that was at stake. On the horizon, they could just make out a narrow stone bridge.

Inside Linda's bag, the will-o'-the-wisp—Elizabeth—was jostling back and forth in the glass jar like a lost soul.

Alex, who was riding in front, was the first to see the sign: CLOSED DUE TO RISK OF COLLAPSE. Exactly. She had ridden out here before, but it had been a while ago now. The collapse was a reality now. You hardly needed a sign to see that. Still, she had a sinking feeling in the pit of her stomach when she saw those words.

You didn't need to be an engineer to understand that the old bridge had seen better days. It seemed to be crumbling before their very eyes, one piece at a time. Alex grimly eyed the holes in the stone structure and turned around to her friends. She saw Sabine's eyes glowing from a distance and shivered. She turned to Anne, who looked tired.

"Do you think you're up to teleporting us across?"

"I can't really control that," Anne replied, looking resigned. "It was a fluke that it worked the last time."

"Okay." Alex eyed the downed bridge with determination. "Then we proceed, one horse at a time."

"Are we going to make it?" Linda looked around nervously, hearing the hoofbeats approaching.

"Yeah, are we going to make it?" Lisa squirmed anxiously in the saddle as Starshine scratched with his hooves.

"Which sounds better—making it across or winding up down there?"

Everyone followed Alex's gaze. Together, they saw the chasm unfurl below the bridge. The sound of rocks coming loose and falling into the ravine made them gasp.

"Okay," Linda said quietly. "One at a time, but quickly!"

Their hearts were pounding so hard they could practically hear each other's heartbeats in the muffled silence that arose in front of the bridge. Even so, all four of them nodded.

"NOW!" Alex yelled, picking up speed across the bridge. She shut her eyes tight and didn't open them until she could hear that Tin-Can was across.

Lisa and Starshine successfully jumped over the broken bridge. It was a small but dramatic jump which made the bottom drop out of her stomach and the soles of her feet tingle.

"Hurry!" Lisa cried to Linda and Anne. "I don't know how long the rest of the bridge will hold." Rocks were crashing down faster now, in bigger chunks. Lisa's temples were throbbing and she had a cold, metallic taste in her mouth.

As Lisa looked back across the ravine, she saw Linda galloping toward her, preparing to make the jump. Lisa's eyes also met Katja's white gaze as the three Dark Riders began closing in on her friends. Lisa quickly looked away until she heard the familiar sound of Linda's voice softly praising Meteor. They had made it.

"Anne! Now!" Lisa yelled.

Anne urged Concorde ahead and they flew across the bridge. The rocks from the top of the bridge started coming loose just as Concorde's hooves hit the ground safely on the far side.

"Come on!" Alex yelled to gather the others with her.

They were leading the hunt, but they couldn't treat themselves to a look back. Anything, but not that. So they kept going, through the quickly thinning woods, which opened up into a clearing. Their pursuers were still right on their heels, rushing straight for the rocky ravine they had barely managed to cross just seconds earlier. Sabine, Jessica, and Katja were all jostling for position, pushing each other aside on their menacing horses.

None of them seemed willing to be second.

They could see Scarecrow Hill beyond the clearing. The black, gnarly branches reached toward them in a ghostly greeting.

Just behind the other two, Sabine took a running start toward the rocky gap. She rose up in her saddle with a growl as she kicked her horse on both sides with her spurs. Her horse whinnied and kicked backwards, but then kept moving forward with its rider.

"Come *on!*" Sabine bellowed, jumping over the gap where the bridge had been, just as Jessica and Katja had done. Her bellowing became a frightened yelp as the stones suddenly started crumbling away into the ravine before the Dark Riders had a chance to make it to safety. Anne turned to look back and saw the horses' legs moving, the riders' shocked faces as what was left of the bridge gave way underneath them and they all fell, plunging downward along with fragments of the collapsing bridge. The terrible sound of stones and bodies falling into the ravine drowned out all other sounds. Then the three of them were gone, vanished into the ravine, and everything else became oppressively quiet.

36

The first thing that struck the Soul Riders as they rode up the steep slope to Scarecrow Hill was how deserted the place was. All they could hear was the faint whistling of the wind as it lifted the scarecrows that hung all over the enormous tree. They looked like they were almost flying. The black sheets of cloth were fluttering desolately back and forth over the wooden skeletons for bodies. The scarecrows' arms were like tree branches, just as skinny and gnarly.

"They look awfully alive," Anne remarked.

"But they don't scare us," Alex said. "Maybe the birds that want to eat the apple."

"I can't believe we managed to lose Sabine and the others," Linda said. "Do you think . . . do you think they survived?"

Anne thought about that. The floundering bodies falling and falling after all three tried to force their way onto the remnants of the bridge. The horses that were still galloping in midair as the bridge gave way. The fatal clattering of rocks rolling. She shivered.

"I don't actually know," Anne said. "I did see them fall. It looked awful."

"Who knows," Lisa said. "I don't think they're truly human, not . . . not like us. It'll take something more than a ravine to take care of them."

Linda remembered Mr. Sands's diaries. Eternal life in exchange for eternal loyalty to Garnok. Of all the unbelievable things that existed, even though she had never believed them. She nodded slowly.

"Well, it will definitely delay them at any rate. We need to pick the apple now!"

Tin-Can snorted as if he agreed.

They stopped at the top of the hill, just at the foot of the enormous, contorted tree. Everything was all remarkably quiet, even the horses. The scarecrows moved menacingly in the wind.

"Do you see?" Lisa said. She sounded winded, not just from the fast-paced ride there. There was something else making her pulse race, something big and intangible. She could hear the music swelling inside her now, a grand melody that made her want to clench her fists in the air, against the flapping scarecrows that were crouching down in the presence of the power of the melody. It was a melody so strong that everything else faded away alongside it. She started humming and felt the song rising toward the gnarled branches. Something gleamed and she glanced up, curious. The rising morning sun barely broke through the clouds and made everything sparkle. Lisa gasped and pointed up into the tree for the others to look.

They could see the one, solitary apple, gleaming and golden, towering way up near the top, hanging from the biggest, knottiest branch. The sun shone down on the apple. The music inside

Lisa grew stronger still. Could everyone else hear it? Or was it just her?

A thought rose out of the melody. Was she supposed to pick the apple?

"Do it," Alex said, looking Lisa right in the eye. The others nodded in agreement. Lisa felt flushed. She took a deep breath and climbed her way up to the top of the tree. She plucked the apple with a hesitant, slightly trembling hand.

"Good job," Linda smiled. "Now it can do some good!" She stopped and pulled out the glass jar containing Elizabeth. "Do you see, Elizabeth?" she said. "We succeeded! We did what you said!"

Lisa smiled back and passed the apple around so everyone could see how it sparkled in the sunlight. But when she looked in the jar, her smile faded.

"Oh no!" she said. "Elizabeth isn't very clear at all anymore!"

"What?" Linda blurted out and peered more carefully into the jar, her face alarmed. The others and their horses crowded around Linda's outstretched hand. All they could see was a faint flickering glimmer, the color watered-down and sort of panting, as if Elizabeth was gasping for air.

"She's starting to disappear," Linda said, choking up. "Oh no, what do we do?"

"All right," Anne said. "Now we're really in a hurry!"

They rode back toward the darkness together, away from the sun and the enormous tree. The leaves rustled more the farther they entered into Goldenleaf Forest. Was that the wind moving through the trees or—something else?

They would find out soon enough.

37

With Elizabeth's light fading in the glass jar, they rode on. This should have been a victory ride, four giggly, relieved girls flying along. Fortified by the assuredness of having won, at least for the moment. The apple was in safe custody in Lisa's saddlebag. Despite their accomplishment, it was hard to feel victorious. The only thing they talked about was Elizabeth, who seemed to be losing her luminosity.

"What if she dies?" Linda said worriedly. Lisa felt a twinge. She pictured the real Elizabeth in front of her, riding ahead of them on Calliope and telling them to follow her, to dare to believe in their own powers.

Now Calliope was dead, and Elizabeth's light was fading. Lisa thought it felt like her light might die. She sniffled and grabbed the reins.

"Maybe we could ride to Fripp," Anne suggested. "He could help us!"

"To be completely honest, I have more faith in Pi, actually," said Linda, who had ridden up alongside Anne on the wide trail. "She's the one who transformed Elizabeth. She should be able to undo the curse."

"Hey, I bet you're right," Alex said, and Anne also had to agree.

All four of them were quiet, thinking about Elizabeth and how much she had helped them. They each had a special bond formed with her by this point. Before she had been transformed, she had almost started to feel like a second mother, a safe, wise person who could hold your hand when storms where raging in the world and everything was unfamiliar. They thought about Elizabeth, and they remembered what she had said as they walked up to the Secret Stone Circle for the first time.

My girls, Elizabeth had said. *Now is when everything begins in earnest.*

"We'll ride to Pi." Lisa's voice sounded scratchy, as if she hadn't spoken in a long time.

"Yes," Alex agreed, picking a twig out of Tin-Can's mane.

As she rode into the lead on Tin-Can, Alex's hair was the same shade as her horse's coat. There was something proud about her. She breathed perfect fearlessness as she led them over stock and stone, closer to the place they had left in a wild panic only the day before. Alex reminded her a little of Elizabeth, Lisa thought.

"We'll ride there, show her the apple and grab the book. In and out, zoop!" Alex continued.

"Do you think the apple is really going to help us?" Linda asked, shivering as she thought of the darkness that had drawn in over them the last time they were in Cauldron Swamp.

"It has to," Alex said firmly. Linda wished someday she could sound that decisive.

"That sounds like some old fairy tale," Anne said, "The Witch and the Apple."

"The apple is our only chance," Alex said. "Our only chance to get the book and help Elizabeth. I think we should go for it." She glanced up from under her untidy bangs. "Before we go in there, it's important that we sync with each other. No one can lag behind.

That's super important. And, Lisa, don't look down at the swamp this time!"

"I promise," Lisa said. She felt a shooting pain as she remembered the spooky light in the swamp water. She didn't want her mother to be diminished into a ghost, a mirage, a hollow echo from the dark water. She wanted to remember her the way she was, alive and vibrant, so much more alive than everyone else. Not just a pawn in a shadow play by evil powers. She knew that the creature she had seen in the swamp wasn't her mother. She would keep her true mother to herself, deep in her heart, where she kept all her lovely memories, just like she had collected stamps when she was little.

She lived on in there, *Isa's mom*. Lisa slipped her cold hand deep down into Starshine's bright blue mane. He snorted and she felt his body heat spread, from her hand all the way to the depths of her heart.

Linda was riding behind Lisa. She had been unusually quiet, but a cautious smile now cast over her lips.

She felt invincible. Not by herself, but because she was with the others. They could lift each other. Together they didn't need to be afraid, because they could conjure up a power that made their fears vanish out into the dark nooks. Together they belonged at home in the light. She thought about Pi's face when she had hissed, "*The moon?*" in Linda's face.

Yes, they were powerful. They mustn't forget that. And now they had the apple for assistance as well.

The fall leaves swirled in a golden shimmer around them as they rode along at a gallop. Then they rode into the woods, back toward what they had previously fled from not long ago.

Back to Cauldron Swamp.

38

Cauldron Swamp felt so much bigger this time. Riding over all the meandering wooden bridges took time. It gave them time to lose heart, build up their courage, and then lose it again. Dusk arrived and then the sun set over Cauldron Swamp. The whole swamp was shrouded in a dense darkness.

Pi's wooden house towered in the distance. It stood on thick pilings on the sandy hill. The house had a sloped roof, Victorian stickwork detailing, mullioned windows, and window lights. The curtains were drawn and the air was teeming with ill will. Whoever lived here did not want visitors.

"This really is the ideal house for a witch," Lisa said.

It was true that the house was crooked and dark, but at one time it must have been a cozy place to live. It had two stories and a spectacular view of the swamp and the forest. With a little good will, you could imagine a sparkling lake, an inviting summer cottage where all the windows and doors were thrown open wide to let the light in. Here, right at the end of the wooden bridges, atop the pilings that connected the house to the swamp, there was a large veranda, perfect for eating breakfast on sunny mornings. But the sun never shone in Cauldron Swamp anymore. The veranda was full of big, bulky iron cages now and cauldrons that had been left there to rust. Linda tripped over a broom. They left the horses on the veranda and picked their way through all the junk to the front door.

"What are those iron cages for?" Anne whispered to Lisa.

"I don't know," Lisa whispered. "But I saw something like that in the lab at Dark Core. Although these ones look rougher and rustier. Ugh."

Meteor whinnied loudly and tossed his head. Starshine stamped his feet in place and looked unhappy.

"I wonder what she does out here, actually," Alex said, warily eyeing the drawn curtains in the windows of the house.

One by one they gathered in front of the heavy front door. They were standing so close together that they looked like one single, large figure, shrouded in shadows.

"Okay," Linda said and gulped. "Let's do this."

She knocked, three determined knocks. Then it was quiet, but it wasn't the silence of absence. It was more like the kind of silence that comes when someone is trying to hide. Something fluttered behind one of the black curtains.

Linda knocked again. Four hard knocks. She put one ear to the door, listening attentively.

"I hear something," she whispered.

Yes, inside the cottage, someone was moving. Slow, shuffling footsteps. It sounded like a broom moving slowly across the floor.

The girls remembered the roots that Pi the witch had for legs and feet and shuddered.

"The apple!" Lisa whispered. She yanked it out of the bag and held it out in front of her. Was it a present? A peace offering? Bait? She didn't know, but she knew one thing. The apple needed to be visible when the door opened. *If* it opened.

Then, finally, the door slid open with a creak. No one stepped forward or said anything. Everything was filled with a hesitant silence.

"Hello?" Linda hollered. Her voice echoed in the dark home. She felt grateful for her friends' body heat. They stepped closer, together, into the pitch blackness. It smelled stuffy and putrid, like a bag of wet swimsuits and beach towels that had been stuffed into a closet at the end of the summer and forgotten. But somewhere in the musty air, she stood waiting for them.

Short, hissing breaths were coming closer, toward the lamp burning outside the door.

When Pi stepped out of the shadows, all four of them took a step back. The stench of rot was everywhere now, and there was no way to defend against it. A crooked hand, half-atrophied wood, half-nightmarish claw, reached out toward them.

Lisa took a deep breath and held out the apple.

"Here!" she blurted out. "Do you see, Pi? We picked the apple! It's ours now."

"The apple . . . ?" Pi wheezed. The specter of genuine astonishment behind the mask was palpable. She extended her hands toward the apple, but then backed away.

"What do you want? Do you think you're on the right track, little girls? Do you think the druids wish you well? Think about it. At one time, I thought that, too. Actually, they don't care about you. Don't you understand that? They think only of themselves, not of you." Pi's voice was a low, hoarse whisper. The roots that had at one time been her feet were now running wild and lashing against the threshold.

Linda cringed at Pi's words. They really hit home, hit the part inside her that had doubts. And yet, even so, she did it. She stepped forward.

"The book," Linda said, looking directly at Pi. Somewhere behind the mask there was little left of what had at one time been the druid Pi. She planned to address that part of her now. Or at least to try.

"We need it and we need it fast. You know why, Pi, don't you? The moon magic won't wait for us. Nor will the magic of the sun, or the lightning, or the stars. In the name of the druids, of what was once yours, we demand the book of the Light Ceremony from you. You have lied to yourself and others about where you're keeping the book, but you are no longer entitled to it, Pi. Not now that you have gone over to the other side. And one more thing . . ."

She pulled out the glass jar containing what was left of Elizabeth. The pink light revealed Pi's gruesome wooden mask. It was reminiscent of a big owl with enormous eyes and a sharp, angry beak. Pi winced when she saw the jar. Then she recovered and chuckled.

"Elizabeth," she said in a deep, raspy voice. "There you are!" She ran her long scratchy claws over the glass, making a screechy sound. The girls grimaced. Linda took a step forward.

"You must break the curse," she said. "Make Elizabeth human again. And then we want the book." Her voice was slow and determined. Almost friendly.

The apple gleamed urgently in Lisa's outstretched hand, right next to Pi, who eyed the apple with her shining eyes.

Pi nodded slowly. Her breathing sounded even more labored now. Just as wheezy and bubbling as before. She trembled inside the wooden mask, but the owl's grotesque face remained stiff. The girls stood in the doorway, not daring to move from the spot. Finally, Pi walked back into the darkness—they heard her dragging footsteps and wheezing breaths—and then she came back with a thick, dusty book that looked old. It was beautifully bound with gold threads and ornate lettering.

"Here," she said. "Take it and get lost. Scram and never come back again."

Linda took the book and held the jar up again.

"And now you need to help Elizabeth," she said.

Pi laughed.

"If your precious little Elizabeth was as clever as people said she was, then she never would have brought you here. Plus, she should also have known that I only deal in the kind of magic that destroys and deceives. I don't dabble in repairing or restoring things anymore. The fact is, I couldn't restore Elizabeth even if I wanted to. And believe me, I don't want to."

Linda's eyes filled with tears of rage. She made one last attempt at coaxing Pi, but then realized it was useless. Pi was going on now and talked in a loud, monotone voice. She wasn't even listening to them.

"I'm sick of her and the druids. They haven't done anything but freeze me out. They have their own agenda and will do anything to get their way. They're just using you. Did you think the druids cared about how things turned out for you?" Pi laughed a dry, wheezy laugh. "You ought to do like me and avoid them. And forget everything they filled your little heads with."

"Come on!" Alex hissed from behind Linda. "Take the book and run!"

The light in the glass jar flickered, weaker now than ever, almost completely transparent. Linda slowly backed away with her arms protectively around Elizabeth and the jar.

They were halfway out the front door when Pi caught Lisa. She felt the sharp wooden claws pierce her jacket, scraping her back. An enormous owl flapped its wings right above Lisa's head, preparing to attack. She screamed. The owl swooped down at Lisa, grabbed the apple in its massive claws and flew over to Pi. It hooted and landed on Pi's bony shoulder.

"Ah good, Hel," Pi said. "Thank you for sharing your catch!"

Something shifted in Pi as the owl landed with the apple. She seemed to grow, stretching taller, looking stronger. Her voice was steady, not scratchy anymore, when she hissed, "I changed my mind. Give me back my book!"

"Not on your life!" Linda yelled. She backed out the door and raced with the others back down the footbridge toward the horses. Pi shrieked and her owl imitated her cry. She wasn't shuffling anymore. Now she moved after them quickly and supplely.

"The apple made her faster," Alex cried. "Come on!"

The owl flew after them, ripping at Anne's hair. Anne flailed around wildly and flung herself up onto Concorde with the owl's nasty claws still in her hair. Concorde got a running start and then eased into a gallop. A big tuft of her long, blond hair ripped out, caught in the bird's claws, and she screamed in pain. But the owl had flown back to its owner, who stood whining about the moon and false druids. Then Pi raced after them with her owl, Hel, above her like a flapping storm cloud—but the girls were already on their way down the bridge. They galloped as quickly as they could with the sickening stench of old swamp water in their noses and the owl's flapping wings right behind them.

They managed to escape, Alex on Tin-Can, Linda on Meteor, Lisa on Starshine, and Anne on Concorde. They escaped, just like the last time they were here. But this time, they didn't plan to come back.

Elizabeth's flame flickered in the glass jar.

39

This time they couldn't afford to rest for the night. They had to get back to Fripp and the Secret Stone Circle and they had to do it fast. So they rode through the night and into the morning as the dawn was approaching. The horses sighed heavily and hung their heads. Their riders, too, were fairly slumped over as if all the air had gone out of them. Many hours later they saw the sun shining over Silverglade. They were just able to make out the outlines of horses and riders out in the field.

"Has it really only been a couple of days since we were last here?" Linda said with a slightly sad sigh. "It feels like another lifetime from now."

"Calliope was alive then." Anne's eyes were wide and full of grief. "And Elizabeth was . . . well, Elizabeth. I just can't wrap my head around it."

A tear rolled down Lisa's cheek. She looked up and saw that Linda was crying, too. In spite of everything, despite the heaviness in her chest and all the problems that remained, crying helped make everything feel ever-so-slightly better. They all mourned the loss of Calliope, Elizabeth's beautiful, beautiful mare who had deserved a better fate.

And they were all equally worried for Elizabeth, who seemed to be gradually leaving them.

The sun continued to shine on them after they rode past Silverglade, closer to the chain of mountains that would take them to the Secret Stone Circle, but they couldn't feel any of its warmth. They rode into the dusk and nightfall, and no one dared to check on Elizabeth in the glass jar. What if the glow had faded completely?

It wasn't until the stone formations towered before them that they took out the jar holding Elizabeth. Her light was faint and elusive—but it was there. And Linda, who was holding the jar, thought the flame became a bit stronger when they saw the pink runes. When the light in the glass jar fluttered, her heart fluttered with it. Maybe they could still save Elizabeth!

They dismounted from their exhausted horses and let them graze among the runestones, and they walked over to the small figure who was waiting for them.

"You got it! You really did it!" There was no mistaking Fripp's genuine happiness. His round, black, glossy eyes twinkled as he looked at the book and stroked it gently with one furry blue paw. The gold letters danced under his gentle touch, twinkling like the stars in the night sky.

Of course it wasn't just any old book. It was the book of the Light Ceremony, a special book full of ancient magic. Without it the Soul Riders wouldn't get any further in their requisite training. He had been worried. There was no point in trying to conceal that, but now they were here, and they brought the book.

The Secret Stone Circle looked even more secret in the garb of night, somehow. An owl hooted and the moon went behind a cloud. Only the stars stood watch above them. The girls were tired after their long ride, but Fripp was darting around like a blue blizzard and chuckling happily.

"Finally," he mumbled. "Finally everything can begin."

"Uh, not really," Alex said apologetically. "Something happened with Pi . . ."

"Yes?" Fripp said absentmindedly. He continued running his paw over the cover of the book.

"Elizabeth," Linda said, pulling out the glass jar. There was a faint flicker from the will-o'-the-wisp. "There was a terrible accident. There was no saving her horse, but here she is, at any rate."

Fripp reluctantly looked up from the book and took the jar.

"A will-o'-the-wisp," he said, looking for a long time at Elizabeth's face, which could still just be made out in the gleam of light.

"That is unfortunate, of course, but I'll do my best to deal with it. Although that might take a while. . . how long as she been in this condition?"

"Almost two days," Alex said. "Please, tell us that you can make her herself again!"

"I'll ask Avalon the druid to summon a friend here who is the foremost authority in Jorvik when it comes to transformations," Fripp said. "That's all we can do. But I promise that we'll do everything, truly everything that we can. So try not to worry. You need to get some sleep now so that you'll be able to get through tomorrow. We'll learn all about this then." He tapped on the Light Ceremony book, which gleamed in his firm grip.

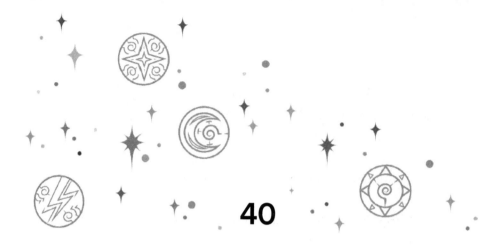

40

The next morning Linda was the first to wake up. She snuck out of bed and was just about to slip on her shoes and go outside when she got a surprise. Elizabeth was standing there in the doorway, smiling her Mona Lisa smile, holding a big cup of tea in her hand. It was as if nothing had happened, as if this was just any old morning. And Calliope stood beside her, peacefully munching grass. Linda felt the happiness welling up inside her and wanted to dance little pirouettes.

"Elizabeth!" Linda rushed over to her and hugged her. "You're back! And you're yourself again! And, oh, Calliope!"

"Of course I am." Elizabeth's eyes sparkled in the sunlight. "It's not that easy to get rid of me. You did know I would come back, didn't you?"

"Yes, Elizabeth," Linda replied, petting Calliope's neck with a happy smile. "I knew that."

Then the sun went behind a cloud above them and a chilly breeze picked up. It blew over the druid houses, collapsing them like paper. Elizabeth's gray cape flapped in the breeze and then she was gone. Only her cape remained. Calliope brayed and reared. Linda stood close to her and stroked her soothingly. She was startled when she noticed something dark trickling down onto her hand. Black oil? Mud? No, it was water, mucky, sludgy water! The stench of swamp turned her stomach. Calliope broke free from her hold and galloped away, but got stuck in something—she got stuck in water that was rising around her.

"Calliope! Elizabeth!" Linda screamed as she watched the black, goopy water gushing everywhere: out of the collapsed druid cottages, out of Calliope's delicately arched nostrils, over the grass and the stones. The ground crackled and gave way. Now Linda wasn't with the druids anymore but somewhere else. She swam, coughed, spat, tried in vain to get to the surface, but everything was dark, gushing water.

A weak voice echoed, bubbling through the masses of water. *The more powerful the magic, the bigger the side effects.*

Linda's own voice was intermingled, rising and falling along with the bubbles in the black water: *Don't you understand? We caused this!*

The water rose over her, black and shiny like oil. First it drowned out her words, then her. And there were others drowning in the water. She couldn't see them, but she could hear their voices, their desperate cries for help. They were women, men, children, and animals, dogs barking, and foals neighing. *Help! Help!* Everything was black water now. It ran down into her lungs. She couldn't breathe. She . . .

Linda sat upright in bed, gasping for air. She was soaked with sweat and her heart was racing so fast that her whole body was shaking. Her screams had woken her up as well as the others. Alex had sat up with such force in the bottom bunk that she had banged her head.

"Linda!" Lisa and Anne came rushing over to the edge of her bed. "What is it?" Lisa stroked Linda's sticky forehead.

"I had a nightmare," Linda whispered. "Elizabeth was there, and Calliope. And then the dark water washed them away and me, too.

Listen, something is about to happen! Can't you guys feel it, too?"
She took several jerky breaths. Then she straightened up and said.
"Come sit down, you guys. Hold hands and close your eyes. I need
to test something I've never done before."

All three came and sat next to Linda on her bed. Linda took
hold of Anne's hand on the one side and Lisa's hand on the other.
Lisa held Alex's hand and Alex held Anne's. There was a crackling,
like from electricity. They all jumped but kept holding hands in
an unbroken circle. Linda closed her eyes and let the black water
rush into her. Everything came back to her: the masses of water,
the cries for help, the desperate neighing, the gushing, drowning
sensation. And then the same words as last time, in the same order.

The stronger the magic, the bigger the side effects.

Don't you understand! We caused this!

Linda's breathing was labored now. She was gasping for breath.
She opened her eyes, let go of the girls' hands, and exhaled. The
other three exhaled with her.

"Okay, you can look now," Linda said.

The others were staring at her.

"What WAS that?" Alex said. She was holding her pendant in
her hand. It had become extremely hot.

"My dream," Linda said hoarsely. "Or more of a vision. What
you saw is going to happen. I'm sure of it. And it's going to happen
soon. We have to tell Fripp and the druids!"

They dressed quickly and raced off to the Secret Stone Circle,
where Fripp was waiting with another man in a cape similar to
the one Elizabeth had had, although longer and wider. They raised
their heads and simultaneously burst out with their greetings when
they spotted the girls.

Their horses stood at little way away, grazing. Linda had time to
think that Meteor sounded very calm. His whinny was muted and

friendly, no screams of panic like in Cauldron Swamp. That had to be a good sign, right? But her heart was still racing and she had a cold, clammy feeling, as if she had just found herself in freezing water. She shivered and strode quickly over to Fripp and the man with the friendly brown eyes.

"This is the druid Avalon," Fripp said. "He is going to help me teach you the Light Ceremony today instead of Elizabeth."

"Forget the Light Ceremony!" Linda blurted out. "There's going to be a flood somewhere! We need to stop it! Now."

"A flood?" Fripp said, scratching his head. "No, no, we haven't seen any signs of that. The druids watch all the water sources in Jorvik around the clock since abnormal energy flow is often evident in the waterways. We would have heard something. So, gather around and we'll get started."

Linda couldn't shake the stomach-churning feeling of drowning. Her heart was pounding just as fast as during her vision. Everything felt wrong. She looked around at her friends to see how they were reacting. They looked bewildered, to put it mildly.

"But . . . we saw it, too!" Anne burst out. "We *saw* it. Water everywhere, people screaming for help, foals whinnying in fear."

"I'm sure you did," Fripp said. "Linda is so strong in the moon's circle that she doesn't just have visions about the future but can also share them with those of you in the sisterhood. But you need to know one thing. Visions are never absolutely certain depictions of something that is definitely going to happen. They show one *possible* future. In this case, it was something that might happen further along in time. Not now, because if that were the case, we would already have been aware of it from the druids."

The girls eyed each other skeptically but didn't say anything. Linda swallowed the hard lump in her throat, but in spite of everything she was breathing a little more easily now. What if Fripp was right? That the visions were further ahead in the future, so far ahead that they might never come to pass?

"So," Fripp continued. "We'll start the lesson now, right, Avalon?"

Avalon nodded. Then he opened the book of the Light Ceremony and began to read. The grand words and his beautiful, melodic voice slowed Linda's pulse. She let go of the dark visions and listened to the story of the Soul Riders and the Light Ceremony, the story of herself.

"Almost first was the light, but before it there was a girl on horseback, Aideen. She brought light to the island, and life and hope poured forth out of the cold emptiness. She carried the light within her and in the torch she held in her hand. In the Light Ceremony, we conjure up the girl's power, her goodness, and inextinguishable inner light. We journey through time and space, but always return to ourselves, for there is the power. If this book has reached you, then you have been chosen. Soon you will be initiated in the Light Ceremony and become Aideen's and the light's foremost protectors in the battle against Garnok.

"A word of warning: the Light Ceremony must not under any circumstances be performed by anyone who is not a Soul Rider or closely allied with Aideen's secret druid order. Such action would entail mortal peril.

"You who now hold the book in your hand—"

"The book in your hand?" Linda objected.

Avalon looked up and shrugged. "In the past, great care was taken to ensure that each chosen girl would read the book herself, from cover to cover. She would sit here in the Secret Stone Circle and read the whole Light Ceremony book, regardless of the weather. After many long meetings, Elizabeth and I managed to convince even the eldest and stubbornest of the druids to realize that it might make more sense to do a quick review followed by some hands-on practice."

Even Linda looked relieved. Avalon continued reading.

"You who now hold the book in your hand have been chosen. Our efforts are now your efforts. Your strength is an invaluable tool in our fight."

The glass jar with Elizabeth in it, which was sitting on the ground, flickered. But the glow was so faint that it was hardly visible. It was hardly a sigh. Elizabeth was withering right in front of their eyes. Lisa was about to say something but was cut short by a sudden noise. It was the sound of galloping hooves, and it was coming closer.

Everyone turned around. They saw a druid come riding up at high speed, heard the horse's rapid, snorting breaths, and saw how its hooves ripped up the grass.

"Look!" Alex said, pointing to one of the runestones. It glowed a bright, vibrating pink as the druid and his horse thundered past. Then the light went out and the stone became gray again.

Linda stood frozen, taking in everything that was happening. She opened her mouth, trying to say something, but nothing came out.

Fripp mumbled something and turned to the sky, almost pleading. A shadow fell over Avalon's face as the druid leapt off the horse and hurried over to them.

"What . . . ?"

Linda stood as if frozen on the spot, feeling the dark water inside her gush forth again. This was the icy cold sensation from the nightmare, the sense of reality being peeled away, layer by layer. She already knew what the druid was going to say.

"The big dam at Winter Valley is failing! If it breaks, everyone who lives in Winter Valley is in danger, humans and animals alike! The Soul Riders need to ride there right away and try to mend it!"

"But how . . . ?" Fripp began.

Linda cut him off. She had tears in her eyes and her voice was trembling as she said, "*We* did this with our magic by traveling through the portals. Don't you understand? We caused this!"

They looked at each other in horror.

"What have we done?" Anne whispered.

It took a moment before Fripp was able to get them to calm down a little, and then they gathered around him. His face was somber, and yet he still radiated a calm that made Lisa's racing rabbit pulse beat a little more slowly. She grabbed Anne's hand and squeezed it. Anne squeezed back.

"Soul Riders," Fripp said. "Your powers are being tested now. And unfortunately the situation has become critical, but believe me: you have what it takes to stop this. Trust in yourselves and each other—and please, try to stay calm."

They turned and looked into each other's eyes. All four of them stood with their heads held high, although their legs were trembling and their minds were spinning.

Would they succeed? How do you keep calm when all you can feel is panic? And would they reach the dam in time?

Alex's voice was a little unsteady, but she was half-smiling as she said, "Well, at least it's not like it can really get much worse, right?"

She was right, Lisa thought, glancing over at Starshine, who was tossing his head impatiently, ready to be off. *Let's do this.*

"Come on," she said. And the others followed her over to the horses.

Fripp stood and watched them for a long time. Finally, as the sound of their hoofbeats faded away, he turned and walked away.

Everything was quiet again.

Acknowledgments

Ever since *Soul Riders: Jorvik Calling* came out, I have—practically every day, actually—been astonished at how wonderful you all are. Yes, YOU! My readers. You who contact me on social media, send drawings and fan fiction, come up to me at horse races and shows and book fairs and say hi. You who time and again have asked when the next book is coming out. You're the best, and you deserve all the thanks in the world! I hope that you enjoy the continuation of the Soul Riders' story every bit as much as I have.

Just like last time, I had a wonderful team that helped me the whole way.

Many thanks to all the talented people at Andrews McMeel Publishing, including Dave Shaw, Spencer Williams, Chuck Harper, Courtney Watkins, Jackson Ingram, and Jean Lucas. I'm so grateful for all your hard work!

Thanks to my team in Sweden: Anton Klepke, editor and dramaturge extraordinaire. Thanks to Marcus Thorell Björkäng for his continued confidence and invaluable assistance. Thanks to Marcus Olsson, who came in very late in the game with yet another assist, providing many astute and pertinent observations. Thanks to Ulrika Caperius, publisher extraordinaire and fellow horsewoman. Thanks to everyone at Bonnier Carlsen who has made me feel so welcome.

Thanks to Star Stable for letting me be part of your lovely StarFam. A special thank-you to Clara, Karin, Juliana, Jane, Matilda, Meli, and Lauren—you guys are amazing and I'm so lucky to be working with you!

A big thank-you to Marie Beschorner and Tara Chace.

Thanks to Agnes, Elsa, Pärla, Marcus, and Dylan. A person couldn't have a better family. I love you.

An especially warm thanks to my dear friend and fellow author Anna Bågstam Ryltenius and her family who opened up their home to me for several broiling hot weeks in July when I was extremely stressed about deadlines and inflexible schedules. Many of the most important scenes in the book were written on your porch at Fornudden, south Stockholm, wearing just a bikini, dreaming in vain of Jorvik's chilly autumnal winds.

Thank you all. Thank you. Thank you. *Thank you.*

First published by Bonnier Carlsen Bokförlag, Stockholm, Sweden.
Published in the English language by agreement with Ferly.

Andrews McMeel Publishing
a division of Andrews McMeel Universal
1130 Walnut Street, Kansas City, Missouri 64106

www.andrewsmcmeel.com

20 21 22 23 24 BVG 10 9 8 7 6 5 4 3 2 1

Paperback ISBN: 978-1-5248-5618-2
Hardback ISBN: 978-1-5248-5619-9

Library of Congress Control Number: 2020936705

Made by:
Berryville Graphics
Address and location of manufacture:
25 Jack Enders Blvd.
Berryville, Virginia 22611
1st Printing—7/20/20

Writer: Helena Dahlgren
Synopsis and concept development: Marcus Thorell Björkäng
Language editors: Anton Klepke and Marcus Thorell Björkäng
Editor: Jean Z. Lucas
Cover design: Malin Gustavsson
Cover art: Marie Beschorner
Art Director: Spencer Williams
Production Manager: Chuck Harper
Production Editor: David Shaw

ATTENTION: SCHOOLS AND BUSINESSES
Andrews McMeel books are available at quantity discounts with bulk purchase for educational, business, or sales promotional use. For information, please e-mail the Andrews McMeel Publishing Special Sales Department: specialsales@amuniversal.com.